SEP 1 3 2021

Praise for *Mayflies*

'*Mayflies* is one of those novels to press into the hands of friends. Beautifully written—wise, funny, poetic, alert to time, place and the ordinary human . . . I adored this book.'   —Carol Ann Duffy

'*Mayflies* is entirely unexpected; a joyful, warm and heart-filling tribute to the million-petalled flower of male friendship. This book will last beyond these feverish times: it's not just a reminder that culture makes the worst things bearable, but a beautiful example of it in action.'   —*The Times*

'Life-loving and elegiac.'   —*The Observer*

'A delightful nostalgia trip of enduring teenage friendship . . . an affecting and evocative picture of an era and a relationship.'
                                                                   —*Daily Telegraph*

'An assured and self-contained piece of theatre, in which love of many kinds is tested, *Mayflies* is rich in allusions, gracefully written, yet vigorous . . . This is a book of high artistic ambition, and a reminder, were it needed, of the seriousness that fiction can address . . . O'Hagan's achievement is not to flinch from reality, nor to wallow in misery, but to fill the pages with roaring life, right up to the last kick of the ball.'   —*The Herald*

'O'Hagan has written a tight, delicate and soulful novel . . . about the power of enduring friendship.'   —*Sunday Times*

'A rare thing: a life-enhancing novel about death. It will stay with you and you will want to read it again.'   —*Scotsman*

'Stop all the clocks, cut off the telephone and read Andrew O'Hagan's new novel. *Mayflies* is a lifetime book.'
                                                                   —*The Australian*

ANDREW O'HAGAN

· · ·

Mayflies

McClelland & Stewart

First published in Great Britain by Faber & Faber Ltd. in 2020.

LIBRARY AND ARCHIVES CANADA CATALOGUING IN PUBLICATION

Title: Mayflies / Andrew O'Hagan.
Names: O'Hagan, Andrew, 1968- author.
Identifiers: Canadiana (print) 20200389025 | Canadiana (ebook) 20200389068 |
ISBN 9780771018916 (hardcover) | ISBN 9780771068133 (EPUB)
Subjects: LCGFT: Novels.
Classification: LCC PR6065.H18 M39 2021 | DDC 823/.914—dc23

Jacket Design: Luke Bird
Jacket art © Matthew Brookes / Trunk Archive
Typeset by Faber & Faber Ltd
Printed in Canada

McClelland & Stewart,
a division of Penguin Random House Canada Limited,
a Penguin Random House Company
www.penguinrandomhouse.ca

1 2 3 4 5   25 24 23 22 21

Penguin
Random House
McCLELLAND & STEWART

for
Keith and Joy Martin

Think where man's glory most begins and ends,
And say my glory was I had such friends.

WILLIAM BUTLER YEATS

Summer
1986

I

Tully Dawson made himself new to the world, and ripe for the glories of that summer, by showing he was unlike his father. It wasn't a matter to fight over: some families are made up of strangers and nothing can change it. But I think it always bothered Tully that Woodbine couldn't cheer him on when he came by the football field to watch the game. The old man would only shake his head in a know-all way and stare at the Firth of Clyde with an injured look. Tully had named him after the cigarettes; they all had their nicknames, those reluctant fathers. They sat at home opening cans of lager and cursing our Saturday nights. I suppose we could have drifted over to the touchline and asked his opinion, but being young is a kind of warfare in which the great enemy is experience. Our cheeks burned and we watched him walk towards the unstained light of the harbour.

Nineteen eighty-four was the end of old Woodbine, or 1985, when the strike ended and the Ayrshire men returned one by one to the pits, met at the gates by women giving out carnations. The miners had fought hard, but they were all sacked within a month. 'He takes his shame out on us,' Tully said. 'I suppose Thatcher never really got it about the enemy within.' And that comment was pure Tully. You could imagine how his whole spirit, as well as his famous good looks and his green eyes, came from a dream of the freedom that existed just beyond his dad. But the photographs tell a sadder story – the saddest one – because Woodbine had green eyes too.

Irvine New Town, east of eternity. Tully was twenty years old and a lathe turner. He impersonated Arthur Seaton from *Saturday Night and Sunday Morning* by taunting his boss all week and drinking pints of Black and Tan all weekend. He looked like Albert Finney, all slicked-up hair, but in Tully's case spiked with soap. At that time, he had the kind of looks that appeal to all sexes and all ages, and his natural effrontery opened people up. He was in a band, obviously. They had sprung into existence the previous winter. They were called the Bicycle Factory, another *Saturday Night* reference, and would later flirt with success and change their name several times as Tully went from singer to drummer. When people asked why he was so often the best man at weddings, it was clear they hadn't known Tully Dawson in his prime. He had innate charisma, a brilliant record collection, complete fearlessness in political argument, and he knew how to love you more than anybody else. Other guys were funny and brilliant and better at this and that, but Tully loved you. He had the leader thing, when he was young, the guts of the classic frontman, and if any of us got together we instantly wanted to know where he was. Some people gain that status with power or with money, but Tully did it with pure cheek. His brighter language made older people seem dull. His dad wanted to constrain the future with robotic disappointment, drinking all day at the

Twa Dogs, and Tully was ready for flight. He wasn't so much the butterfly as the air on which it travels. And that summer he was ready for an adventure beyond the Ayrshire hedges.

• • •

I wasn't meant to go to university. We weren't that kind of family. Very soon, we weren't any kind of family at all. My dad wandered off in search of himself – 'You might begin by looking up your own backside,' said my mother, Norma – then she decided that the life of the single mother was not for her, and flitted to Arran. I think they had a slightly exaggerated sense of my self-sufficiency (I'd just turned eighteen) yet it was consistent with their behaviour all through my childhood, falling apart or bolting. My mum and dad imagined I would love swanning about in a council house by myself. In fact, I spent more and more time at Tully's, and within a few weeks I felt I was finished with them.

'I've divorced my mum and dad,' I said to Tully one night at the pictures. It was *Mona Lisa* for the umpteenth time.

'Don't be daft,' he said. 'They'll be back – like Arnie.'

'Nope. I'm not having them back. It's the solo life now.'

'No way.'

'I'm serious. They can pay the bills for a few months and then that's that. They never wanted to be in a family and they've tortured each other for years. I'll stay until I go to uni. That's the end of it, man. They fucked it.'

'Stay at mine whenever you like. If you don't want to stay just come over for your dinner. My mum loves you.'

'Thanks, mate.'

He leaned over and kissed me right on the forehead.

'You're in charge, Noodles. Do your life your own way.' I didn't know I wanted approval until Tully gave it to me. I didn't know life could be like that. It was part of the teenage dream, to find a pal who totally noticed you.

'Do you think Bob Hoskins is a family man?' I asked.

'In dreams,' Tully said, staring at the screen. 'Everybody is, in dreams.'

That was just the latest change: the divorce. I'd always been bookish. I was one of those kids who bumped into lamp posts on the way back from the library. I read all the books they had, including the Zane Greys and the Mills & Boon. I read bird-watching books and tomes on French wine and the history of scent. I didn't know what to do with it all, yet it somehow embroidered an image of the future.

I'd gained courage from a lovely teacher, Mrs O'Connor, who taught English at St Cuthbert's, a Catholic secondary in the middle of a housing estate. Poor old St Cud's. The nuns, with the grace of God, fought a hard battle against the popularity of Buckfast Tonic Wine, and readied us for a world in which piety might make up for a lack of basic arithmetic. Each year, the boy who wasn't expelled and the girl who wasn't pregnant became joint dux, and the football team added to its fame for rioting in nearby towns. The idea at home had been that I'd get out of school as fast as I could and get a job. And so, the year before that final summer, when I was seventeen, I'd gone for an interview in the office of a fence-building firm down by the railway station. To be honest, it was a Portakabin, or a kennel if I'm more honest, and it smelled of ancient socks and roll-ups.

The day of the interview, I arrived wearing a borrowed suit with a book jutting out of one pocket. It was a hot day for once. I wore some fat old tie of my dad's – I think the tie was older than I was – and my hair was slick with a gel called Country Born.

'What d'you want?' the foreman asked. He had a scoundrel's face and there was something swampy about his shirt.

'I was at the Jobcentre. You advertised for an office assistant.'

'We just want a wee lassie to make the tea.' I saw the calendars of topless women on the walls and took a deep breath.

'I can make tea,' I said.

'What's that in your pocket?' I pulled out the paperback. I swear to God it was a tattered copy of *Nausea* by Jean-Paul Sartre. 'Oh, for fuck's sake,' he said. 'Away you to university or something. Wasting my time.'

'It's only a book,' I said. 'It's about existentialism.'

He grimaced. He wheezed. And a part of my library-haunting self will always be stranded there, in a cabin without air, in a world without God, as that foreman howls and gasps and slaps his knee. In a moment, he was bent double, coughing hard, as I retreated to a sticky door plastered with images of Samantha Fox.

In my life at that time, Mrs O'Connor was the voice of reason. I remember watching her as if her entire ethos, her confidence in the face of adversity, her femininity, might travel over the classroom like her perfume, and refresh me. She stood tall and resplendent in a red cardigan and glowed with her love of metaphors. She had a tenderness towards weirdos, a kind of therapeutic belief in the value of being extravagantly yourself, and I often sought her out, even when it wasn't the English period. The school was full of kids who'd forgotten their books and hated lessons, and she stood at the front of the room with a volume of Shakespeare held up, daring one or two of us to suspend our disbelief and make a plan. The day after my failed interview I told her I couldn't even get a job as a fencer's dogsbody, and she sat me down at one of the desks. 'Look,' she said, 'you love observing people and talking back, but the truth is you've read more books than I have.'

I can still see her red hair with the light behind it, the sun pouring through the window of the classroom where she plied her trade in sensitivity.

'You must have read *some*,' I said, 'to end up in this dump.'

'I've never read like you do,' she said. 'Henry James. E. M. Forster. Stuff like that. Why are you going for daft job interviews? You have to go and study at the university. Why aren't you doing sixth year studies?'

I looked up at her. 'Things are . . .'

'Rough at home?'

'I didn't say that.' I waited a second and she took my hand. Nobody had taken my hand since Mary Stobbs in the nativity play in Primary Two. Mary was bold but Mrs O'Connor dealt in something even more mysterious – kindness. 'My mum and dad have got zero to say to each other and they live in different

8

parts of the house.' She nodded. I told her they weren't cut out for giving advice, and that was fine. I wanted my own life anyway. I should go and find it. No drama. They'd done their bit. I got wafts of her perfume and scrutinised her face for signs of ridicule. But she looked at me calmly.

'Listen, I don't care what the shrinks say. Some people's lives are about their parents and some aren't. I know I shouldn't say this, but just leave. Pass the exams and go. Don't look back. You're a weirdo and weirdos have to get out.'

'Thanks very much.'

'Honestly. You listen to Shostakovich. So do I, but I'm not seventeen. You take bundles of records out of the library. The other day you mentioned Edith Sitwell. Nobody in the history of this school has ever mentioned her before. I scarcely knew her myself. I know my Shakespeare and I love books, but Edith Sitwell? She had a long nose and she wore a lot of rings and . . . you cannot become a fencer's office assistant, do you hear me? You'll die. You're too strange and you like the writing of Jean Rhys. You like . . . Norman Mailer and Maya Angelou and you have to be with people who . . . see that.'

That evening, Tully phoned me during his night shift. 'Just phoning to make sure you're all right,' he said, 'and to tell you you're a dick.'

'Thanks. What's happening?'

'I'm going mad in here. Zombies all over the factory floor.' I told him about the teacher who was standing up for me and he said I should take all the help. Having Tully on the case was like having an older brother. As he spoke, I saw all the things

9

I'd written on the back of my hand from the day's lessons and conversations. It was like I was on the edge of a big plan, and Tully was all for plans and schemes.

Whenever I smell pine floor cleaner, I think of Mrs O'Connor. After what she said, I began coming to her classroom after school, for a few minutes at first, then half an hour, and pretty soon I was adding to my Highers, sitting at the front for two hours each evening, drilling down on Thomas Hardy and Shakespeare and Yeats, 'Sailing to Byzantium' and 'The Wild Swans at Coole'. We discussed gyres and tragedy. We made a project of *Antony and Cleopatra*. She also helped me with form-filling and took me through past papers for the other subjects, too, keeping a light on in that classroom, in the middle of that estate, in the middle of the Eighties. The cleaners were out in the corridors mopping the floors and the smell of Scots pine travelled under the door and became the odour of those perfect and unexpected hours. I fancied we were high up in a forest where the air was clear and no one could damage your hopes or trouble your freedom.

After the results came in, I went to school for the last time. She was sitting with a huge pile of jotters. 'Ah, James,' she said. 'I gather you got a place.'

'Strathclyde.' She jumped up from her desk and hugged me right next to the blackboard. '*Susan*,' I said.

'Mrs O'Connor to you.' She was smiling. I didn't know what to say. It can take a whole lifetime to know how to thank a person.

'It's good,' I said, and she sat down again and took up her

pen. I went to the door and slipped past it before popping my head back round.

'Forgot something?'

'You know she had brothers,' I said.

'Who?'

'Dame Edith Sitwell. The poet with the rings.'

'Away ye *go*, James,' she said.

'They were called Osbert and Sacheverell.' We both smiled. 'There's a couple of good Scottish names for you.'

She threw her head back. I could still hear her laughing as I made my way down the corridor and smashed out into the sunlight.

2

It was Tully who thought up the trip to Manchester. The festival was advertised in the *NME* and John Peel had talked about it on the radio. We met in the Glebe. In those days, the patrons were pissed before first orders, and on every surface there were crumpled betting slips and stuffed ashtrays, full of stubbed cigarettes and bookies' pens. Ex-workers stared at the television, then into their flat pints.

We sat in the back bar at sewing tables rescued from a local factory. There was something heroic about Tully in his thirst for life. He bridged the old with the new and was on a mission to be morally alert. It was just the two of us that night. I walked through the fag smoke and saw him in the corner. He was wearing his 'We Are All Prostitutes' T-shirt and playing dominoes with a guy called Stedman McCalla. Now, the other men in the bar were heroic to Tully and me: they were sacked workers, mainly, guys who were struggling in a town that had just been designated an unemployment black spot. But Tully had unearthed an irony: they were victims, these veterans of the fight against Thatcher, but he was the first person I knew, and perhaps the only one, who saw they could also be victimisers. Tully understood that difficult things did not cancel out other difficult things. He had a taste for ambivalence, and I'd never met anybody before who possessed that so naturally. Steady McCalla was a Jamaican barber who had lived in Britain since 1959, when he'd arrived, aged twenty. He was a big man to us: he knew about reggae and he'd come to Southampton on the SS *Begoña* from Kingston, passing through, I still remember him telling us, Cartagena, then Puerto Cabello, and Port of Spain. He described the black funnel of the passenger ship. He told us about a spicy horse stew they ate when the boat left the Port of Vigo, the shebeen below decks, and his family's journey via Lambeth in London, where his cousin lived, to Glasgow, and the setting-up of a barber's shop in West Nile Street.

'Was it always like this?' Tully asked. 'Full of racist fuckers?'

'They don't know what it is they're doing,' Steady said. 'They're children. They're pickney. And children are rough.' Tully almost pestered him for information. When they'd first come to Scotland, Steady's father got a job working for the Corporation buses, but the union complained.

'You hear that?' Tully said to the guys at the bar. 'The Transport and General Workers' Union said they would all go on strike if men from Barbados and Jamaica were given jobs on the buses.'

One man turned and shook his head. It was the kind of complexity you never heard about round our way until Tully spoke about it. Steady drank a half-pint of beer and a rum and Coke every night in the Glebe, and none of those men, so far as I saw, ever spoke to him. They never included him or turned in his direction, but Tully made a point of going right over to him, offering him a drink, asking if the seat beside him was free. I'm sure Steady didn't want company, most of the time. But Tully needed those in the bar, those stalwarts, to know that they could cause pain, too, and that we all have our own wrongdoing to contend with. And Steady – who seemed old to us, though he was only in his late forties, with a sprinkling of grey in his moustache – was the best storyteller any of us had ever met and a figure of solid originality.

'Hey, Steady,' Tully said that night. 'I was telling Noodles the other day that your old man was a born footballer.'

'He was that,' Steady said. 'He had the touch, you see.'

'Like my old man,' Tully said.

'My papa could have gone professional. In a different life he could have played for a team, I am telling you. I grew up admiring all the sportsmen, especially the ones that did big overseas. I'm talking Lindy Delapenha, the footballer. Or Randy Turpin, the Fifties boxer. When they won, and when they scored, they were British, and when they lost, they were Caribbean!' He let out a huge bark and knocked on the table. After the dominoes, Steady waved us away to get on with reading his book.

'I just like the way he lives,' Tully said, at our new table in an empty corner, flicking through the *NME*.

It showed the brothers from the Jesus and Mary Chain sitting under a Gibson guitar. 'We can go and see these neds at the Barrowland,' Tully reasoned, 'playing for fifteen minutes with their backs to the audience, or we can go to Manchester for what is certain to be the best gig in history' – a celebration of punk rock, to be held at the new exhibition centre, G-Mex. 'It's ten years since the Sex Pistols played at the Lesser Free Trade Hall. And the night before G-Mex, the Shop Assistants are at the International.'

'Is that in Manchester as well?'

'Aye. So, there's that on the Friday, then on the Saturday it's New Order, the Smiths, the Fall, Magazine. About six other bands. I don't want to be funny, but if we miss it we might as well be dead.' He grabbed his jug by the dimples and slugged from it as if he'd just invented common sense.

'How much?' I asked.

'It's thirteen quid, Noodles.' (He called me Noodles after the Robert De Niro character in *Once Upon a Time in America*. Noodles was the childhood pal of the gangster Max, a name Tully occasionally took himself.) 'Don't worry about it,' he said. 'I have presented the options. I now rest my case. We're going to Manchester.'

Two years makes a big difference when you're eighteen. Tully was an employed twenty-year-old and he paid my way a lot. We agreed about the arrangements and drank several more glasses before Tully suddenly stood up. He walked over to the fireplace, where flames roared up the chimney despite nobody benefiting and the weather being fine. Quite casually, he threw into the fire a handful of firearm blanks that somebody in his factory had given him, then he pushed me by the arm over to the bar, and told me to watch. After a few minutes, loud eruptions in the fireplace caused the men at the bar to jump. It went off like a night of fireworks and the barman looked straight at Tully. We stepped back. The punters covered their mouths. 'Don't you two come back in here!' the barman was shouting. 'I mean it – you're barred!' That was pure Tully, too. He stood there with his arms out, the picture of innocence, the very soul of anarchy, and as we scrambled to the door we saw Steady in the corner, patting his chest with an open hand and nodding as if something agreeable had occurred.

. . .

As luck and menace would have it, the manager of the Job-centre offered me a job that week. It was only a summer thing. They'd seen me looking at the boards and decided, after a brief, eloquent interview during which I failed to mention Karl Marx, that a person so interested in poetry might be safer off the streets. The gig didn't last long, Tully made sure of that, and he would later describe it as my period being a junior commandant in the SS. 'On the other hand, I feel you might be able to corrupt it from the inside.'

'It's Irvine Jobcentre, Tully. Three dossers and a dog. Hardly the nerve centre of international capitalism.'

Wearing a tie and a sneer, I manned the Job Information Point. Not that we had any jobs: Thatcherism had passed through the town like the plagues of Exodus. We'd had blood and frogs, and were waiting for boils and locusts. One day, I was busily sorting through the box of non-jobs and arranging non-interviews for the long-term unemployed, when one of the executive officers, Mr Bike – a man with his shirt tail hang-ing out, a limp in his conscience, and a face fairly barnacled with acne – demanded that claimants who'd been out of work for more than two years be called in. 'What's he on about?' I said to the colleague next to me. She was painting her nails under the desk.

'The Final Solution,' she said, blowing her cerise fingertips. 'Over two years on the dole. Tebbit or some other bastard came up with this thing: they have to prove they're "actively looking for work".' She curled her digits, making quotes in the air. 'And if they can't prove it they get their benefit cut.'

'Shite.'

'They're "reducing" the unemployment figs.' And when she did the air quotes this time she reversed them into two Vs. 'Up yours.'

The first day of those interviews we faced a row of sleepy faces. Word came down from Mr Bike that we were to tell the claimants nothing. 'If they come in and say they're busy looking for work we have to accept it. But if they say they aren't, we can nab them.' I was already forging a plan to thwart him when I went into the interview room with the glass of water he'd demanded. There was a yucca plant and a coffee table bearing an aggressive box of tissues. The girl with the nails and I were posted outside with a clutch of ballpoint pens, checking people in and helping them fill in their forms. But we took pleasure in mangling Bike's message.

'Tell them you're obsessed with the jobs pages,' said my colleague, Rosa Luxemburg, the great insurgent, whom I now loved.

'That's right,' I said. 'And they can't touch your money. And it is your money.' Even a school-leaver with a vague interest in the Decadents could see it was a low moment in the annals of common decency.

'Are you tipping them off?' Bike asked me later that week.

'Not in the slightest.'

'We can come down on them like a ton of bricks if we discover they're at home sitting on their arses all day.'

'Nice work.'

'I've got my eye on you,' he said. 'I'm not sure you're cut out for this.'

• • •

Woodbine kept himself out of the way. He'd get home from the pub and go straight upstairs to the bedroom, where he kept an armchair, an ashtray, and a small black-and-white portable. He never objected much to me coming over after work and spending a lot of time at the house, as if it was just more chaos, more of Tully's way of doing things. Downstairs, Tully's mum, Barbara, and I formed a club, a do-it-yourself alliance, where we made a festival of the circumstances.

I phoned her one day from the office to ask if she had any Oxo cubes. She said she had two. Tully and I had agreed to meet at the bottom of Caldon Road at 6 p.m. and steal as many vegetables as we could on the way home. People had patches in their back gardens. It wasn't dark and we weren't very talented as thieves. Tully's method was a model of bravado and devil-may-care: he would open the gate, cough quite loudly, and walk up to the fenced-off beds and howk a turnip or a brace of carrots. I would be in the next garden over, fishing for a radish, and often a living room window would suddenly shake with banging from the inside as the part-time growers caught sight of us.

I'll never forget that soup. We dropped a huge load of vegetables on the kitchen table and Barbara couldn't believe her eyes. She borrowed an extra scraper from the woman next door. We laid newspapers on the floor for the peelings and peeled the veg with the radio up, Barbara chortling, getting two onions going in her biggest pot. 'We'll all end up in the jail because of you two,' she said, drying her eyes with the corner of her sleeve. Above us, on the wall, a picture of a crying boy offered comfort, or creepiness, depending on where you stood. Barbara had painted its frame with gleaming white gloss. Tully made the point, to general agreement, that it seemed excessively Scottish for every meal to be overseen by the image of a poor child in distress.

At one point, Woodbine came down the stairs and walked into the mayhem of peelings. 'It's like a Chinese laundry in here,' he said.

'It's Jimmy's broth,' Tully said.

I was sitting there in a shirt and tie and Tully still had his overalls on and Barbara was standing at the sink.

'Happy families,' Woodbine said.

Later, she carefully carried a tray upstairs to him, hoping he'd take some soup before the pub. She came back to watch telly with us, Tully and I taking turns to do the ironing and drop the items in a plastic basket.

I had never had a family like that. As the summer came, Barbara took to ringing me to make sure I was coming in for tea that night. She would see us off upstairs before ten o'clock to listen to John Peel's show, knowing our habits, and when I said every few days that I'd better go home to my own house, she would say fine, before laying out the plans for the days to come and what we'd eat and what we'd watch. Together, Tully and Barbara had made a quiet project of including me as my parents vanished. It never felt like a crisis, or in any way odd, because they called it staying over and framed it as part of the bid for good times. Tully's sister Fiona would sometimes be there with her boyfriend Scott, and she said the house was never livelier. 'You three should have your own show,' she said.

'It's the Marx Brothers,' Tully said. 'Mum's Harpo.'

I met Barbara on the stairs one night. Tully was asleep in his room and she was waiting for Woodbine to return. I fetched a glass of water and sat on the top step listening as she spoke about her husband, saying he used to be like Tully, a singer and someone who knew all the jokes and was great at telling them.

'Do you worry about him?' I asked.

'Oh, he's a pure pest,' she said. But she didn't mean it. She joined her hands, as if in prayer, and touched her lips with them. 'He goes out like this and you don't know if he's fallen down a hole or been hit by a bus, or what.'

'My mum never worried about my dad . . .'

'She must've at one time.'

'No.'

'Well, maybe he didn't love her enough.' She said it very sweetly, from knowledge: like it was the only kind of evidence that mattered.

'I never saw any love between them. Never once. Never saw them kiss each other or laugh together or plan a holiday. Nothing like that. I imagine they were put on earth just to make it smaller than it is.'

'That's a harsh comment,' she said.

'I know.'

'But it is weird of them just to go away like that.'

'Unbelievable,' I said. 'But they take no pleasure in family. They lost all the telephone numbers of their relatives in Glasgow, their aunts and uncles, their cousins. Lived by this sort of carelessness all their lives.'

'You're so young to be talking like this,' she said.

'I hope I'm not upsetting you. It's bad to upset people. Especially at night. You've been so kind to me, Barbara.'

'Oh, don't be daft,' she said. She clapped both my arms. She moved her hands up to my shoulders and onto my cheeks, and I turned my face, I think automatically, and pressed it against the palm of her hand. It was a few seconds' impulse, and felt natural and slightly wrong. 'Don't be daft,' she said again, pinching my ear and withdrawing her hands into the pockets of her dressing gown.

'You've got such good fun in you, Jimmy,' she said, looking into the black well at the bottom of the stairs. 'Let it rule the day. I've seen people's lives ruined with disappointment, people who wanted to go places.'

'I don't know,' I said. 'This is a place.'

She leaned against the stippled wallpaper, the Anaglypta, the stuff encasing our lives, and a shadow fell over her face as she looked at her watch. 'It's dark,' she said. She shook her head and talked for the better part of an hour. She recalled for me the younger Woodbine, back in the East End of Glasgow, in the days when he was hopeful and easy to love. She spoke of their first house, a 'room-and-kitchen'. In spite of everything, she seemed to say, remembering the good times was a duty of care. 'Ewan has these . . . episodes, the doctor calls them, when he loses it completely,' she said. 'He can get delusional. He thinks he's somebody else or has important tasks.'

'That's terrible,' I said.

'That's why I can't sleep. You never know.'

3

Tully had outside enemies, mainly the neighbours, who hated his music nearly as much as he loved it. On £27.50 a week for shaving a heap of metal, he'd built a record collection and a life of his own. His guitar was an instrument of torture to those around him, except to Barbara, who loved whatever he did. His bedroom was plastered with Killing Joke posters and one of a huge crucified Christ under the words 'If You're Gonna Get Down Get Down and Pray.' Again and again, we'd watch *The Godfather* or kitchen sink classics. A stack of videotapes stood next to a small amp on which he'd Tippexed 'Jobbies and Shites'. We knew the words to the films so well we'd often watch with the sound down, speaking the lines until Woodbine banged on the wall.

• • •

The trip to Manchester was brewing when Barbara had me over for a more formal dinner. In most families round our way, dinner was a secretive affair, a ritual to be executed around six o'clock, when a swift heating of pies, a resentful peeling of potatoes, and a stirring of beans would be carried out in an atmosphere of self-pity. But that night Barbara insisted there would be a bottle of wine. It was a nice evening, with the window open: kids played on the waste ground next to their terrace and you could hear the traffic roaring along the bypass. When Tully's dad came to the table, he laid his cigarettes next to his plate and took his specs from the pocket of his cardigan. He glanced at the picture of the crying boy, then he looked at me. 'What's that on your hand?' he asked.

It was covered in ink.

'Just things I noted down,' I said. 'It's a bad habit.'

'So you're going to the university after the summer?'

'Yes, Mr Dawson.'

'To study what?'

'English and Russian.' I don't know why I blushed, but it felt appropriate. He held his knife like a pen and seemed for a second unsure what to say. His lips moved a little with no sound. I could see Tully staring down at his mutilated curry pancake. His hair was flat (he only spiked it at weekends) and he wore a jumper with buttons on the shoulder. The atmosphere intensified when Barbara put some more mash on her husband's plate and left the spoon sticking up in the Pyrex dish.

'So I get less to eat than him?' he said, pointing to Tully's plate, 'because he's working?'

'Oh, Ewan!'

'These boys are taking over the house.'

There was a clang of cutlery.

'What you talking about, you old bastard?' Tully said. Barbara waved a dish towel over the table and poured more Concorde and that was signal enough. She asked me very

24

formally if Russian was a useful language to have and I told her things were changing in the Soviet Union. 'Maybe you could go there at the end of your studies,' she said. 'And if you still want to be a writer you could write the story.'

'Like John Reed,' Woodbine said quietly. 'He saw the Bolshevik Revolution. He wrote *Ten Days That Shook the World*, didn't he?' Tully glanced at him and I saw there was a touch of admiration along with everything else. He'd inherited much more from his father than either would ever be able to recognise. Woodbine's priorities were clear. He'd been a shop steward and a fan of Rangers FC.

'You want to watch yourself in the Soviet Union,' he added. 'Gulags. Spies.'

'He's only going to Strathclyde,' Tully said.

'One small step for man,' I said.

'You and your foreign travel,' Woodbine said, lighting one. There was still food on his plate but he pushed it away. 'Moscow. Glasgow. Manchester.' He turned to me and pointed with his lighted fag. '*The moon!* It's all a con.' He then talked about a brother of his who had worked for twenty years in the North Sea. 'You don't know anything about life until you've worked on the rigs.' He went out to the pub after that and left the three of us to wait for *Brookside* and an Arctic Roll.

'I've always meant to ask you, Barbara,' I said. 'Why is Tully called Tully? I mean, it's not his nickname, and it's usually a surname?'

'You're going to think I'm daft,' she said, 'but, when I was pregnant with him, I had a library book . . . a sort of romance,

25

you know. And the main guy in the book, the hero, was an Italian dancer called Tullius, who made it big in Monte Carlo.'

'Christ's sake, Mum. Noodles is going to think you're mad.'

'Well, maybe I am mad. They all called him Tully in the book. And I said to myself, "If this child's a boy he's getting called Tully. And he's going to be a brilliant dancer and take me to all the big casinos."'

She lifted her mug of tea and winked.

'That's worked out well,' Tully said.

'He was born with a caul around him. Did you know that, Jimmy? It's a special event for a baby to be born like that.'

'Shush, Mum,' he said.

• • •

Some days at the Jobcentre were like Darwin on springs. 'Survival of the lippiest,' I said to Rosa, who had come to work sporting red hair. Mid-morning, a mining engineer came in with a child in his arms. He said he'd been trying to get a position as an assistant in a local pet shop and they told him he didn't have enough experience. I informed the mutt-zoo manager, on the phone, that telling the engineer he was underqualified to change fish water was like the local minister telling God he was inexperienced.

'I'm going to c-complain to your b-boss,' he said.

'Knock yourself out.'

The day improved after that. One woman, five feet high with pink spectacles, who came in for her interview with Mr Bike, told me she wanted to work for NASA. I asked her if she'd written to the people at Cape Canaveral. 'Aye,' she said, 'and they havnae written back to me yet.' I felt there was a lot of weight on the word 'yet'. The lady admitted she had no experience in space aviation but was determined. 'I feel sorry for aw they astronauts that got blown up and I think they need new people, brave people.'

'Well, you are brave, Mrs Gunion. No question. When you go in for your interview, please tell my colleague what you have just told me, and perhaps add that you've looked into training opportunities in things . . . related to your chosen field. They're not allowed to cut your benefit if you're going after a particular career.'

'Well, I am,' she said. 'I willnae settle for anything else.'

'Right.'

'I love space.'

'Good for you.'

'It's ma dream. They cannae punish you for having a dream.'

'Well, they shouldn't, Mrs Gunion. That's for sure.'

'I've got aw the information.'

She was soon in the room with Mr Bike. My eyes were on the door. He would be asking her questions about cosmic gases, loving his job, testing her knowledge of landing gear and pressurised suits. 'So, Mrs Gunion, long-term claimant, you're in a space shuttle returning to Earth. The trip normally takes four hours at 17,500 miles per hour. We want you home thirty minutes later than scheduled. By how much are you reducing your speed of re-entry? Come on. You have one minute and can't use a calculator.'

It was my last day at the Jobcentre. It wasn't supposed to be, but I was sitting at my desk, contemplating the liquidation of Mr Bike, when Tully burst through the doors with an evil grin on his mug. He wore a green ex-army shirt, Levi's with turn-ups, brothel-creeper shoes, and more bangles than a Maasai bride. He ripped a card from the computer-assembly nonsense on the wall of jobs and slumped in the chair in front of me. *'It's a dog's life if you ask me,'* he said, quoting from one of our films, 'but I have a deep desire, much deeper than you can imagine, to play goal attack for the Irvine netball team. Any vacancies?'

'Let me have a look, sir.' I started flicking through the cards in my box. The film-reference game was going into full flight. *'You're not much good at netball, are you, Jo?'* I said. (*A Taste of Honey*.)

'No, I'm bad on purpose.' (The same.)

'But hold on,' I said. 'There's a sporting life opportunity here. Head of Keepy-Uppy at a school in Cowdenbeath.'

'It's a hard life if you don't weaken,' he said. (*Saturday Night*.)

He slumped back in the chair. 'You get more wisdom from one of those flicks than from the whole of Wullie Shakespeare.'

'Oh, you don't half love a cloth cap,' I said.

'I'm telling you. *Billy Liar* is better than *Hamlet*.'

'If you say so, Tully.'

'It is,' he said, smiling. 'Nicer people.'

Tully pulled five tickets from his back pocket. 'Check these, sucker.' They were white with black writing and my eye fell on the words 'Standing Area', 'Greater Manchester Exhibition Centre', and '£13 in advance'. I think my mouth dropped open before I looked up at the eager expression on his face.

'They came,' I said.

'Five tix. You, me, Tibbs, Limbo, and Hogg.'

'*You're a good man, Mr George.*' (*Mona Lisa.*)

'Here's yours,' he said, handing me a ticket. 'A present for passing your exams. Your education continues in the Rainy City.'

'Thanks, man. I can't believe it.'

'You're here to work, not gab, Mr Collins.' That was Bike, creeping up behind me in his unacceptable trousers. His plooks were angry and his eyes were pit-bull grey. 'The Enterprise Allowance Scheme,' he said, slapping a heap of white leaflets down on my desk. 'A wonderful project, already proving effective, aimed at getting your average layabout to start his own business.'

'*Don't let the bastards grind you down,*' Tully said, sitting in the chair opposite with one leg up on the desk.

'Who's the comedian?' Bike asked.

'A rare member of the full-time employed,' I said. 'A scholar and a gentleman. May I introduce my dear friend Tully Dawson, Professor of Dirty Tackles at the University of Mince and Bollocks.'

'Get your manky feet off that desk,' Bike said. 'It's government property that is.' With a despising look, he handed me a bundle. 'Take these leaflets and distribute them down the shopping centre. It shouldn't take more than an hour.'

'*I always was a liar, a good 'un and all,*' Tully said, and Bike just looked him up and down with narrowed eyes. He stood there with his legs apart and his arms folded over his Rotary Club tie, a born joy-crusher, an Eighties wretch. Every time he grinned a door slammed on some poor bugger's life.

'Quick march,' he said.

'Mussolini,' Tully said and popped his lips. Bike ignored him and started walking backwards, tapping his watch.

'The Job Club starts at 2 p.m. on the dot,' he said, 'and you're taking the seminar.'

'The seminar?' Tully said with a sneer. 'What – how to lick a stamp?'

'I'm watching you,' Bike said.

'I usually charge extra for that,' Tully said. I gathered my things and took the leaflets. I knew it was all over as we walked towards the exit.

'Two o'clock!' Bike shouted.

'How about you go and fuck yourself, ya Tory dick,' Tully shouted back, as I pushed him into the corridor.

We walked through the sunshine in search of Greggs pies and a can of Vimto. He carried the leaflets and I carried the pies, and we swerved round a congregation of Bible-thumpers at the entrance to the shopping centre and threaded through the schoolgirls on their way to What Every Woman Wants. Tully told me he'd found Woodbine outside the living room, in the middle of the night. 'He was shadow-boxing,' he said, 'and kind of butting his head against the banister. Then he ran up and down the stairs, drunk.'

'Really?'

'Another night, a while back, he thought he was on night

shift. He was out there burying old light bulbs in the garden.'

'Light bulbs?'

'Like a psycho.'

'Is there nobody who can help him?' I asked.

'I think he likes it.'

Going along the side of the Trinity Church, we hopped a fence and went to a favoured spot by the old graveyard. There was a high wall there and we sat on it with our legs dangling. The pies were hot but the Vimto was cold as we passed it back and forth, looking down at the River Irvine. 'Do you worry . . .'

'That I might become him?'

'That'll never happen.'

'I'm not so sure,' he said. 'Got to avoid it.'

Behind us, in the graveyard, lay the bones of Dainty Davie, friend of the poet Burns. We stayed quiet for a second, then I remarked on it. 'His name was David Sillar,' I said. 'Like Silver. A schoolteacher. This is a ghost town, man.'

He sang a line of the Specials song. 'Not like Manchester,' he added.

'We'll see. Every town's a ghost town.'

'All right, Morrissey.'

'I'm just saying we don't know what it'll be like.'

'Well, I definitely know,' Tully said. 'And Manchester is the business. I'm talking Ian Curtis and Shelagh Delaney.'

When I look back I detect a shudder in Tully's hopes for himself. The Manchester trip was only ten days away – ten days! – and he needed it to be glorious. I knew he loved his own band but I hadn't recognised the level of hope he had invested in it. He wanted the cover of the *NME* and a Peel session and a tour of Britain in a Bedford van. At that time, there was no other version of tomorrow that appealed to him. That July, it's the hope and the humour I remember first, but then the shudder, the sense of catastrophic consequences if his father's life was to become his.

The river was fast down there, with high flats on the other side. 'Did you see the look on that clown's face?' Tully said. 'The king of plooks back in your office.' We dreeped down the wall and made our way along a sunny path by the water, finding a spot by a hawthorn tree that stood on the bank, its colours fading. 'It's hard to believe a guy like that was ever young. He's like some Reggie Perrin dude with his mental tie.'

'Imagine having Norman Tebbit as your hero. What quagmire of depravity must you come from to think like that?'

Tully wiped his hands on one of the leaflets while spitting crust. 'No way, man. Where do you get that lingo? "Quagmire of depravity." Maybe they should hire you to improve this poxy shit.' He looked at the leaflet on top of the pile and we egged each other on.

'*Have You Got a Bright Idea? You Could Earn £40 Per Week.*'

There was a dazzle on the water. It was clear as silver bells beyond the nettles and the buttercups and the washed-out pinks dropping from the tree. Algae snagged on the rocks. We were full of fresh air and we had our tickets.

'I'm not going back to that Jobcentre dump,' I said.

'Nah. It was quite an Ian Curtis job, though. He worked in a place like that.'

'An unemployment exchange. No wonder he went the way he did. They gave me my wages today. I'm not going back.'

'Too right you're not. Enterprise, *my arse.*' High on the day's winnings, we dealt the remainder of the leaflets over the railings, laughing our heads off, and away to the Irish Sea went this flotilla of white lies. 'Boldly going where no man has gone before,' Tully said, 'the Starship *Enterprise* and its crew of wanks.' The papers drifted quickly away on the current and soon the river was clear again. I sometimes wake in the night and picture one of those leaflets floating peacefully to Nova Scotia.

4

Our friend Lincoln McCafferty had moved into a flat in Paisley. He shared it with two schizophrenic social workers and it was the dirtiest place we'd ever seen. For one thing, there was no bathroom. You had to go to the pub downstairs if you were desperate, which was okay because Limbo was in the Cotton Arms every hour it was open, manufacturing pee. His flat was a horror show of Victorian plumbing and zero sanitation, with just a single cold tap in the kitchen. It would be unfair to say the flat resembled a cave, unfair to caves – some of them have decent drawings – but it was a slum, surviving a number of bombing raids but struggling against the devastations wrought by Limbo.

He loved the flat on a point of principle. What it lacked in amenities it made up for in a huge stereo stack system with a double tape deck, housed in a smoked-glass cabinet, all of which came from a local electrical store called Stepek. He put together mix-tapes on that stereo, making them for everybody, so long as they didn't want any 'disco shite', revered the Exploited and agreed to pay upfront in cans of Kestrel or Breaker. If he did you an especially sought-after tape – John Peel's Festive 50 without the chat, for instance – you'd pay him in Red Stripe, with a possible bonus in Jack Daniel's.

Naturally, the tapes varied in quality, usually beginning well with Limbo carefully pressing 'Record' just as a track began, but by the end – when certain of his multiple down-payments had been tasted – your tape would turn into a rasping opera of Red Lorry Yellow Lorry and assorted feedback, punctuated with susurrations from the beloved DJ and liberal uses of the word 'fuck' as Limbo pressed the wrong button and broke unheralded into the programme.

It was the night before the journey to Manchester. Limbo's flat was the mustering point, or the scene of the first devastations. When Tully and Tibbs and I arrived from Paisley Gilmour Street station, he stuck his head out of the landing window and shouted, '*Get thee to a nunnery.*' We came up the broken stairs and found him at the door of the flat, wearing a striped T-shirt and a military coat, with a bottle of Eldorado poised before his open mouth. In moments like these, where everything was appropriate, Limbo would often quote from his favourite novel, *Brideshead Revisited*. In drink, he liked to be Anthony Blanche, but with a fierce Ayrshire accent and a Billy Idol-style curl of the lip. 'Hurry up, you small boys,' he said. '*I should like to stick you full of barbed arrows like a p-p-pin-cushion.*' All his life, Limbo was a standard-bearer for the perfectly surreal. For instance, he went to the swimming baths every day to brush his teeth but he never swam. 'Why would anybody swim?' he asked. 'If God had meant you to swim, he'd have given you the shoulders and the buttocks of Mark Spitz.'

On arrival, Tully gave him a slobbery kiss on the forehead

and told him to break out the hash or he'd wreck the place. Tibbs and I followed, Tibbs patting Limbo on the head and taking a slug from his bottle, and me bowing and tumbling my hand like a dandy before the Sun King. Limbo pushed me down the hallway after Tibbs – Tyrone Lennox, the apprentice postman, a bright and merciless comedian with a fringe flopping over his pale blue eyes, was somewhere to the left of Joseph Stalin. He felt that Celtic Football Club was the saviour of mankind. This was the cause of much consternation in others and much pride in him. He carried a Rucanor bag up the stairs, a bedroll jammed between its straps. He didn't own much, but he owned the room.

There was a two-bar fire and a smell of gloss paint. 'This is the un-living room,' Limbo said, squatting on a blue milk crate to build a joint. 'People have died in this room, long, long ago in the mists of Gothic time, before Lulu.'

'It's fuckan mingin in here, so it is,' Tibbs said, looking disgusted.

'I thought you'd be used to this,' offered Limbo, 'coming as your mammy does from a long line of impoverished *taigs*, over here to steal our totties.'

'Stop talking shite and hurry up with the doobie,' Tibbs said, grinning at the opposition and tossing his fringe out of his eyes. Without ceremony, or fear of objection, he drew out a tape from the pocket of his Harrington and stuck it into the stereo system. A master of the elaborate wind-up and the swift political assassination, he waited. He owned every single record and every T-shirt ever produced by Factory Records.

'I was fuckan listening to that,' Limbo said.

'Get it right up ye,' Tibbs said. 'Do you think I've taken two days off my work and am missing a regional meeting to spend my time listening to the New York Fuckan Dolls?' It wasn't really an argument. 'Yankee pish,' he added. Limbo gave him the finger while the music of A Certain Ratio came jigging into the air.

'Please, whatever you do – don't be shy,' Limbo said, as Tully took a slug of his Eldorado. 'Please make use of the facilities. In this establishment there's only one rule – if anybody draws a swastika on my forehead while I'm asleep, I'll fuckan kill them.'

'Seems fair,' I said.

'I can't promise anything,' Tully said. Lenin looked down from the wall above the electric fire and Tibbs began dancing and doing air trumpet in front of him, chugging the joint and spewing smoke like the battleship *Potemkin*.

'*I dunno, work tomorrow*,' Tibbs said, slipping into the film-reference game. But Limbo had his own films. As was customary, he came back with a quote from the lower regions of *The Exorcist*. In any given situation, he felt the horror classics best said what had to be said.

'*D'you know what she did, your cunting daughter?*' He sat on the floor hugging a cushion, sneering for an imagined camera.

'Who else is coming to Manchester?' he asked.

'It's not who's coming, it's who's there,' Tibbs said. 'Friedrich Engels and Pat Phoenix from *Coronation Street*.'

'And Piccadilly Records,' said Limbo. 'We're going there

straight away. Soon as we get off the bus, man. I've looked it up.'

'Magic,' Tully said. 'Best independent record shop in Britain.'

We were all obsessed with record shops. The major churches of the British Isles, with their stained glass, rood screens, and flying buttresses, were as nothing next to some grubby black box under Central Station, or some rabbit hutch in Manchester, which sold imports, fanzines, and gobbets of gig information.

'Soon as we get off the bus,' Limbo said again.

'Abso-fuckan-lutely,' Tibbs said, before adding the words, 'England is getting rode.' The room erupted into song.

'Getting rode, getting rode, getting rode. England is getting ro-o-ode. England is getting rode. Getting ro-o-ode. Get-ting rode!'

'Whatever you say,' I said, sitting this one out.

There were differences. I make much of the camaraderie, but it's often differences that keep the conversation lively, especially among the similar. Most of the boys were older than me – it showed in the money – and we'd all gone to different schools, some Catholic, some Protestant. We all lived on housing schemes, except for Limbo and another pal, Caesar, who lived in Spam Valley. Limbo's father was a professor of architecture, and hopeful, I think, that Lincoln would follow him into the ranks. Sadly, or hilariously, Limbo's current living arrangements could only sneer at such hopes.

Last to arrive that night was David Hogg – cropped,

peroxided hair, and wearing a sixteen-eye pair of Doc Martens, a biker's jacket, and a Test Dept T-shirt. Hogg's stock-in-trade was contempt: he gave us all the finger as he came in, then slid down the wall. Even as a boy he wasn't fully comfortable with those he spent time with: he thought we were idiots, which was reasonable enough. I think he was the first person I knew to speak with a kind of upswing at the end of everything he said. He lived in Pollok and worked for British Shipbuilders, which everybody still called Fairfields, though that company was long gone. Hogg was nicer in himself than he was outwardly, if you got him on his own. That's what I thought anyway. He was keen to cordon himself off, as though he was moving on, and perhaps he was, with his good watch and his girlfriend. After he'd been in the flat for half an hour, he started wandering around and rootling in the so-called kitchen, taking out spoons and stuff and making a sort of construction with the utensils.

'You bored, Davie?' Tully said.

'I'm just making something.' By now he'd found two tins of paint under one of the beds and an old paraffin heater on the landing.

'He's an artist,' I said, taking the piss. 'Best leave Hogg to his engineering. I think it's a jazz exploration of England in D minor.'

'What's England ever done for any of you?' Tully asked.

'George Orwell. Factory Records. *Brookside*,' Tibbs said.

'Test Dept,' Hogg said, opening one of the tins.

'Hammer Horror,' Limbo said, 'and the Magna Carta.'

Hogg stayed in the flat by himself when we went to the pub. The whole of Paisley smelled of vinegar and the evening was almost warm. But weather is one thing and regulars are another and you could say it was hostile to groups of lads in the Cotton Arms. In fact, if looks were bullets, it was the St Valentine's Day Massacre: the four of us sauntering in with similar haircuts and jeans and all confident-like. The barman lashed a dish towel over his shoulder and poured four pints of Tennent's, his eyes on us, then we carried them over to a table. Photographs of old mills and weavers' rallies were hung around the walls and above the bar ran the legend 'Pain Inflicted, Suffering Endured, Injustice Done'. At the other tables, men scowled and licked their chops in preparation. The women wore so much jewellery they jangled every time they lifted their drinks, their glances quite pitying and the gold so brassy it was almost red. Bad vibes can be an excellent spur: they can make you exist a bit more vividly in a strange room, at least that was my thinking, my hope, as some gigantic guy blocked me on my way to the bog. A neon sign for Schlitz played havoc with his angry eyes and his nightmare shirt. 'This is *oor* pub,' he said.

'Em, by whose decree?' I asked. 'This is a *public* bar.' He looked at me for what felt like 150 years. Then he sniggered, snorted, huffed, and swayed, before wetting his middle finger and sticking it in my ear.

'Aye, but – wi' private security,' he said, wiggling his finger.

'Look, mate,' I said, my heart thumping. 'We're just out for a drink. Not looking for any trouble at all.'

'But we are,' he said. 'We *love* trouble.'

'Em. I totally sympathise.' Nervous laughter. 'Trouble has its own, em . . . charm. Undoubtedly. I mean, personally, I can't understand why anybody wouldn't love trouble. It's just such an underrated—'

'Stop. Talking. Ya. Dick.'

'Of course—'

'Shut. It.'

He inspected me and flicked my collar, like a lion toying with a dead gazelle. He inclined his head and I thought, This is it, he's going to nut me. At any second his large head would be crashing into mine, and I'd be out forever. Smithereens. 'What are you, anyway?' he said. 'Some kind of university study group?'

'No, just—'

'Shut. Up.' But while he stared, his rictus became a smile. 'I'll let you off,' he said eventually, and tapped my shoulder as he left. Such is the mercy of kings, gods, psychopaths, and lions, so savage in fury, so benign in forgiveness.

It marked no obvious change in the pub's atmosphere. Broiling and pissed-up like the Rangers end on a Saturday, it seemed to grow hotter with delayed violence, and we were surrounded by ill-wishers of every stripe, looking over. Tully, being a specialist in the reversal of obvious outcomes, took on the threat by standing up on a chair and performing what I can only describe as a deconstruction of the Glasgow pub song. He did it with his eyes closed and his hand on his twenty-year-old heart.

'Aw, *je suis*. Origami. Vertigo,' he sang.

'Who the fuck is that tube?' said the guy with the angry eyes.

'Aw, *je suis* . . .'

'Would somebody just lamp him.'

'Aw, *je suis*. Origami. Vertigo.'

Tully in his happy hour. He sang it about twenty times, and the atmosphere in the pub gradually changed and people started to laugh. I'd never seen a performance like it. He had the Glasgow singing style down pat, the well of sorrow, the swell of sentiment, the average passion raised to a wobbly vibrato.

'Aw, *je suiseeeeeeee*. Origami-i-i-i-i-i-i-i. Vert-i-go-o-o-o-o.'

Originality is a gambler, and Tully stepped down from his chair the best sort of hero, the best sort of hero in those parts, a comedian. The lords of extinction were suddenly on our side and the drink flowed and the ashtray was full.

'I've worked out a plan, so I have,' Tibbs said.

'For what?'

'The weekend. There's tomorrow and there's Saturday. The bus gets into Manchester just after two.' He spread a few beer mats on the table. It was like General Patton planning the advance of the Third Army through France. 'We go to Piccadilly Records. We hit the town centre for a few beers. We get some grub on our way to the International Club and we go and see the Shop Assistants. I don't know where we sleep. So that's tomorrow. On Saturday we go round the shops.'

'Fuck the shops,' Tully said. 'I want to see Manchester.'

'Obviously,' Tibbs said.

'What time at G-Mex for the gig on Saturday?' I asked.

'All-dayer, but nothing will happen before two,' Tully said. 'And we're going to have the daftest time anybody's ever had in history,' he said. 'Then we go to the Hacienda. Then we lie down and then we die.'

. • • •

At closing time we went back to the flat with chips. On the way up the street, Limbo was drunkenly advertising his cultural programme. 'I want to announce the forthcoming publication of my first novel,' he said. 'A masterpiece of sadistic philosophy. It will blow the lid off the literary world. It is called *The Sausage*.'

'Eat your heart out, *A Clockwork Orange*,' Tully said.

At this Limbo pulled a Curly Wurly from his pocket and tore it open with his teeth as he staggered towards his building. No light on the stairs, a kerfuffle of boots in the hall, and then Hogg, standing in the middle of the living room with a joint in one hand and a dripping paintbrush in the other. Over the walls and the ceiling he'd repeatedly daubed the word 'Nag, Nag, Nag' in yellow paint. A naked light bulb was overhead and you could see the blobs of paint in Hogg's hair and down his legs and over the floor. 'How about it?' he said. 'I am the Jackson of Pollok.'

5

At the back of the bus, wee Tibbs was offering a lecture on Margaret Thatcher's poisonous relations with South Africa. 'If she doesn't agree to sanctions,' he said, 'I hope every African nation boycotts the Commonwealth Games. What are the Games anyhow but the burning embers of British imperialism?'

'That'll be bad for Edinburgh,' Hogg said. This was a very adult comment, so it led almost instantly to a general onslaught on his recently purchased car. Limbo called it the Poser Mobile and Tully called it the Shaggin' Wagon and Hogg was defensive. 'It's a silver Capri,' he said, 'a perfectly respectable motor. You're all jealous.'

'It's a dick-mobile, David,' I said. 'If you're going to drive a Capri you might as well grow a moustache and call yourself Gavin.'

'That's horribly true,' said Limbo. He wasn't saying much. He was reading a copy of the *Daily Record* as if it was Plato's *Republic*. He was also drinking quite heavily from an unpronounceable half-bottle of vodka.

'And you can fuck off,' Hogg said. 'None of you clowns has even passed your test. And you have the cheek to slag off my motor.'

'Fuck your motor,' Tibbs said. 'We're talking about South Africa. And I'm saying the world should jump on Thatcher's head if she still opposes sanctions.'

'And I'm saying that will fuck up the chance for Edinburgh to make a few quid.' He was still nettled. 'None of you pays any taxes.' He nodded to me. 'He's just out of school, Limbo's a fuckan layabout.'

'Why, thank you, sir,' Limbo said, not looking up.

'And Tully and Tibbs—'

'We pay our taxes!' Tibbs interrupted. 'We don't earn what you earn. But you'd probably side wi' the National Coal Board.'

'As I was saying,' Hogg continued, 'you're not adults.'

The egocentric strategies of childhood don't always go on to become adult traits, but I think we all believed, pretty instinctively, that they would with Hogg. We could see him on a hill somewhere, looking down on us with his finer knowledge and his hire-purchase Capri, but our senses agreed that the loss was his.

'To fuck with Edinburgh,' Tibbs said. We settled back and looked out the window at the passing high-rises, and Tibbs again took his G-Mex ticket out of his jacket pocket to examine it. 'I wish Manchester was in Scotland,' he said. 'I mean – the Fall, New Order, the Smiths. It's a nuclear fuckfest of musical talent.' He turned the ticket over in his hands and then he kissed it right in the middle.

Tully stood up and beamed over the back of his seat. 'He's like Willy Wonka holding the golden ticket,' he said.

'Charlie,' I said. 'It's Charlie that gets the ticket. Wonka is the weirdo who owns the factory.'

'Capitalist pig,' Tibbs said.

We talked a lot about the festival and Tibbs obsessed every now and then about what he was calling 'the plan' – where we'd go, in what order, and what we'd see and how. He'd rehearsed the list again and augmented it, but it was sparse of practical contingencies, like eating, sleeping, and washing, and remained heavy on verbs associated with drinking, seeing, and finding girls who might be up for a snog.

Only three of us brought bags: Hogg, Tibbs, and me. Thinking about it now, I see how young we were, wanting our clean T-shirts. The bags were a pain all weekend, lying under tables, being left behind. Hogg and I had matching tartan duffel bags, his red and mine green. His was full of tapes and snacks. Mine was full of toothpaste, changes of clothes, and a book I never took back to the library. Tully had a toothbrush in the top pocket of his leather jacket and Limbo had no items at all. 'Jesus,' Tully said, 'you're like a caravan of gypsies with all this crap to drag around.'

'Not me,' Limbo said. 'I travel light.'

In Limbo's flat, I'd done my best under the freezing tap with a lump of Imperial Leather. The result: I was sleek as a week in Saint-Tropez. The situation: both ears were scrubbed, the neck was pristine, and the excess lather was holding up the quiff. I wore jeans with turn-ups and a Harrington my mother had got me from Kays Catalogue, plus a white T-shirt, and black suede shoes I'd borrowed from Tully.

A conversation began about which instrument Karl Marx would play if he was in the Fall. It grew instantly heated. 'He'd play the glockenspiel,' Hogg said. 'Because he's German and it's about banging metal. An industrial sound, and that fits with what he says about the means of production. Definitely the glockenspiel.'

'You're full of shite, so you are,' Tibbs said. 'That instrument . . .'

'Glockenspiel.'

'Aye, that. Marx would never play it. Totally bourgeois piece of shit. And Mark E. would never have it in the band. He'd sack him. Even if it was Marx and he agreed with him about the proletariat and all that, he'd boot him out. He could play the bass. A good, solid bass player in the Fall, that's Marx.'

'Glockenspiel.'

'I'm going to put your head through that fuckan window if you say it one more time,' Tibbs said. 'There isn't one good song featuring that thing.'

'Wrong. John Lennon uses it in "Only a Northern Song".'

'It's a hippy contraption.'

'Glock—'

Hogg jumped out of the way to avoid Tibbs's fist. Both were grinning. 'I'm actually going to batter you, Davie.' It had always been a comical fact about Tibbs: he mentioned violence but he never remotely engaged in any. It was part of the comedy of teenage life to threaten people with 'a doing' you couldn't really imagine. 'It's the Catholic laziness ethic,' Tibbs said when I questioned him about it. 'You see it in football quite a lot. We like to get angry but we're too lazy to fight.'

We were soft as Tunnock's Teacakes, sentimental as sherbet.

Tully tried to lighten the mood by introducing the subject of Sheila Grant and the rape storyline on *Brookside*. At the time, we were all addicted to the Liverpool soap opera and it took up a fair amount of our conversation. Limbo suddenly perked up. 'I'm with the popular newspaper columnist Joan Burnie,' he said. '*Brookside* is not just soap opera. It is social commentary of the highest order.'

'Hear, hear,' I said. Limbo had gone all academic. I was never sure if he did this in tribute to his father or just as general mockery.

'It seems obvious,' he went on, 'that *Brookside* speaks to the national mood in terms of the decimation of our communities, and it addresses our latent, vicious attitudes towards women and other vulnerable groups.'

'Shut your face,' Tibbs said. 'This is serious.'

'How come nobody thinks I'm serious when I'm serious?' Limbo asked, twisting round when Tully slapped the back of his head.

There was much shouting, a bottle of Merrydown cider was doing the rounds, then Tully announced a brand-new Top Three, our main method of assessing character. 'Name your top three best films starring Robert De Niro.'

'Too easy,' I said. '*The Godfather, Part II. Taxi Driver.* And *Once Upon a Time in America.*'

'Only a wearer of arseless chaps would leave out *Raging Bull*,' Tibbs said.

'Good point,' Tully said, stubbing out a fag.

'Top three best goals ever scored by a Scottish player,' Tibbs said.

In unison: 'Archie Gemmill.'

'Too obvious,' he said.

'Have there *been* three goals?' I asked.

'Fuckan traitor,' Hogg said. (Still not over the motor.)

'Check it out,' Tully said. 'Number one . . . the other Gemmell.'

'Celtic versus Inter Milan, 1967 European Cup Final,' Tibbs said.

'Aye,' Tully replied. 'I hate the Pope's Eleven, but that was a brilliant goal.'

Tibbs stood up and put his hands out, swaying with the bus. He was excited and when Tibbs was excited he flushed like a newborn. His eyes were staring out so blue at the memory of a world-shaping triumph. 'After going down one-nil,' he said, 'Gemmell's goal totally demoralised the Milan players and led to the Celtic victory.'

'Fine,' Tully said. 'That's number one. Number two is Kenny Dalglish's goal for Liverpool against FC Bruges in the 1978 Cup Final.'

'That's never a best Scottish goal,' Tibbs said. 'It's not even one of the best from Dalglish.'

'Is it your Top Three or mine?' Tully asked.

'What about Kenny's goal for Scotland in the World Cup play-off at Anfield against Wales?'

'Shut it, Tibbs!' Tully threw his arms up then slouched

back against the window. He looked round at the rest of us and said, 'What a prick. It's my shout.' When it came to football lore, Tibbs could enter a reverie. He wasn't even on the bus any more. He was on some celestial pitch that lies deep behind Kenny Cloud Nine.

'I declare this Top Three null and void,' Tully said.

'I'm talking about 12 October 1977,' Tibbs went on. 'Scotland were one up from a controversial penalty before Martin Buchan – by the grace of Mary – sent in a beautiful cross which Kenny headed into the net.' Tibbs crossed his arms and walked with great concentration down the bus, explaining to the other passengers, most of whom averted their eyes and held on to their bags, the effect of this goal on world events. 'This particular header,' he said, 'sent Scotland to the 1978 World Cup in Argentina. Now . . .'

'Here we go,' Tully said.

'. . . though this was one of my favourite Scottish goals ever,' Tibbs continued, 'it inadvertently led to the rise of Thatcherism and all its horrors.'

'Oh, take me to Cuba,' Tully said. 'Lay me down in the Bay of Pigs.'

Tyrone Lennox was on a roll. 'In 1978,' he said, 'Ally MacLeod whipped the whole nation into a patriotic frenzy so he did, which ended in ignominy and humiliation. The aftermath of the Argentina campaign is widely accepted to be the main reason the Scottish devolution bill failed in the referendum of March 1979. This led to the Scottish Nationalists withdrawing support for the minority Labour government and a subsequent vote of "no confidence" led to the election won by Margaret Thatcher.'

He was a juggernaut of reason.

'Open-and-shut case,' Tully said. 'Goal makes Dole.'

Cheers.

Looks of amazement.

'You're all wrong,' Hogg said. 'The best Dalglish goal was against England at Hampden in 1976.'

'Right through the goalie's legs!' Tully shouted.

'Precisely,' Hogg said. 'A miracle.'

'I think that goal led directly to the independence of Djibouti,' Tibbs said, smiling, 'and the election of Jimmy Carter as president.'

· · ·

Everybody needed to pee when we got to Gretna Green. Limbo was lively again, so there was piss-fencing at the urinals. Tully wanted Lucozade and came out of the garage with a small bottle and an armful of cheese and onion crisps. I was lying on a grass verge staring at the sun. He chucked me a packet. 'What you thinking about, Noodles?'

'I can't wait to get there.'

'I know, man, it's going to be bananas. No way was I missing it, not for anything. Even if they wanted me to stay . . .'

'Who's "they"?' I asked. He rolled the Lucozade bottle between his palms and frowned as he shook his head. 'Forget it, man.'

I stood up. 'Where will we sleep in Manchester?'

'I'm sure they've got park benches. Your old pal here'll take care of you.'

Loyalty came easily to Tully. Love was the politics that kept him going. I wanted to read for a while and he winked when I said I'd find a seat on my own. 'Stay free,' he said. The sun was behind him, and when I wiped the grass off my hands and went to climb back on the bus, it blocked him out and glinted off his bangles. I looked over at the trees. Everything was new and everything was fresh. The service station was surrounded by Scots pines; a breeze came through them and you could sense the border. I don't think the pines registered then, but they do now, reminding me of the English classroom, Mrs O'Connor and her red hair, Yeats's 'Sailing to Byzantium' – and those final trees, somewhere in the future, where we climbed the hill and the scent said *memento mori*.

6

The fields gradually turned to red brick, the road giving out to streets, to multiple signs and office buildings and people walking by. When I thought of England as a child it was always of somewhere on the other side of the afternoon's horizon, a kind of sweet-tempered, wholly imagined Arcadia, where people read books to their children and baked cakes for them. It wasn't really England at all, but a sort of fantasy of well-being that came with the word 'foreign'.

We came into Manchester like air into Xanadu. The place was a state of mind to us and we saw cascades of glitter in ordinary things. Portland Street was wide open and the buses – '*Macclesfield*', '*Cheetham Hill*' – rumbled past as we crossed the road and turned the corner and tried to establish our bearings. Piccadilly Records was part of a dowdy strip next to Piccadilly Gardens, but it felt like the headquarters of high taste, full of nodding young worshippers flicking through the bins. It was just after 3 p.m. when we came in, and Limbo was talking to no one in particular. 'If Jesus Christ had done cool stuff,' he said, 'like if he'd starred in *The Driller Killer* or directed *I Spit on Your Grave*, then I would be like John the Baptist, telling everybody to sign up.'

'You are the pagan Pope,' Tully said.

'Better than no Pope at all,' said Tibbs.

The guy behind the counter frowned as we entered. He was playing a song by the Ex about the Spanish Civil War and Tibbs went to shake his hand and the guy avoided it by straightening up and clasping his hands behind his head. He was cool and his jacket had nothing of the home catalogue about it.

'*Live on your feet*,' Tibbs Lennox sang, smiling and bobbing. He pointed in the faces of nearby customers. '*For* no one *is a slave*.'

'Safe,' said the shopkeeper-guy. 'But we're all out of Kaja-googoo, if that's what you boys are looking for.'

'Very funny,' Tibbs said.

'Where you lot from?' asked a guy leaning on the counter. He had mirror badges on a white denim jacket and a feather earring.

'They're from Rottenrow,' Tully said to him. 'I'm from Los Angeles.'

'Here for G-Mex?'

'They are,' Tully replied. 'I'm here for the ale. For the revolution. And for hot dalliances with the ladies of the vicinity.'

The shopkeeper rolled his eyes and reached for the turntable, putting on a new single by the Wedding Present.

'He got a D in home economics,' Limbo said to the customer. He rubbed Tully's hair just to show them that we knew how to be friendly.

'Watch the barnet, ya dickpiece,' Tully said.

'He's a bit on the touchy side,' the customer said.

'He doesn't know the capital of France,' Limbo said, pointing at Tully. 'He's king of the remedial class. The Funny Farm. Very sad.'

'Shut it,' Tully said.

'What you doing tonight?' the customer asked.

'Shop Assistants,' I said. 'At the International.'

The customer flicked his earring and gave a look to the shopkeeper-guy. 'Foof,' he said, as if we'd just fallen into a swamp.

The shopkeeper looked on, bored senseless by way of profession.

'Shambling post-punk garbage,' he said.

Tully looked at him. 'Jesus Christ, mate. Are you trying to sell records, or what? I congratulate you on being the World's Worst Capitalist.'

'You're welcome,' said the shopkeeper-guy. At that point, Tully turned to a girl with black lipstick who was flicking through the LPs.

'Do you know any good pubs round here?' he asked. 'We're only here for the beer.'

'Different from Scotland. Pubs shut at three,' she said.

'What?'

'English drinking hours.'

'Shit, I hadn't thought of that,' I said.

'We need to set ourselves up,' Tully said impatiently. 'Make a plan. Find out where the drink is and find out where this gig is tonight.'

The boys spread over the shop like a contagion of acumen.

The LPs in the bins had handwritten comments by the staff. 'No other sound matters,' one of them had scrawled and pinned to a Velvet Underground album. 'The truth. The dark-ness. More.' On a UK Subs record they had written, 'Vulgarity rules'. The walls were covered in posters Blu-Tacked next to adverts for used guitars and bands seeking singers. 'Influences: Dolls, Ziggy, Morrissey.' Limbo leaned against a Hüsker Dü poster and slugged from a quarter-bottle of whisky. I was inspecting the run-out groove on a single when he started blethering and guffawing like a madman and sort of dancing. Nothing made sense. 'Like James Dean, like James Dean, like James Dean, you're a penis.'

'Ah, modern poetry,' I said. 'Is it Ezra Pound?' He lunged across the shop and got me in a headlock, pressing the bottle on me.

'You're boyishly handsome yet tensely American,' he mewled, 'but would you survive in the trenches, *mon frère*? I fear not. Get a large dug up you.'

'Is he saying *dog*?' asked Feather Earring.

'I'm afraid so.'

'Sorry to geg in, lads,' the shopkeeper-guy said. 'But could you just eff off now out of the shop? You're causing chaos.'

'Thought that was the point, mister,' Limbo said.

Ignoring the shopkeeper's main point, or embodying it, Tully leaned both arms on the counter to explain in florid detail how Prince was shite. Hogg was, by this point, rum-maging in his bag for money, ready to spend a week's wages on German imports by Einstürzende Neubauten. He placed an example on the counter, *Wrench*, the bootleg of a gig in Japan where the band tore up the stage with power drills.

'Forget the Purple One,' Tully said to the shopkeeper, concluding his case, 'this guy prefers bands who make their own instruments.'

'Commercially available instruments,' Hogg replied, very solemnly, 'are a panacea to the assumptions of the bourgeois class.'

'A bit like your Capri,' Tully said, heading for the door.

'Fuck off.'

Hogg wasn't getting much joy from the shopkeeper, but he hung around for another minute or two, scavenging for status, I chose to imagine, or hoping for a sudden, late flowering of admiration. Receiving neither, and fed up with the guy's attitude, he swung his bag of self-defining treats and left the shop.

I walked up to the counter. Limbo was buying a badge. He was hopping on the spot with mysterious anticipation. Taking the money, the shopkeeper rolled his eyes. 'I've heard it all before,' he said. 'Weekend punks on the lash.'

Limbo wandered to the threshold, then turned around. 'Dear sir,' he said. 'Please do me the honour of getting a dug up you!'

I was the only one of the Scots left in the shop. I'd deliberately hung back to talk to him and get information about where to go. I lifted one of the fanzines from the counter and flicked through it, then paid in silence. I always got nervous in record shops. The last two customers left and the shopkeeper seemed relieved.

'I'm sorry for all the ruckus,' I said.

'Don't worry about it. It's the Festival of the Tenth Summer. Was always going to happen.'

'Are you involved in it?'

He gripped the black counter and smiled for the first time since we'd come in. 'I was one of the advisers,' he said. 'And you wouldn't believe the meetings. Organisers talking about postmodernism. Talking about praxis. And when it comes down to it, it's just a horde of pissed lads like you lot roaming around the city.' I smirked as he shook his head and started shelving records behind him.

'So, where do we go?' I asked.

'Mess about for a bit, then go to the Britannia Hotel.' He shook his head again and I thanked him.

• • •

I felt I was already one of the necessary people of the city. Standing outside the record shop, in the warmth, in the haze, I could see the warehouses and department stores overlooking Piccadilly Gardens. I tried to picture the workers inside those buildings, and wondered if they too were excited for the weekend. The hedge across from me was somehow greener than the average hedge and the road was busy with buses and Manchester was everything. I just paused for a second, standing there, and realised I was 'in it', part of the city right then, and part of the history we were here to celebrate. Whether illusory or not, a huge democratic feeling arrived on the air and I breathed it in before going in search of the others.

They were just down the street, in Spudulike. Problem: they didn't allow drinking inside the shop and Limbo had found a possible supplier of cider. 'What if I pour it into paper cups?' he asked the girl at the till, while making signals to a home-less-looking man outside the window.

'Nah, mate,' the girl said. 'I'll get the sack.'

'Just forget about it, Limbo,' Tibbs said. He turned to the girl. 'I'm Tyrone.' When they got talking, he asked her if she preferred *A Taste of Honey* or *This Sporting Life*, like it was a crucial question for everyone. He didn't get far with that so he asked her if she knew the location of the venue for that night's gig.

'Come again?' she said.

'The International Club. That's tonight. Tomorrow we're heading to the Festival of the Tenth Summer, at G-Mex.'

'The tenth what?'

'Anniversary of punk rock,' he said. 'But that's tomorrow. Like I say, tonight we're heading to the International.'

She pondered. 'Oh, I know . . .' She looked over her shoul-der and shouted to the middle-aged lady decanting the coleslaw. 'Mavis, these lads are heading to the International in a bit. That's in Rusholme, aren't it?' She didn't wait for a reply and told us she went swimming near there. 'It's in Anson Road,' she added. Tibbs then chanced his arm and asked for her phone number but she just stared at him.

'Come on,' he said.

'Shurrup and go and eat your spud,' she said. 'Lovely eyes, though. I know what you Scottish lads are like.'

'Okay,' he said. 'I'm not being cheeky, but can we stay at yours tonight? We're out-of-towners without a pillow between us.'

'You must be mad.' She lifted a few dirty trays before going behind the hatch to join Mavis.

'I'm definitely on my own in this world,' Tibbs said.

Soon Tibbs, Hogg, Tully, and I were driving the plastic knives and forks deep into the slurry of our Styrofoam boxes. But Limbo could not be told – it was a general rule in our lives – so in fifteen minutes or so he returned to the shop, not with the promised cider but with a bottle of red wine, which had emerged from his negotiations with the dosser outside. He was grinning as if this happy outcome had been written in the stars. The wine said Fitou on the label and it was already open.

'Guy had his own corkscrew,' Limbo said.

'First-class service,' said Tully, his box lid squeaking as he closed it. Then he climbed out of the booth and sauntered up to the serving hatch to charm the girl for cups. He also got her phone number.

'Fuckan dimples,' Tibbs said.

Tully set up two cups in front of us. I can still see them: the two cups full of Limbo's wine now sitting forever on the table.

'What's Fitou?' I asked.

'It's red wine they produce in Motherwell,' Tully joked, gulping from one and then sipping from the other and passing them round.

Suddenly there was a figure standing by our table. It was

Bobby McCloy, alias Dr Clogs, an Ayrshire comrade. He was unexpected.

'Okay, fuckwits. Here we are in Manchester,' Dr Clogs said, 'home of the Hacienda. What's the script?'

'Jesus Christ, Clogs,' Tully said. 'How did you know where to find us?'

'It doesn't take Sherlock Holmes,' he said. 'Piccadilly Records. I knew you were on the ten o'clock bus. Your mother grassed on you.'

Top marks to him: he'd found out our whole itinerary on the grapevine and just showed up. He offered very little in the way of explanation. He grinned, and from his inside pocket he produced a noxious sherry-like liquid called Four Crown, a favourite, Tully insisted, among Glasgow tramps.

'Give us a slug,' Tibbs said, taking the bottle.

'And you scored a ticket?' I said, looking at Clogs.

'Had one for months,' he said. He touched the side of his nose. 'Keeping it dark, young James. You never know who's watching you.' He dragged over a chair and sat there like Che Guevara in his jungle threads: camouflage jacket, green army shirt, black jeans, beetle-crusher shoes.

'You're a brilliant fuckan weirdo,' Tully said.

Our friend believed chiefly in the Birthday Party and Kraftwerk. His other main obsession was the Apple II computer humming in his dad's garage. He dyed his hair black, as many did, and had small tolerance for the small-minded, being generally ill-disposed to people in general, or people he wasn't already on bottle-sharing and swearing terms with. He could be entertainingly dismissive in a deadpan way and his stock-in-trade was mockery. Mainly, he was independent. He sat inside the house playing Metroid for the second half of the Eighties, learning how to code.

'Welcome, Clogs, to this band of brothers,' said Limbo. 'We have a plan to deflower the city and not sleep for forty-eight hours.'

'Speak for yourself,' I said. 'I fully intend to repair to that park over the way in a minute and settle down for an afternoon nap.'

'Poof,' Limbo said, knocking back a cup of wine and breaking into a horrible song called 'We Built This City'.

'What's that?' Tully asked, flicking one of the newcomer's badges.

'A rare token of New York's subculture,' Clogs said, unscrewing the cap of his sherry. 'As you well know, it's no optical illusion. If I'm not mistaken, wee man, it says "Patti Smith, *Horses*".'

'Horses, horses – *horseshit*,' Tully said. He took the bottle off him and had a swig. 'You'll be arguing for David Bowie next.'

'And all these badges,' Tibbs added, 'are a complete betrayal of the British working class. Not a single one for the miners.'

'He probably loves Ronald Reagan,' I added, looking into a mess of beans. 'I feel Clogs has strayed very far from the programme and is guilty of crimes.' Tibbs rapped the table and shook his head in mock dismay.

'Thought crimes, so it is,' he said.

'Badge crimes,' Tully said. At which point Limbo got up on the table and addressed the tattie-customers in their loosened ties.

'Oyez, oyez,' he said. 'After careful adjudication by his peers, it is hereby pronounced that Robert McCloy, fresh from the bus, and late, too, is guilty of crimes against decent standards in the sporting of punk badges.'

'Hear, hear,' I said with my mouth full.

'My learned friends,' Limbo continued. 'Though the defendant claims to oppose America in its abuses of international law, he is guilty of badge crimes.'

'Boys . . . boys . . .' Clogs said.

'This is now a proven fact. He shall be taken from this place . . .' – Hogg and Tully grabbed Clogs, pinned him to the chair, and started flicking his ears – '. . . and subjected to the severest punishment allowed by law, that he be held in a box bedroom, and that he be forced to listen to the music of Phil Collins until he be dead.'

. . .

In Piccadilly Gardens, Tully rolled in a bed of dandelions, and then, carrying the dregs of Limbo's wine, he climbed up a statue of James Watt. 'Oi, buddy,' he shouted at a passing stranger. 'What does a gentleman do in Manchester if he wants an afternoon cocktail?'

'Whistle for it, mate,' the man said.

'Thank you, sir. Thank you, indeed. I am presently engaged in shagging one of your premier monuments. Toodle-pip!'

'The Scots steamers,' Tibbs said, standing next to me, 'paying homage to the inventor of steam.'

'Engine,' Clogs said. 'He invented the engine. Or improved it. Something like that.' We watched Tully kissing the master's bronze face and offering the sky a dram. 'Excellent. We have a whole weekend of show-offs and memorials.'

'Hey, Manchester,' Tully shouted over the gardens, his arm crooked around James Watt's neck. *'We had it all, duck.'*

He held up the bottle. The sun caught it.

'*A television set and a packet of fags.*'

I think he imagined everyone below him, all the ordinary people of the city, would know the films he was quoting from, that they'd know them by heart, having somehow lived in them all their days.

7

We saw 'Britannia Hotel' in red neon and a sign saying 'Happy Hour'. I think the Housemartins song of that name was in the charts at the time, because Limbo was singing it loudly as he stormed up the hotel steps, disappearing through the revolving doors into a Valhalla of tartan carpet.

Five o'clock. All pints eighty pence.

'Look, Noodles,' Tully said, hanging back. By the entrance, a bronze figure of a soldier in a Tommy helmet holding a rifle with a long bayonet. Tully touched the soldier's boot and read out the words. '*To the enduring memory of those members of the staff of S & J Watts & Co., who laid down their lives for their King and country in the cause of truth, justice and freedom during the Great War.*' He ran a finger down the names and stopped at one of them, J. T. Dawson. 'No relation,' he said, 'but how would I know?'

A pigeon hopped onto the steps.

'It's weird what Limbo said earlier on,' I began. 'It was a joke but it's the sort of idea that sticks with me. He said I would've been a bad bet in the trenches. Him and Tibbs and Hogg would've been first over the top, wouldn't they?'

'Definitely,' Tully said.

'They'd run into the bullets.'

'Chasing a football probably. Especially Tibbs, kicking it into no man's land. And you'd be in the officers' mess, Noodles, writing a poem.'

'Where would you be, Tully?' He dropped his cigarette and the pigeon scarpered. He put his arm around my neck.

'I'd be shivering in the trench,' he said. 'Shell-shocked.' I leaned back to look at him to see if he was being serious.

'Really? That's how you see it?'

'Yip. There's always one.'

We stood there looking at one another.

'Are you all right, Tully?'

'I just want to get so drunk,' he said.

I didn't properly register what he was saying. At that age, you can't speak about courage or what kind will be required or how much. He looked back at the memorial before staring into the street and taking a deep breath. 'That was my da's story,' he said. 'National Service. Best years of his life, apparently.'

'That's the kind of thing they say.'

'Learning how to box. How to be a man. What sort of poor bastard thinks being stuck in a Malayan swamp is the best gig they ever had?'

'It's an old story, Tully. But your dad tried to make a life.'

'He's from another world, Noodles.'

'But you have things in common. The football.'

'He showed me how to play. It's the only thing we ever did together. I was a wee boy then and it was the only thing.'

He said it with a kind of wishful clarity, and the last few

words were swallowed up as he stepped into the revolving doors.

• • •

Clogs was interested in Australian lager. Limbo was telling the barman it was pish, but Clogs said things were happening down under. A pint of Castlemaine arrived, accompanied by six glasses of rum and five halves of Guinness. We'd each put £10 into a kitty and Tully was the keeper, but also by now the general MC, asking difficult questions of passing strangers and milking their responses. He made six trips back and forth to our two large tables, bringing a pair of drinks at a time, before he sat down and announced that Sarah Ferguson and Prince Andrew could go fuck themselves as far as he was concerned. A more immediate problem was the music playing in the bar, and Tully also took that matter in hand, asking the guy who was serving if we could possibly opt out of Lionel Richie. The barman seemed annoyed by all the fuss but he pressed a button under the taps, and the just-about-acceptable music of the Cure arrived in our wallpapered corner.

'I don't think you'd know the difference,' Hogg was saying to Clogs, 'between William Burroughs and William of Orange.' On several levels, this was an incendiary statement. Hogg had a problem with Clogs that tumbled out at various times and places. 'I'm not trying to be cheeky or anything,' he added.

'I like the stuff you like, let's leave it at that,' Clogs calmly said. But he couldn't quite manage it himself. Of all the boys, these two were the only real adversaries. 'I admit to having certain reservations about your love of sheet-metal music,' Clogs began to say, 'but I'm willing to drop them for the sake of camaraderie and a quiet weekend with the boys.' Hogg returned quickly, as always, with a new controversial subject – favourite films – and he rushed at it with no other wish than to score a massive victory in as little time as possible. Smarting like Stan Laurel, Hogg plucked at his hair and got narky.

'I can tell you for nothing,' he said, 'that the phrase "Make my day" was first used by Clint Eastwood in *Sudden Impact*.'

'Nope, you fuckan bass-slapping halfwit,' Clogs said, 'it comes from an earlier film called *Vice Squad*.'

'Bullshit.'

'On the contrary. Watch the films again.'

'You know everything, Clogs.'

Tully's attention wandered while the boys argued. 'Still thinking about that war memorial?' I asked.

'You're a mind-reader, man.' He took a large gulp of Guinness. 'I'm just thinking about all those names. Like my dad always says, "If you haven't been in the army and come home and built a decent life, you've failed."'

'That's narrow enough.'

'Like, go away and learn how to fight, then stay home and learn how to die.' Something was unloosening in Tully, and he was trying to hold on to it.

'Nobody has to live like that,' I said. 'That's your dad's life you're talking about there.'

'But how do we avoid it?'

'By being right here.'

'And is it enough?'

'We'll see. It's enough for now.'

We looked up. Clogs was spreading his hands and sighing. 'Please bear witness, gentlemen, to the manner in which Hogg here must always appear to win an argument. Am I not civil? Am I not collegiate? Some would call me the king of tolerance. And you'll notice I have not reached for the superior weapons in my armoury.'

'What weapons?' Hogg asked, downing his rum. The doctor took his time and appeared to measure his words carefully.

'It's a well-known fact,' he said, 'that in 1981 you had a perm.'

'You're a fuckan liar,' Hogg barked.

'There are multiple witnesses. You had a proper Scouse perm. I think your mother did it at home, David, out of a box. And you were into robotic dancing. I'm afraid these are the facts. I only deal in facts before the court. You once danced, in broad daylight, outside the shopping mall, wearing a white boiler suit with a circuit board pinned to your chest. You wore gloves. And you had a perm.'

'You're making it up,' Hogg said.

A quiet period ensued when we just watched the bar and the booze began to take effect, though Limbo, whose capacity for drink was mind-boggling and endless, was sailing into his fourth hour of being pissed.

'I hope we get past the bouncers at the Hacienda,' Tibbs said. 'We can't get a knock-back from the best club in the world. We just can't.' With a natural confidence in happy endings, I said we'd get in. 'But how do you know, Jimmy?' he asked. 'Guys get knocked back all the time. And if that happens I'm not showing my face again at the sorting office.' Clogs unfolded a wrap of speed and we each dabbed a finger in the powder and rubbed our gums. A wee bit drunk, then a wee bit high, it was magic to feel you had things to say and people to say them to, and a gentle fog of contentment filled the bar, until Limbo sparked up a joint and was asked to leave. 'You're not doing that in here,' the barman said. Tully took to his feet like Atticus Finch. He asked the barman to consider the special challenges faced by his client, the legacy of Irish depravity, a dicky heart, a wandering sister . . .

'Fucking idiots,' the barman said.

More drinks arrived and a fresh attitude. After fetching over the glasses, Tully moseyed into the foyer, looking for new action. I followed him, and soon we were talking to a pair of girls in ruffled skirts who were attending an office do. The conversation was going badly but not too badly until Tully asked them about *Brookside*. They said they didn't watch it, they hated soaps in fact, but Tully, in that state, wasn't the world's best listener, and he quizzed them on plotlines going back four years, and then insisted they tell us if they thought Bobby Grant would kill Matty Nolan.

'What yer on about?' one of them said.

'Would you like a drink?' I quickly asked. Her friend shrugged, as if it was a good question from a bad quarter. 'Listen,' I said. 'Why don't I go and get you a couple of Advocaats and lemonade?'

70

They looked at each other. 'Why would we drink that shite?' the first girl said. 'Why would we want some yellow twat-drink? Because we're girls? Because we're dolly birds? We'll have two pints of snakebite and black, thanks very much.'

When I returned they took the pint glasses and spoke about us as if we weren't there. 'They're not terrible-looking,' said the second one. 'Especially him, stupid with the green eyes.'

'What's your name?' her friend asked.

'Tully Dawson, at home and abroad.'

'That's him,' I said.

'Indeed,' he said. 'Tullygarven, townland of Ulster.'

'Seen much of Manchester, then?'

'I've seen it all,' he said. 'From the top of a statue in those gardens over the road there. Climbed up with a bottle of red wine.'

'Bit soft in the head,' she said.

'Problem is,' her friend offered, 'they've got no arses. He's got eyes and the other one's got hair, but they've got skinny arses.'

'It's a terrible disappointment,' Tully said, 'because he comes from a long line of fat-arsed truck drivers.'

'And you both talk shite. Thanks for the drinks. And take my advice – beef up your arses.' They tottered off and Tully burst out laughing.

'We could take you out for a meal!' he shouted after them. 'If you like spuds we know the perfect place ...'

'You know how to treat a lady, Tully.'

I went into the gents toilet at the back of the bar. And there was Limbo in a twilight world of hissing cisterns and broken tiles, one hand on the wall with a burning cigarette clamped between his fingers, Limbo, eyes closed and head back, pissing into a trough of deodorising cubes as the light flickered over a cubicle and he sang a few lines from an Orange Juice song.

'President Lincoln,' I said. 'Are you doing all right?'

He dropped his head and turned towards me. 'People have no idea what it takes to be the leader of the free world and the champion of equality,' he said.

'Well, it's a burden, I'm sure. Don't take too much of that speed.' He staggered back fixing himself and puffed on his fag.

'No, seriously,' he said. 'Are we having a good time?'

'We've got to get to this gig,' I said. 'It's twenty past seven. We have to find the International—'

'Those two arguing out there,' Limbo said, 'it's a bit like *What Ever Happened to Baby Jane?*, i'n't it?'

'It's quite funny,' I said.

'And you're all ugly bastards.' He straightened up and burped, flicking his cigarette into the trough.

'Thank you most kindly,' I said.

The foyer was lit like a Chinese restaurant.

'*Beef up your arses!*' Tully shouted at me when I got back. Then he started telling me about the people walking past. He was always good at collecting information and he said the porter told him there were two different work dos – the Arndale Centre's C&A men's department and another place, to do with chemicals. 'The city's just doing its stuff and they don't even know we're here.'

72

'Perfectly possible that they don't,' I said. 'Unless you took out a full-page advert in the *Manchester Evening News*. "Six Scottish Pricks Get Wasted in Major European City." People live here, Tully. They haven't all just come here to see the Shop Assistants and a bunch of bands tomorrow.'

'I know...'

And just at that moment, I swear to God, Mike Joyce and Andy Rourke from the Smiths came down the stairs with another bloke and went through the revolving doors. I thought I was seeing stuff – nobody else in the foyer seemed to notice. I elbowed Tully and he turned in time to see Morrissey and Marr. A lurch in the stomach. The singer was wearing a red shirt and he hit the air like a chip-pan fire. Right behind him was Johnny Marr, light and young as his melodies and smoking a fag. It was like a branch of philosophy crash-landing in front of you. The word 'vermilion' came to mind, and so did his lyrics, all the band's images, and that's how it works when you're a fan who thinks Keats might save the world. In an instant, without a word being exchanged, Tully and I were through the doors and onto the pavement, just in time to see the famous Mancunians stepping into a Rolls-Royce.

We were the only ones there.

'Morrissey, ya fuckan bawbag,' Tully shouted.

Tully the disciple, paying the penalty adulation offers to self-respect. And when we are gone from the world, there will still be spores of delight, somewhere in the universe, recalling the moment Tully Dawson ran down the steps of the Britannia Hotel and spread himself over the bonnet of the Smiths' posh vehicle, his face pressed with contorted affection against the windscreen. He hollered and he sang, hugging the car, his legs spread and his Teddy-boy shoes dangling over the edge, his trousers hitched with the effort, showing a placid innocence of white sock. I stood amazed and Tully turned his mashed face round and grinned for the whole of Scotland. He climbed off and stood back, dancing in the road, when the driver unceremoniously switched on the windscreen wipers and beeped the horn. 'Aye, go for it, ya wanky-car-driving Tory set of dicks,' Tully reasoned.

He blew them a kiss as the car drove off. I walked over and shook his hand. 'What a legend,' I said, and I stooped to pick up a burning cigarette from the pavement. I took a puff. The filter was wet. I passed it to Tully and told him whose fag it was as he had the last drag.

'He cow's-arsed it,' I said.

'Fuck it,' he said. 'I don't mind a bit of saliva. The guy wrote "How Soon Is Now?"'

8

We hopped off the bus in Rusholme and went into Victoria
Wine. Tully bought a bottle of Old England and we stood outside passing it back and forth, leaning against the iron grille,
the sweet sherry almost pleasant. To me, we could have been
at Le Chat Noir, drinking absinthe into the turquoise night,
ready for fame or oblivion. Limbo marched off down Anson
Road, because we were hogging the bottle and he wanted to
see the support acts. 'Away ye go, then, National Party Rapist
of Soweto,' Tibbs shouted after him.

The International was over the road, but we took our time:
it was much too enjoyable being on the street. At one point
Tully, Tibbs, and I were sitting against a telephone box. 'We
could phone somebody, so we could,' Tibbs said. He was
always a bit sweet and a bit childish when he was drunk. He
sat in a blue striped T-shirt and the whole of Rusholme was
reflected in his eyes.

'Like who?' Tully asked.

'Caesar. Or Ross. I think Ross has put a phone in his da's
Lada.'

'Fuck his da's Lada,' Tully said. 'Lad-i-fuckan-da-da. I could
phone my mum and tell her Noodles is leading us astray.'

My head was tingling. I would have sat there all night. Tully rubbed a bit more speed on his gums and shook his head before slugging from the bottle in that slightly desperate way he always had. For a second I floated into privacy: the faraway mood of exhilaration that comes with excess, and I loved the excess, and loved the seeming permissiveness of that night. Who would I call, I wondered, if I stepped into the phone box? And the answer – so free of regret – was no one. I had no one to call and I was quite glad about it. Now that the queue was short, Tibbs walked over the road. 'C'mon,' he said, glancing back.

'In a minute,' Tully said.

I sat on my jacket and felt right in my skin. I'd never felt so part of the world, so part of its weather.

'Woodbine was a good footballer when he was young,' Tully said.

'Your mum told me that.'

'Well, she was telling the truth. He got a trial for City.'

'Manchester City?'

'Aye. The silly bastard.'

'That's amazing.'

He looked away. 'He could've been down here in Manchester years ago.'

I passed him the Old England and he drank it.

'*It scares the health out of me*,' he sang from the Bodines song.

He sighed and looked into the yellow distance. 'I totally love those words,' he said, 'and I wish they were mine.'

It was always the way with Tully: keeping his worries close.

I never pushed him to say what he wanted to say – I knew he was pushing himself – but with all the hilarity of that weekend came a brightening emotion in him. I could see it clearly, the dream of newness tugging him along, the wish to separate from home.

· · ·

Limbo crashing into the world of the anoraks was like a bird of prey arriving for tea at the ducklings' end of the loch. He'd already swooped round the dark circumference of the hall and was now making his way to the front. Feathers falling, he stumbled towards the stage, tipping drinks down his gullet and smoking two cigarettes at once. It might have slipped his mind that he had one going when he lit the second, but Lincoln at play in the fields of the Lord, our friend Limbo at the International, was a mighty, sovereign, ravenous creature in love with more for more's sake.

The venue was like a ratty school gym. Disco lights revolved in high-up gantries and lasers scanned the linoleum dancefloor. The odour of student sweat was mingled with high-tar cigarettes. The tables up the back of the venue were sticky with beer. It was a small place, and from our perch at the bar we could see the quality unfold. Near the entrance, Hogg was talking to a Japanese girl in red braces. She nodded a lot. Dr Clogs and I speculated about whether Hogg might have used the words 'radical Belgian funk' in trying to seal the deal. Meanwhile, a crimson-faced Tibbs, with much pointing and quaffing, was addressing a group of Liverpool lads on the whys and wherefores of Militant, the Trotskyist group causing a bit of trouble for the Labour Party at the time. The words, 'Naw, but . . .' appeared to be the central mantra in his presentation.

I walked off on my own with a glass of water. It was amazingly cold and I felt for a minute it was clearing my mind. As if by some accidental empathy, a beautiful woman appeared at the edge of the crowd. She had coloured rags in her hair, black skin, and the reddest lips I'd ever seen. She looked over. It was only a second and I knew I had no chance, but I began thinking of what I might say to her.

A thump of the bass drum announced the band.

'*Yeeeeeeeeee-ha!*' shouted a voice. The female singer came to the mic, carrying a plastic tumbler and a tambourine.

'Hello, we're the Shop Assistants.' She was wearing a Chinese cap and seemed not entirely devoted to the art of performance.

'*Yeeeeeeeeeeeee-fuckan-ha!*' came the voice again.

It was Tully Dawson, down at the front. The venue was compact enough and the crowd shy enough that a mad boy could be an amplifier.

He loved expressing his admiration for a band by shouting them down. Was it disappointment when faced with the real thing? Was it pride asserting itself? There was no obvious explanation, and, whatever the urge, he handled it with a frenzied deployment of the word 'shite'. It's a largely forgotten pastime, that of abusing live bands, but I've never known anyone else who did it with such obvious brio. Tully could dominate a hall with the heat of his invective. Once, at a

Spear of Destiny gig in Ayr Pavilion, he made Kirk Brandon threaten to end the show. And here he was again, drunk and moshing with his subconscious at the edge of the stage. 'Total *sh-iiiiiiiiiiii-te*!'

The band went shambling on.

He shouted himself hoarse. Nobody minded. Then he came to the bar. 'They're pure shite, aren't they?' he said.

'No. I think they're great,' I said.

'I'm only kidding.' He paused. 'I like to give them a bit of bother.'

'Why, though?'

He passed me a vodka. 'Well, I want my band to be up there being shouted at by some dick.' He turned his back to the bar. 'It'll never happen,' he said. 'I'm stuck forever, man, and only when you're out like this . . .'

He looked at me.

'What's going on, Tully?'

'I'm still glad I came. Manchester. Me, you, and the boys. That's it. Nothing was going to stop me.'

'Mate . . .'

He just bent his head towards the bar and said it loud enough for me to hear. 'My da had a heart attack on Wednesday.'

'*This* Wednesday?'

'Aye. A minor heart attack. But he's young for that.'

'Jesus, Tully.'

'It was like an omen, a few months ago – burying those light bulbs in the garden. His health is all over the place, and his mind.'

'You don't think you should be up the road, at home?'

'Why you saying that? That's exactly what I *don't* think. Don't tell me you find that hard to understand?' He wiped his nose with the back of his hand. 'He's fine.' And with that he lunged back into the sway of bodies. He swallowed his drink in one gulp and threw the plastic tumbler in the air.

I drifted away towards the tables near the back wall and there was soon another voice at my shoulder. 'That's entertainment,' it said.

It was Dr Clogs, and as I turned a green laser cut diagonally across his face. He held a pint. 'You might put in a special request,' he said. 'I believe they do a most excellent "Cherish the Love", or whatever it's called, by Kool & the Gang, a rallying call for the Yorkshire miners.' It occurred to me that though Clogs was young – he couldn't have been more than twenty-two – I thought of him as old, the way he leaned to one side, and smoked his cigarette like someone taking particular measures against pain.

I saw Limbo combing through a thicket of small tables, rescuing drinks. He spotted us up the back and soon arrived with a tray of specimens. 'Taboo and lemonade? Mirage and ginger?' He gestured to the tray with a flowing hand, as if presenting the finest silks of Arabia, and raised an eyebrow. He was a natural actor, Limbo, and he held us for a moment with his cavorting eyes and his impersonation, before letting out this great cackle that made his whole body shake.

'Those drinks are absurd,' I said. 'Can't you make it your business to steal alcohol worth drinking?'

'What? I beg your pardon. Let me understand you clearly,' Limbo said. 'You're saying no to Taboo and Mirage?'

Just then, the beautiful girl came past. 'Excuse me,' I said, leaning out from the group in a sudden upswing of romantic confidence, 'could I offer you an unspeakable drink?' She stopped for a second and was smiling at my daftness and I had to be quick. 'Which one are you, Taboo or Mirage?' I asked.

She inclined her head, like people do when speaking to an idiot. I'd completely and absolutely, without a doubt, fucked it. She put a finger to her lips and I thought she was pausing before issuing the put-down of the century.

'Em,' she said. 'I've seen the ads. I know who I am – Mirage.' She plucked the drink from Limbo's sordid tray and walked off, just turning, as if by the magic of cinema, to wink in my direction before she disappeared.

'Jesus Christ,' I said, 'I need some air.'

'It's overrated,' Limbo said. 'Stop pestering women and giving away my booze. She was nice all the same, so you can be rewarded with a Bols Blue and ice. Come on, you little tease, I know you want it.'

Limbo drank several of his mad drinks and dropped the tumblers onto the carpet. For reasons impossible to fathom, he raised his eyebrow again and adopted the voice of Viscount Montgomery of Alamein. 'You'd jolly better had,' he said. 'I can tell you I've had fourteen Beziques and I feel bloody marvellous.'

The band were struggling with a poor amp. Or several poor amps. 'Pure fuckan mince by the way!' Tully was shouting.

The singer was trying to see where the bombardment was coming from (and why, no doubt) as she twisted the mic away from her mouth after 'Home Again'. She swayed with composed embarrassment, the sort of embarrassment all members of small independent bands had then, a form of shyness, or stage absence, that seemed to go well with their accidentally perfect tunes.

'That was pish!' Tully shouted.

'I think that boy's had too many beers,' the singer said. Then the drums thumped again and the band were off on another spree.

The night seemed to last forever and there was nothing to regret and no direction home. My head was full of Tully's news, but I knew him: he didn't want to deal with it tonight. As the set progressed and the energy lifted off we walked to the front and all stood together by the stage. Tibbs leaned over and handed the fuzzy-haired bass player a CND badge. She pinned it to her jacket and tossed her hair before they went into a cover of Motörhead's 'Ace of Spades'. Limbo was rocking, all his lanterns lit. He was good at being young. The flashy drinks had brought Las Vegas into his face.

'Roll me on,' he said. He turned to us, all portly. 'Onto the stage. Roll me.' Martyr for tunes, vampire for drink, Lincoln McCafferty crossed his arms over his chest and we rolled him towards the guitarist's fashionably buckled legs. In the universe of small humiliations, there can surely be few more effective for the guitar hero than the arrival at his feet of a rotund little Scottish guy high on Taboo. The guitarist, disturbed mid-song, shuffled and kicked as Limbo gripped on to his legs. I say gripped, I mean hugged, Limbo nodding in time to the music and gnawing the guy's jeans.

The Shop Assistants ended their set in a soft meltdown of confidence. That was the habit of the day, the vital register, with those bands. Scattered applause and an air of depletion went with a squeal of departing feedback, immediately giving way to the beat of the Ramones and a huddle on the dancefloor.

Tully and I wandered over towards an open door at the back of the venue. We stood for a moment by a group of shining beer kegs and I gave him water. His hair was stuck to his forehead. His eyes were glassy. His voice was low. He took out half a spliff from an inside pocket. 'I can't believe we saw the Smiths in their Roller,' he said, 'and now this lot. And we've still got tomorrow. I never want to go home, Noods.'

'Of course you do.'

'Let's not talk about it.' He drew really deep on the spliff, he always did that, and I thought it was a sign of confusion – he was dulling himself. He drank like that, too: as if oblivion was a perfect place to be by yourself.

'It's been a blinder already,' I said.

'Totally.' He blew out the withheld smoke. 'Like all the old boys watching you score at Ibrox and the cheer going up.'

Then he was gone again. He stood up and spun round and made the hall come to him as he mounted a raid on the dancefloor.

· · ·

Exhausted, I found a table in the corner and took out the fanzine I'd bought at Piccadilly Records. When I looked up I saw the girl again and she came over. 'I'm bored as a week in Bradford,' she said. 'Is this seat free?'

'I'd be honoured,' I said, already in love with her eyes.

'So you're the guy who reads at gigs?'

Her name was Angie. We talked about derelict housing blocks. She was the first black girl I'd ever met who wanted to talk to me, and she used the word 'street' as an adjective. Everything was street. She was from Hulme and knew all the members of A Certain Ratio. She wanted to know where we'd been that day and I told her all about it – the bus down and Spudulike, the carry-on at the Britannia Hotel.

'Just living it up,' she said.

'With no digs.'

'That's crazy,' she said. 'Street urchins.'

She asked me what I was into. I named a whole lot of things. She nodded along to what I was saying. She had the slimmest hands. I didn't know what to say, so I said I loved James Baldwin. 'Well, you're sweet, darling.' She swallowed my vodka in a single go and kissed me bang on the lips.

'Let's run away to Paris,' I said instantly. I'm sure my eyes were dewy. I had twenty-three quid and a bit of loose change.

'Cute,' she said, smiling like a superstar. We spoke about Soviet dissidents. 'Maybe you'll write a book,' she said, 'like your friend James Baldwin.'

'I'm sorry for saying that.'

'Don't be soft,' she said, tapping me on the nose. 'We're on

84

the same side. For now.' There wasn't a phone in her flat, she said, but she'd be at G-Mex the next day.

'Do you think this is a bad period for dancing?' she said, looking at the action on the floor. 'Like there was the Sixties – tick. There was disco – tick. But what's this?' People were sort of chickening their way round the floor or bowing down towards each other in a slow way. 'Know what I mean?'

'Bad period for dancing, good period for self-consciousness.' She giggled and I'd never seen so much life in a giggle.

'I'm going to like you,' she said. 'Wait there.' She strode off and returned in the company of a man with a strong head and painted Doc Martens. He was the editor of the fanzine I'd been reading and was in a band called the Speechwriters.

'Friendly Mancunians,' I said.

'We're all friendly about 'ere,' he said.

'Not if today's anything to go by,' I said. 'We've been to a few places today where they told us to shut our daft faces.'

'That seems about right,' Angie said. She tapped me on the nose again and began putting on her coat.

'Can I definitely see you tomorrow?' I blurted out.

'Look out for me,' she said. 'It's a test.'

She stood for a minute more. The place was emptying out and staff were collecting plastic glasses. By now, Tully and Hogg were snogging two girls over at the bar while Limbo and Tibbs were crashed out on a banquette. I liked the way Angie hovered. She said the word 'darling' to a few girls drifting by with their coats, like she knew everybody and knew how to be friendly and familiar and the opposite of uptight.

Clogs came over with his hands in his pockets. 'This is Bobby,' I said to the fanzine guy.

'I'm Frank,' he said back. Clogs shook his hand in a grown-up way, like they each deserved respect.

'I confess to a certain amount of uncertainty about where we might sleep,' Clogs said. 'Do you have any advice, sir? We are a meagre group of four. It appears two of our group have apprehended some eyelashes.'

'I'm sure there's more to them than that, Clogs.' I said it glancing at Angie. 'Women aren't merely eyelashes.'

'It's a rhetorical device,' our future host said. (I had a feeling that exact burden would fall to him, English grammarian or not.) 'They call it synecdoche, or metonymy. I'm never sure of the difference. The part for the whole.'

'It reduces them,' I said, warming up. 'Women certainly have eyelashes. But I'm sure they have brains, too, and possibly souls.' I was giving Angie the entire de Beauvoir. She did a little starburst of 'bye' with her fingers and was about to turn.

'I'm going to like you,' she repeated.

'Tomorrow!' I said.

'That's what it's called.'

I wanted to shout some sort of poem as she left.

'You're gone,' Clogs said.

'Angie's a complete star,' said the fanzine editor. I felt for a second he must know where all the broken hearts were buried.

Clogs turned to logistics. 'These nurses, the two over there with our pals. They have a flat over in St Mary's Hospital. Ah, here comes one of the dashing swains.'

Tully sloped up, plastered. 'We're away,' he said. He looked like a man who'd won the pools but was too depressed to spend it. 'The girls said me and Hogg can sleep on their floor but you lot are getting the heave-ho.' While walking away his spirits recovered and he did a wee Michael Jackson shuffle next to some goths.

'Ten in the morning at the Peterloo Café,' I shouted. 'The corner of Albert Square.'

'I hear you, Bubbles.'

He did a double pirouette, ending on his toes.

9

In the taxi Limbo babbled all the way while Tibbs replayed the whole of the Falklands War, bastard by bastard and ship by ship, until he fell into a coma. Then we drove through the streets in a temporary state of peace. 'Looks like Alex Ferguson's for United,' the driver said. 'That's what they're saying anyhow.'

'On the radio?' our friend asked. It occurred to me he should have called his fanzine *Frank* – he was totally Frank. Not like Frank Sidebottom or Frank Chickens, but an ordinary, workaday Frank who was all Manchester.

'I can't see it,' said the driver. 'There are too many Jocks down here already.' Frank laughed. I think the term I'd use now is 'good-naturedly'. Limbo grunted in his sleep and spoke phrases that might have involved nuns or policemen.

'What did he say?' Frank asked. His face told us he was unoffendable. He was taking us to the flat in West Didsbury where they did the fanzine.

The city gave out to rows of houses. Heaps of bricks. Not quite suburbia, but a certain ambience, a ghostly, ruined feeling; we passed tall, smokeless chimneys, and dark waste grounds edged in yellow light. Tibbs was snoring.

'We bumped into the Smiths,' I said, 'at the Britannia Hotel.'

'All of them?' Frank asked.

'All four, and the new bloke. We didn't say much.' I was still dealing with the image of Tully licking the windscreen of their Rolls.

'I would call it an illusion,' Clogs said. 'Let's say a derangement of enthusiasm. The boys had drunk quite a lot of the sauce. We were there and saw nothing of the sort. I'd wager the band in question did not appear, but were to be found hovering in a helicopter over Saddleworth Moor, ready for tomorrow's gig.'

'Not a chance,' the fanzine editor said. 'Take it from me. Steven Morrissey would never be caught dead in a helicopter. He's much more likely to arrive on the 101 bus from Wythenshawe.'

We stopped at a house with a red-brick arch over the door and a wind chime in the garden. 'It's there to ward off evil spirits and the television licence people,' Frank said. All the bulbs were out. We felt our way down the hall and ended up in a room with leather sofas. Using Limbo's lighter, we saw tables covered in jars of stuck paintbrushes, cans of spray paint, guitar cases; there was a lovely scent of turpentine and glue. Frank could see in the dark. He put a record on the turntable and the glow from a candle lit a pot of ferns on the windowsill. There was a whole lot of Artex on the ceiling, a few bottles of Pils on the table, and a girl rolling a joint on a Go-Betweens LP as somebody told their life story. Frank brought in a camp stove to illuminate all the nonsense with its blue flame.

I felt a long way from home – in a good way, in a bad way – and when Tully was gone, the centre was elsewhere. That's teenage love, isn't it – when the party is less fun because your mate *is* the party? I was suddenly aware that I didn't have enough money or directions and that I was every inch the young provincial. The big night would be the next one, and this was just a dosshouse and a piss-up, with no Tully to make it all alive and buzzing and part of the big story. I thought of the girl, Angie.

A vanload turned up from Hulme. One of them was about nineteen and he wore a hearing aid and blue National Health specs, one stem fixed with a plaster. He had a bunch of gladioli, a teddy bear, and many anxieties, a collection he all but wheeled into the living room in a tartan shopping trolley. I think they were all in a band, a fey ensemble, although there was a ginger ruffian who came gnashing at the rear and shook a tambourine in my face before emptying his bladder into a pint tumbler.

Now.

A tumbler of pee, even in a darkened squat, is like Chekhov's gun: it must fulfil its promise to the audience. And just as a visible gun has to go off, a tumbler of pee, left on a fireplace in Act One, is sure to be drunk by a wandering victim in Act Three. And so it was, as *les misérables* were contorting themselves to an acoustic guitar, and others were thinking aloud about the subtle genius of Kenneth Williams, that Limbo descended from his explorations of the upper floors and fell like carrion upon the wretched glass. I'm not saying he drank half of it before he realised, but it went beyond a single gulp.

'Who're your influences?' asked the Morrissey clone. He'd got down beside me on the carpet and was twisting his hair. I think the standard response to that question, at the time, was 'Shelagh Delaney, George Formby, the New York Dolls, and Oscar Fingal O'Flahertie Wills Wilde', but I didn't get far into my list before Limbo came crashing down on the inquisitive student and knocked off his spectacles.

'Got a light?' Limbo asked.

'Certainly not,' said the boy, piecing his fragility back together. 'The gum in cigarette papers is made from animal fat and that's despicable.'

'Can I ride you, then?' inquired Limbo, before singeing his own hair. He was always doing it: a case of too much hairspray and a billowing Zippo. It was put out with a handful of cider and the young man scarpered.

I went to the kitchen and made a cup of tea. Finding a clean mug was an operation best imagined as a sort of journey to the interior, but eventually I brought the teabag to the mug and filled it with lukewarm water. I went back to the main room, where kids were beginning to fall asleep or get off with one another, the music mithering on the stereo. I watched the blue flame on the camp stove. The bluest part reminded me of Esso, the paraffin advert, and an old heater we used to have in the room where my father drank alone. I thought about Woodbine. I understood why Tully hadn't stayed at home that weekend, but it revealed something cold in him, maybe a thing we had in common.

I got up and wandered through the house, bone tired, looking for a place to doss. I found a dark corner under the stairs, and lay down and went to take out my ticket. I wanted to go to sleep visualising tomorrow, the concert venue, the bands. Not Woodbine. Not parents or the ghosts of parents.

The ticket wasn't there.

I searched everywhere using my lighter.

Jeans and jacket. Every pocket. Then I ransacked my duffel bag, the zipped compartment, everything. My panic grew as I slowly realised I wasn't going to find it. The bus down, that was the last place I remembered seeing it, and now, hours later, with tears in my eyes, I lay back, resigned to the worst occurrence ever. Falling into a difficult sleep, I could see the ticket, blown over Hadrian's Wall.

• • •

In the morning I climbed the stairs to clean my teeth. Two girls with Mohawks were asleep in an empty bath. There was sunlight over the rooftops. Water trickled from a rusty tap and my mouth felt like the Second World War. I went back to the landing and stood. The wallpaper was peeling next to the handrail and the wall was damp all the way up. Beneath one sheet was another sheet that was also peeling, a different pattern from another time, and I wondered if it went all the way back to the beginning of the house. I imagined there must be stories. When I craned my neck to see further up, it was CND posters all the way. And somewhere on the upper landing, amid a gentle hiss of spray-painting, I could hear Dr

Clogs leading a seminar on the deficiencies of Sheena Easton as a recording artist.

I couldn't stop thinking about the lost ticket. What was I going to do? It was the end of my life if I didn't get into G-Mex.

In one of the rooms, under a hill of torn envelopes and Letraset, Tibbs was still comatose on his Cub Scout bedroll, his Rucanor bag for a pillow, his jacket on backwards and up under his chin. I nearly lost my footing on a slope of copier paper as I bent to give him a shake.

'Fuck off,' he said. Sleep was not kind to Tyrone: he was one of those people who woke up looking like the angels had glued his eyelashes.

'I've lost my ticket,' I said.

He stretched. 'You're fuckan kiddin'. Where?'

'If I knew that it wouldn't be lost, Sinbad.'

'Shut it. My bonce is gowpin'. What you going to do?'

'Kill myself,' I said.

'Jesus,' he said. 'This is bad . . . I wonder how Tully and Hogg got on with the two nurses.' Then he copped on. 'I'm sorry for you, Jimmy. It's sold out, but maybe you'll be able to buy another one off a tout.'

'The money *they* charge? I'm done for.'

He nodded sagely and wiped his eyes.

• • •

Our diminished party of four smoked on the bus into town. Limbo didn't believe in hangovers and said the rioting in

Portadown had fuck all to do with freeing Ireland. 'It's just a bunch of wee neds trying to impress their pals.' Tibbs had a copy of the *Guardian*. 'Sanctions Deadline Issued to Thatcher,' the headline said.

'Fuckpigs.'

I shook my head and tutted at Tibbs. 'That's no way to talk about Her Majesty's government. After all they've done for you.'

'They murder British Shipbuilders on Monday. They fuck British Rail on Tuesday.' He snapped the paper open as if shooing a fly. 'Look,' he said, '*An order believed to be worth about £90 million is expected to be announced by British Shipbuilders. The contract to build 24 small ferries for Denmark will provide two years' work at the state-owned Sunderland Shipbuilders and Austin & Pickersgill yards.*' He shook the paper again. '*The work will not mean an end to a plan to axe a total of 925 jobs at the two companies.*'

'How to dismantle a people,' Clogs said.

'Exactly. They're all scum, so they are. Then this . . .' Tibbs pointed to the story next to the one he'd read out. 'British Rail broke even last year, right? It had a difficult time during the strike, but it made a profit the year before, eight million, best since the early Sixties, right?' He punched the *Guardian*, that's to say the messenger, before Limbo took it off him and rolled it into a loudhailer. 'And what do the Tories want to do?' Tibbs continued. 'Privatise the fucker and shunt all the profits out of the industry.'

I went into my duffel bag for a T-shirt. Brand new: from

Glasgow. We were always getting things printed at this little shop in Hope Street. I rolled on some deodorant and pulled the shirt over my head and tugged it down to show the boys: Truman Capote and Marilyn Monroe dancing at the El Morocco nightclub. I'd never been to New York. Nobody had. But the people I grew up with felt glamorous watching films, listening to records, or reading books written by people who unfolded their lives, who told of the time they loved and the time they died and the time they danced at El Morocco. We loved black-and-white stills depicting the comedy and the tragedy of private life, or of public life gone wrong. The main characters in my childhood believed in realism in art, they loved quoting from it, but they also loved its very opposite, pitching themselves as far from reality as they could, knowing fine well that life would be all too real on Monday.

• • •

A Russian samovar stood on the counter at the Peterloo Café, gushing hot water while the night-shift workers brooded over their runny eggs. They had slices of white bread plastered with butter, and sleepily stubbed them into their plates, soaking up the yolky mess and wolfing it down between puffs on their fags. It was a silent ritual, sluiced about with tea. It seemed to me Manchester was a place of miraculous routines. I don't know why. It wasn't much different from Glasgow on the surface, not at all, but a powerful atmosphere was seeping into that Saturday morning.

Tully bowled in looking like he'd recently emerged from a

ten-stretch at Strangeways. His hair was flat and his face was wan from a long and desperate night of knock-backs, a night of doom, he went on to tell us, where the best he got was a handful of Quality Street at the nurses' station. 'She was tight as a badger's arse,' he said, slugging my tea, 'and she made me go over to the hospital with her, so she could talk to her pal who was on night shift. Then – nothing. Slept under a table with their pishy dog. What a nightmare. I thought they were the nympho nurses.'

'What gave you that idea?' I asked.

'I'm familiar with the literature. And I know my *Carry On* films.'

'Of course.'

'Anyhow. Turns out they're nuns from the Order of Perpetual Refusal. Hogg got a snog in the corridor and I got the bum steer.'

'Where is he?' Tibbs asked.

'He's across the square phoning his mum. He slept in a dining chair all night with his face on the table. I don't suppose he'll be telling her that.'

Tibbs was loving this. He took pleasure in the common curse of our romantic failures. 'Jimmy got a knock-back as well,' he said.

'No, I never.'

'The black lassie?' Tully asked.

'You wouldn't understand,' I said. 'She's called Angie. Different class. It's a continuing conversation.'

'I saw her kiss you,' Tully said.

'Different class,' I repeated.

And then I told him the ticket news. He raised both eyebrows. 'Noodles, you didn't look after your ticket?'

The traditional Scots method of dealing with a person in crisis is first to make them feel worse and then to help them. He saw the dread on my face and blew all the air out of his lungs before observing tradition to the letter. 'What a fuckan spanner,' he said, unzipping his breast pocket and taking out his ticket. 'Here. Take mine.'

'Don't be daft,' I said.

'This is the second one I'm giving you. And you'd better not lose it or we're both Fuck McFuck of Fucked Alley.'

'But I can't have this. I need to find another one.'

'Just leave it to me,' he said. 'Those bureaucrats or bouncers on the door won't know what's hit them when we turn up with the verbals.'

'The verbals? They'll demand a ticket, Tully.'

'Well, they can take it out of this coupon,' he said, pointing to his face. 'You go with the legit and I'll follow you in, talking shit.'

'Jesus, man. Are you sure?'

'We'll be fine,' he said. 'Nobody on the planet is stopping us getting into this gig. Forget about it.'

He could do that – clear the decks with his confidence. I kissed him smack on the cheek and put the ticket in a buttoned pocket. But what would *actually* happen? I had confidence in his confidence, but what if the guys on the door said no?

Limbo hadn't noticed any of this: he was busy making a

97

breakfast sandwich of red and brown sauce. A bit of film banter crept in.

'*Go on, sup up,*' I said, from *Saturday Night*. '*Get that stuff down you.*'

Tully took my mug and downed the canal water in one.

'*It's thirsty work falling down stairs.* And look . . .' he said. The night hadn't been a complete dead end. Outside the nurses' flats Tully had run into a guy who was wandering around selling speed and he bought two wraps.

'Capital!' said Clogs, leaning over from the next booth as Tully unfolded the first one behind a standing menu. 'To dab, perchance to dream.' Limbo showed sudden interest. It was rough stuff, but beggars and gift horses, et cetera.

'Top three characters from *Coronation Street*,' Tully said as he snapped some change on the table and nodded politely to the waitress.

'Past or present?' I asked.

'All time.'

'The Popular Culture of Manchester, 1960–1986.' That could've been Tibbs's specialist subject on *Mastermind*. He rubbed his hands, then dropped his finger on the table like a depth charge, set to explode with precision and truth. 'Albert Tatlock. Ken Barlow. Mike Baldwin.'

'Sexist pig,' I said.

'Tatlock's up there,' Tully said. 'But *Barlow*?'

'Elsie Tanner. Ena Sharples. Hilda Ogden,' I said. Tully borrowed one of my T-shirts and nodded vigorously when his head popped through.

'There's no arguing with Sharples.'

'Baldwin owns the factory,' Tibbs said, 'so he's obviously a class traitor. But he's a wind-up merchant and he's funny, so it's fine.'

Tully lifted the remainder of Tibbs's Coca-Cola, using it to spike his hair.

'There's this photograph of Violet Carson, who played Sharples,' I said. 'She's dead now. In the photograph, she's standing on a balcony over Salford, and it tells you everything you need to know about everything.'

'I've seen it,' Tully said. 'It would make a great album cover.'

'All vanished now.'

'I can't believe you lost your fuckan ticket,' Tully said.

'In the midst of success we are in failure,' I said. 'Is that in the Bible?'

'No, but it should be.'

10

We had hours to kill before the big show at G-Mex. The others scattered, looking for records and clothes. Tully and I got in a minicab to Salford. He wanted to visit a shop on Great Clowes Street. At first he wouldn't explain, saying it was a surprise, but then he did, unfolding a piece of paper from his pocket. The address had come from Steady McCalla, the Jamaican guy who drank in the pub back home. The week before we left, Steady had spoken to Tully of an old friend of his in Salford, a barber like him, with his own business, and he wrote down the address. 'Go and see my brother Paul,' he said. 'He'll give you a few beers, you and your friend Jimmy.' Tully had kept it up his sleeve.

There was a striped pole above the barber's shop but also a sign on the door saying 'Back Never'. We weren't sure how to interpret that and decided it was a joke and that he must have just stepped out for a while. We walked up the street and went into a furniture shop that seemed empty of staff and customers, a long showroom of three-piece suites and beds. Near the middle, Tully flopped down on a mattress. I lay beside him and we chatted undisturbed for about twenty minutes, covering all the incidents from the night before, resting our heads on huge pillows wrapped in plastic.

'This ticket . . .'

'Don't worry about it,' he said. 'We could talk our way into the White House.'

Tully folded his arms over his chest.

'What I told you last night at the International,' he said eventually, 'I hope you didn't think I was like, "Shut up and don't tell me what to do."'

'That's exactly what you did,' I said.

'Well, just a bit. It's complicated, man.'

'I know. Your da is your da.'

We were talking to the ceiling, the water-damaged tiles.

'It's hard to explain,' he said.

'Of course it is,' I said. 'Not everybody can do my thing. Not everybody can go ahead and divorce their parents.'

'*Nobody* can do that, Noodles. Only you.'

'Divorce is underrated,' I said. 'Round our way, I mean. If you want a new world you've got to ditch your parents. That's number one.'

He punched me on the arm.

'I'm not kidding,' I said. 'It's the humane option. Dr Freud was much more extreme and a complete head-banger, when it came to all this.'

'Kill yer da,' Tully said. 'Marry yer maw.'

We turned our heads on the plastic pillows. In unison: 'Fuck that.' And when the laughing died down he grew reflective. 'He blames me for being younger than him. Blames me for the Miners' Strike. Hates me being in a band. He resents us for wanting to go places and I can't speak to him and now he's dying.'

'He's not dying.'

'And I came here, because . . . I can't figure it out.'

'You don't have to figure it out.'

He turned. 'Am I a bad person, Noods?'

'Fuckan evil,' I said, and he broke into a perfect grin.

'There's more to it—'

A sales assistant appeared at the foot of the bed. He was wearing an orange badge saying 'ELS Furniture & Carpets. 50 per cent off!' 'Can I help you, lads?' The guy was Irish and not as we expected.

'I'm not sure it's the right bed for us,' Tully said, raised on his elbows. You could tell he thought there was something unlucky about the guy. 'Ah, we're just going, mate. We were having a wee rest, know what I mean?'

I swung my legs round. The assistant had spiked black hair and his tie was tucked behind the third button of his shirt. Tully took it as a sign. 'Not going to G-Mex today?'

'Oh, is that what yous are down for. You're from Scotland, right?'

'Aye. You're not going?'

'I want to, like. Really, really badly. It's just I don't have a ticket and they've got me working in this feckin hole all day.'

'This one here, he lost his ticket. You'll get in, mate,' Tully said. 'It'll be a rabble down there. It's run by Factory Records. It's bound to be a mess.'

'D'yez think?' the guy said. It was as if a switch was thrown in his head and he seemed so excited he went a little cross-eyed.

A look came into Tully's eyes, too. If conformity had a look, a facial expression, it would be the opposite of the one he wore now. 'These arseholes,' he said, 'the bosses. Did they give you your money?'

'My wages, like?'

'Aye. Have they paid you yet this week?'

'They have. I get it on a Friday. Yesterday. There's no feckin customers. This dump'll be closed before you know it.'

'D'you know what? Run!' Tully said. 'Just fuckan run for it, mate.'

'Wha'?'

'Run and never come back.'

The boy's face was a picture. Snaggle-toothed, with a little fuzz on his top lip, and ears like the handles on the FA Cup, he walked in a circle and stepped forward and pressed his knees into the edge of the bed. Tully was offering him a dozen reasons that he might have offered to himself, and his voice faded for half a minute, telling it like it was, as I looked at the young man and tried to imagine the years ahead for him. He bit into his lip as Tully spoke, and I saw him in another world one day, maybe twenty or thirty years in the future, marching for peace or sitting in a boardroom or reading to his children. He would never know about the look on his face at that moment, his eyes that Saturday.

'Everybody's going,' Tully was saying. 'Come to G-Mex, you'll get in. And then get to fuck away from this place, as far as you can go. Mate, I'm telling you. Before they get their hooks into you, before they ruin you, just run and don't come back!' Tully was standing on the bed now. 'Vamoose! Scarper! How no'?'

I stood on the bed, too. 'That's right,' I said. 'What's your name?'

'Fergus!'

'That's you, Fergus,' I shouted. 'King of Salford!'

'The whole fuckan country needs you, Fergus,' Tully shouted.

'D'yez think?'

I looked at Tully and Tully looked at me. Then we both looked at Fergus and shouted as we jumped on the bed.

'Go to G-Mex!' Tully said, bouncing higher. 'You've got to!'

'Take. Over. The world,' I shouted.

'Fuck selling beds,' Tully said. 'The whole *country*'s asleep. Go . . . to the festival and then . . . fuck off somewhere else. This is it, Fergus!'

'Go on,' I said.

The guy was nodding and started jumping on the spot. He let off a fart. 'I will,' he said. 'I feckin hate it here. G-Mex! New Order!'

'Go!'

'Selling stupid feckin beds to lazy bastards.'

'That's right, Fergus. That's fuckan right,' Tully said, pointing at him and egging him on and bouncing at the same time.

He jumped up on the bed next to us, a big grin on his face. Then Tully bounced to the next bed and the next one, still shouting. 'No stopping you, Fergus! This place is dead, mate. Dead, dead, dead.'

'Dead, dead, dead,' the boy shouted back. His arms were all over the place and I imagined him again in a car one day, driving home.

'Go! Go! Go! Go! Go!'

We jumped all the way to the front of the showroom. The sales assistant showed us all his mad teeth and he rubbed his hair and ripped off his badge. On the last bed nearest the door, Tully and I were bouncing and hitting each other with the pillows when young Fergus leapt onto the warehouse floor. I've never seen an expression like it. 'Yer great lads!' he said. Then he went out through the glass doors and stood on the street, looked both ways, and ran for it. Tully fell down on the bed.

'No way, man,' he said. 'No way.'

I thought of Fergus running all the way to G-Mex. Then I thought of him running the World Bank or taking a flight to Mexico.

• • •

There was no sign of the barber at his shop. Tully asked me for a pen and some paper, so I slung my duffel bag down on the step and got them out. He wrote a note saying that Paul's old friend Stedman in Ayrshire had sent us to say hello and that we'd see him another time. I can still picture Tully's words written out to this gentleman we'd never met, the sheer hope and personality in them. 'We'll get you to fix our hair next time and if you're in a faraway place we send you the best wishes in the world. If you ever come to Scotland please depend on us for music and good times in *La Lucha*.'

We went from there to the canal. The development was just starting then, bridges coming down and cranes everywhere. Old warehouses stood at the edge of the water decked with faded words. 'Manufacturers', said one, above broken windows; like a white shadow on the bricks, the word 'Rubber'. We sat on the bollards and Tully suddenly grew dark again, after all the hilarity.

'You okay?'

'That guy,' he said. 'The way he got totally excited. Left that fuckan furniture shop, right there and then.'

'Top class,' I said.

'Dead-end job – gone, just like that.'

I felt he was trying to say more. Then he did. 'All those guys where I work. They're waiting to buy their houses off the council. Is that all there is? A guy in our factory topped himself. He did a total Ian Curtis from the beam in the canteen.'

'Jesus, did he?'

'Aye. Three weeks ago. Dead.'

'I'm surprised you didn't say anything, Tully.'

'I dunno. It upset me.'

'And he did this at work?'

He nodded. 'Start of his shift.'

'You should get out of there, mate. Go to night school, take the Highers, go to uni. Do something you care about.'

'Maybe I'm not cut out for anything else.'

'Bullshit. It's happening.'

'Something's changed, Jimmy.'

'Look at that guy in the furniture shop,' I said.

'I know. That was a masterpiece.'

'No question,' I went on. 'Soon as we get back. Take the books from my place. All of them. I'll be in a small room anyway. Take the Highers. We'll sort it.'

'Sometimes I think I'll die in there, like the guy in the canteen. I can't rely on the band to get me out – not really. And you can't just live for the occasional gig and a few nights down the Glebe.'

'It's over,' I said. 'We have an agreement.'

'That teacher helped you, didn't she?' he said. 'She got you. And you're never coming back, Noodles. You're off.'

'I know how to do it now,' I said. 'We can go at life differently.'

'Night school.'

'Then you're free. Or in a better prison.' We shook on it. He changed his life as he looked towards the canal and saw the cranes and the sun over Salford. A guy walked past carrying two Kwik Save bags and Tully flicked a butt into the dirty water. Seagulls went for it. We stood up and wandered. You couldn't walk much further: 'Salford Quays Project Team', it said on a board, blocking the path. We sat back down on the bank, watching flies dancing over the water, and time vanished. I won't attempt to cover all the things we said there, but it felt like a big conversation.

'Your dad will be all right.'

'I hope he will. But it's not my fight.' He turned. 'That night we made the soup. You could see when he came into the kitchen that he sort of hated us.'

'It must be hard for him,' I said.

'But all he had to do was look at my mum's face. She loved us being there and the soup was magic.'

'True.'

He reclined on his elbows and looked at the sky. 'He's got this crazy fuckan pride in being a victim,' he said. 'And now he is a victim. That's how it works. You complain long enough and then the heart attack arrives.'

'He can't control that, Tully.'

'He spent the strike slagging off the other miners. He never shifted a single one of his prejudices. And recently, while we were making things nice at the house he was upstairs boiling with anger. The way he turns up at the football field all raging and full of spite about the boys trying to get a clear shot at the goal. Violence, man. At some level they pass that on to you, the violence. Unless you say no.'

'Well, you are saying no. You're leaving that factory.'

'I've felt it all in my head, Noodles.' He paused. 'Fathers like ours think they're brave. I'll tell you who's brave – Steady McCalla. You know what they call him in the Glebe? "That Hamilton Accie", after the football team, to rhyme with Paki. Jesus Christ: he's never been to Pakistan. And that's our fathers talking like that. That's them, socialists lumping people together and talking about "darkies". It makes me sick. And they have nothing on Steady. Nothing as thinkers. Nothing as cooks or book-readers or fathers or anything, those men – white, working class.'

'You're right, Tully. But . . . we defend the workers.'

'I defend their rights, not their prejudices.'

'Tibbs would be troubled by this conversation.'

'But he doesn't have a dad like mine, or yours,' Tully said.

'That's true. Tibbs'll be the last man standing.'

A terrible truth was exposed, for two boys who loved those films, those trapped men, those rebellious women. 'I can't wait to get home and start again,' Tully said. I think it was a moment of pure honesty, and maybe we were adults for the first time, sitting by that canal in perfect daylight under the moving cranes.

. . .

Salford wasn't as far from the centre of Manchester as we'd expected, and we walked back. Along the way, near a round-about, Tully made us enter a car repair shop, a petrol-scented dump watched over by a guy in a shiny suit. I stood by the door while Tully went up to the counter. 'I want to spray my TR7 red,' he said to the guy. 'Do you have anything red? I mean really, really red, like a randy baboon's arse.'

'Em, okay,' the man said. He glanced at me as if there might be help available in dealing with the lunatic before him.

'I mean so red you could see it from space. I mean that really randy red, you know like a small dog's penis?'

'Right, yes. We have this.' The man reached into a stack of cans. 'Obviously, these are just for testing the colour. Is that what you mean?'

'Red as the apple in *Snow White*, mate. Red as fuck, basically.' Tully nodded vigorously as if the art of negotiation was all he knew. 'As red as Diana Ross's lips in that picture by Andy Warhol.'

The shopkeeper again looked to me for help.

'Is this guy for real? What's he talking about?'

'I'm afraid so,' I said. 'And I've no idea.'

'You'll have to book the car in for a full respray.'

'Can I not just do it myself with hundreds of cans?'

'It wouldn't look good, mate,' the man said. Tully focused on the stack of cans and inspected the colours while stroking his chin. Raphael or Matisse might have struggled to show such a deep interest in the peculiarities of colour.

'I'm talking red. Powerful red,' he said. 'What do you think, Jimmy?' He turned to me. 'Soviet, right? Good and proper *red*.' I was creased by the door as he lifted a can. 'I feel we're getting closer. Maybe this.' He held it aloft and nodded with a face fairly lit up with menace.

'*Randy baboon.*'

He'd quickly folded away the conversation from earlier, the factory, the depression, the fears he harboured about his life, and returned to the banter, as if to prove that every mood has its instantaneous opposite. Tully was always like that – he could switch it off. But embarrassments were subtle, and he often took quick revenge on his thoughtful moments. The words by the canal had to be recuperated, for now, in a dashing return to his usual style; each painfully expressed ambition for himself, each hope and regret, to be parcelled up and shelved by a sudden return of Tullyness.

As we made our way down John Dalton Street, he told me

we were a bit early to meet the boys outside G-Mex, and any-way he wanted to find a certain shop. He wouldn't say more, but led us down a few side streets and eventually we came out beside a building he said we'd passed that morning. It was an Army Careers office with black signage over the window. 'Here it is,' he said, grinning wildly, as if nothing in life had ever bothered him. He walked straight up to the window, removing the can from his pocket. I stood back while he lifted his arm and sprayed in huge red letters, 'Fascist Pig'.

He dropped the can and turned. 'It's our turn to run, Noodles!'

But I thought the graffito a tad unfinished. As he sped past me, I ran up to the window, lifted the can, and sprayed an 's' to make it 'Pigs'.

There was commotion inside the shop. I stood back for a second to admire our work and then tossed the can and pelted after Tully.

11

To my lost parents it was all Perry Como and Nat King Cole. They liked easy listening, cardigan music, and rock 'n' roll didn't touch them. They spoke of ration-book torch singers, Ruby Murray, Alma Cogan, and Anne Shelton, women they'd seen on their first television sets, lipsticked and mild, those broken balladeers, dressed to the nines in yellow crochet. My mother once told me Debbie Harry looked dirty, and I asked her if she meant it in a bad way. She preferred clean women who came blinking into the limelight, doing angst in a cocktail dress. 'That was when a song was a song,' she said. 'And that Indian rubbish or indie rubbish or whatever it is you play would drive a person mad.'

G-Mex was the old Manchester Central railway station. The building was newly renovated that year, ready for its first big concert, and young people poured in from Deansgate and Piccadilly to reach this long, arched building, a Victorian palace of small windows with a white clock up high that said 2 p.m. On the steps outside the venue, there remained a sense of arrivals and departures, and most of us stood wearing new T-shirts. A crowd was gathering. The sun was shining. The beers came out. The decade was ripe. 'I think we saw that girl you were with last night,' Hogg said to me.

'The girl from last night?'

'The girl from last night.'

'What, the girl from last night? You're saying you saw her?'

'Aye. In Portland Street. Just walking by with these other lassies. Her from last night with the hair things.'

'Fuck, Hogg. You saw her?'

'Definitely her. On their way to G-Mex.'

Across from where we stood, outside the Midland Hotel, I saw a woman feeding ice cream to her dog and there was an aeroplane high overhead. I saw policemen chatting on the steps and there was a total sense of July. I had a word with Tully and we discussed tactics about the missing ticket and he said it would be fine. He was all reassurance. 'Manchester's not for amateurs,' he said with a nod, cuffing me round the ear. 'Come the revolution, all the tickets will be free, anyhow.'

We went up to the doors and I swept through with the ticket, a guy gruffly ripping it in half as I shuffled my duffel bag onto my shoulder. I looked back to see Tully beaming all handsomely and shaking the hand of a man on the door. 'Hey, mate,' I heard him say. 'My pal's gone ahead with my ticket.'

'He's got your ticket?'

'Standing. I promise you, mate.'

'You taking the piss, son?'

I thought it best to take a sharp left into the hall and disappear, just in case the doorman tried to call me back. 'Easy, when you know how,' Tully said a few seconds later as he shouldered his way through the crowd. 'Now, what's it all about, Sunshine? Let's get completely blootered.'

Then to drinks in plastic cups. In my mind the venue is huge, but it was the high, arched ceiling that made you think so. A few thousand people came straggling in wearing black denim and T-shirts, scarlet beads and considered hair. Most of the punters were standing, but there were bleachers, too, and we managed to nip behind the barrier and jam our bags under the bottom row. The concert had already started, some band onstage that we didn't care about, Orchestral Manoeuvres in the Dark. I drew from my jacket a worn copy of my birth certificate and flattened it out on the bar when the guy asked my age. He looked like a roadie for ZZ Top. 'I think you'll find, Mr Barman, sir,' Tully said, leaning over, 'that the fellow before you comes from a long line of school refusers.'

'That's true,' I said. 'Multiple convictions.'

Clogs joined in. 'I'm afraid so. Grievous crimes. These people came from the bottom rung of Glasgow society, crazed with Catholic proclivities and holy water, resistant to all the usual customs of civilisation—'

'Mate . . . I've got a busy bar here.'

'It's all there to see.' Clogs lifted the certificate. 'Look, sir. Father a journeyman tramp, mother a toothless hawker. Names marked with a cross. They lived for years off the Communion host and free school dinners.'

'Right,' said the barman. 'Three pints of cider?'

'Make mine a double,' Limbo said, squeezing in. 'It's thirsty work concealing your hatred of that abysmal band. Some guy jumped on stage and whacked the singer on the head with a beer tray.'

'That's bad,' the barman said, pouring the pints. 'We're short on trays.'

'Right over the napper,' Limbo continued. 'Deserves him right, dancing like that. Bunch of musos. What does that mean, anyway?' He spat out the words. 'Orchestral. Manoeuvres. Is it a sex-with-violins thing?'

I thought I caught sight of Angie, up in the stands. I walked a few steps, heart going and all that. This was pathetic. You meet a girl and you talk to her for twenty minutes and you think it's a wedding. But I was sure I'd seen her up ahead of me, and it all felt uncanny, like she was the spirit of something. And then there were too many people in the way and I lost her. Wee Tibbs joined us now with a look of general awe. Limbo passed around the drinks. He had made a special effort with his hair that day. It stood up in epic liquorice fronds, held in place, he told us, with nearly a full can of Bristows he'd stolen from Boots while touring the town. Two girls, heavily back-combed, came up to our group with a paper cup, asking for donations. 'What's the charity?' Tibbs asked.

'We are, you great wazzock,' one of them said. She took his pint and poured half of it into her cup, then they drank it down and gave us the finger. Time went quickly. A few vodkas and a flurry of denunciations aimed at the Queen or the Pope, and then the Fall were coming on, except it wasn't the Fall, it was Derek Hatton from Militant. He came onstage with the aid of crutches and a grin the size of Toxteth.

'At last!' Tibbs said. 'About time they took a Marxist off the subs bench.'

'Send him to focking Siberia,' a Brummie goth standing next to us said. Tibbs looked at him like the guy was asking for a smack.

'Shut it, ya dick,' he said. 'Hatton stuck up for the miners, so he did, when most of the country was toasting Thatcher for beating them back.'

'Nah, mate. They were right to expel him. He's a nutcase.' Tibbs stepped forward, spread his feet and put his index finger to his chin, a bit like Napoleon on the brow of the hill at Austerlitz.

'Hey. I'm a lover not a fighter, man,' the guy said.

'You're a fuckan tosspot blackleg prick is what you are.'

Tibbs then turned to the stage and hollered in agreement with whatever inaudible thing Hatton was saying. 'Go on, Derek!' There was booing from the crowd. Hatton made a few football jokes and offered good wishes from the people of Liverpool, but the crowd wasn't having it. 'What's the matter with you idiots?' Tibbs shouted, wheeling round and pointing his plastic cup at the stage. 'That guy stood up for working people while you lot were in your bedrooms wanking off to the *Sun*.'

'He reasoned,' said Clogs.

'Stood up to the Tories, so he did!' A space was opening up around him and he downed his drink for the benefit of the spectators. In Tyrone's world, there wasn't time for negotiations. It was better to release all your demons at once, like one of our faves, Peter Finch in *Network*. 'Wake up, you fuckan bastards. You cowards! I know what else you are – total slaves.

This man shakes a fist in the face of corrupt power and what do you do? How do you show your solidarity? By booing! Telling you . . .' He was having the time of his life. He took Limbo's cider off him and chugged it down before dusting off the denouement. 'Yeez are pricks. Fuckan hippy, maw's-beads-wearin', gladioli-spunkin', picket-line-crossin' pricks, and that includes you, hen.' A pale young woman wearing a New Order T-shirt had passed in front of him holding a purple drink and a packet of Quavers.

'Leave me out of it,' she said. 'I thought he was the guy from *Brookside*.'

'Now *Brookie*'s getting it!'

As if on cue, the gap closed up and John Cooper Clarke appeared onstage to do his 'Fuck' poem.

• • •

The future was daylight. The Fall were onstage and the singer was arched over like the venue, gasping for England. It was late afternoon. What a crowd. No one really knew what was going on in the next heart along, but we heaved forward as if we all misunderstood in the exact same key, and there he was, Mark E. Smith, the Fine Fare Baudelaire, school jumper, ramping up the eff-offs and gripping the mic by the knob, sloping about the stage. He didn't sing the words, he inebri-ated them. The guy in front of me was rubbing his gums with speed. He licked the wrapper, and then his pal, jacket say-ing 'UK Subs', sent arcs of white spittle over the heads of the crowd into a great happy nowhere of disdain.

'Totally fuckan magic,' Tully said.

Tibbs had wandered off to shake Derek Hatton's hand. He said the world was full of tossers but when he came back ten minutes later he said Hatton was a tosser, too. We felt maybe the handshake hadn't gone well. In the meantime, space had opened up for Limbo. I felt the entire hall responded to him. He drained the cups and got cigs off everybody. He had spoken much nonsense and staggered about and he was now at rest, sitting at our feet, a twelve-skinner between his fingers. The festival was patchy and there were little islands in the day when you could sit around. The Fall left the stage in a blaze of signature disgust and expletives, at which point Limbo, still sitting, offered the group of us a theory that the blue light in *Halloween* is surely the colour of heaven.

'Nah,' Tully said. 'Heaven be black. Everybody knows that. Ask Clogs.'

'Gratified to be consulted,' Clogs said, reaching down and taking the joint and staring into the middle distance. 'Yes. The colour of paradise, or the matter of God's decor. It's a useful topic any day of the week. Especially today. I make no reference to the Bible, a self-help book for thanatophobes—'

'*Que?*' said Limbo.

'People frightened of death. I gain little from them, and draw your attention to science fiction, particularly to the work of Philip K. Dick, who believed such astral utopias to be red, or maybe turquoise.'

'Red!' I said, turning to Tully.

'*Randy baboon*,' he said. I'll spare the details, but we next discussed what the paints in the Dulux colour range would be called if we were in charge.

What we had that day was our story. We didn't have the other bit, the future, and we had no way of knowing what that would be like. Perhaps it would change our memory of all this, or perhaps it would draw from it, nobody knew. But I'm sure I felt the story of that hall and how we reached it would never vanish.

'What does the E stand for in Mark E. Smith?' Tibbs asked.

'England, I presume,' said Clogs.

• • •

It felt hot in the early evening. Proper heatwave hot, inside the hall. There were black-and-white banners overhead saying 'Festival of the Tenth Summer', and they began to drip condensation, as if all those summers had come at once. The teenage tribes of Britain became close as the evening arrived. Everyone was leaning towards the stage, emotional and ready for the arrival of something we couldn't exactly place. And up in the seating area they waved their arms and I felt the magic of association. It was like a wave of empathy and trepidation all at once and I wanted those people to be cared for.

Then I definitely saw her. Angie. A few minutes before six o'clock, standing at the outer rim of the hall, I could see her waving down at me from a bank of seats. She radiated alertness, with a smile as strong as the feeling in the hall. She waved again and blew me a kiss, holding up a huge paper cup. I made my way closer. I had a standing ticket and the barrier to the seats was now too well-policed. But she ran down and stroked my face and kissed me. I just beamed at her and said nothing. 'Make sure you come to the Hacienda,' she shouted with a hand curved round her mouth.

'I wouldn't miss it for the world,' I replied.

'Bingo!' she shouted and ran back up.

Then the Smiths came on.

Aubrey Beardsley in white jeans: Morrissey in his prime. The singer wafted into view and sold his drowsy reticence like a drug. The band was at its height, romantic and wronged and fierce and sublime, with haircuts like agendas. Morrissey came brandishing a licence, a whole manner of permission, as if a new kind of belonging could be made from feeling left out, like nobody knew you as he did. Time takes nothing away from it, those thousands of heartened teenagers taking the roof off and giving out to a gawky frontman from Stretford. Tully found me and pushed me down to the stage. Over the speakers the sound was scratchy, but every word and every guitar lick felt like a statement only they could make, and only we could hear, those songs rolling from the stage to irrigate our lives. 'That's what it's all about,' Tully shouted and he kissed my cheek as we sang.

I could see Limbo at the very front, whirling out of his skin, holding up a smoke and shouting about panic on the streets of Carlisle. Then he was near us and wagging his finger in time to the music, a wonderful look on his face, singing about a vicar, about Joan of Arc, and throwing plastic tumblers into the air. Our hair was soaking wet. The Ayrshire boys appeared from all corners of the hall, and we hugged and the music soared and it seemed like a huge animation of the things that mattered to us then. Tibbs and Hogg, Limbo and Tully and Clogs. The full brass of being. Who knew what time incubated or what life would demonstrate; we were there, beyond navigation, floating through the air. We beamed to the rafters and jumped shoulder to shoulder. And the words we sang were daft and romantic and ripe and British, custom-built for the clear-eyed young.

The singer threw a spotted shirt from the stage and a group of lads tore it to ribbons and waved the bits like trophies.

'He's bigger than Jesus,' Tully said.

'You reckon?'

'A bit funnier.'

'Definitely funnier,' I said.

They say you know nothing at eighteen. But there are things you know at eighteen that you will never know again. Morrissey would lose his youth, and not just his youth, but the gusto that took him across the stage with a banner saying 'The Queen Is Dead' is a thing of permanence. We didn't know it at the time, but it was also, for all of us, a tender goodbye, and we would never be those people again. 'Check Limbo,' Tully said in my ear, and I looked to the edge of the stage where the boy himself was spread over a speaker, climbing. Nobody at that age needs more than what Limbo McCafferty had in abundance. He had vitality. He had the spirit of resistance in that single moment. And as the final encore bristled and rose to perfect confusion, Limbo appeared on the stage, going past crewmen and bouncers to take up residence by the drums, dancing and smiling for eternity, the crowd cheering him on and spiriting the light in his direction.

12

In a chip shop in Chepstow Street, Dr Clogs gave the punters a lecture on the chief properties of vinegar while Limbo fondled the *Daily Express*. Tully was going through the bands we'd just seen, telling us which were great. He reviewed the whole gig while we waited for deep-fried essentials and concluded that New Order ruled the cosmos. 'I expect a knighthood for getting you in without a ticket,' he said to me.

'I know, mate. You could charm the birds from the trees.'

'All in a good cause,' he said.

Outside the chippy, Hogg was talking about German bands. It wasn't much of a crowd-pleaser, but one girl, not local, asked him if he'd heard of the architect Mies van der Rohe, so they started snogging. You know how it goes: from shy and undateable to swaggering and post-coital, in seconds. Hogg was soon holding her hand as if their intimacy was a matter of domestic wisdom and harmony distilled through the years. They were still talking about architecture when Dr Clogs appeared like a dark aura from the shop and was captured by the sight of the young Hogg in love. He listened, then threw a chip. 'This at last is the perfect union,' he said. 'Gropius *and* gropes?'

'This is Annika,' Hogg said.

'She's got blue hair,' Clogs said. 'Blue as Lincoln's heaven. Which is to say, blue as Limbo's heaven. But limbo, the place, comes before heaven, or instead, if you can't get in. If you know what I mean.' He appeared for a moment to be delving into his poke of chips for crumbs of sense, then he glanced up again. 'And she's got plastic earrings. I suppose they're all the rage above the clouds.'

'She's from Cologne.'

'Of course she is,' Clogs said.

'She's studying transport engineering at Salford.'

'Lovely.'

We sat with our backs to the lighted window, our hair still damp from the gig. It was about eleven o'clock and Tibbs was asleep, lying with his head on his bag and mumbling to himself. Airless night. Sauce on the chips. 'We better finish up,' I said. 'We've got to get to the Hacienda. We're missing stuff.'

'Hold your horses,' Tully said. 'Tibbs is having a nap.'

Dr Clogs still leered at the obnoxious lovers. The German girl meshed her fingers with Hogg's and retreated behind him, head on his shoulder. 'I think there are a few things you should know about your modern lover,' Clogs said.

'Is he speaking with us?' she asked.

'Ignore him.'

'Mr Hogg once had a demi-wave.' The doctor said it and threw a chip into the air and stepped backwards to catch it in his mouth.

'I fuckan did not, Clogs, ya prick.' We all cracked up at that. If comedy is the science of specifics, there was genius in the word 'demi-wave'. 'Say that again and I'll fuckan lamp you.'

'He was Robot Dave,' Clogs said. 'He believed in tomorrow. We all did. But David took it to extremes. He liked Japan.'

'Shut your fuckan face, Bobby. I mean it.'

'The band, I mean.' Clogs was enjoying himself. 'In those days he expressed his futurism mainly via the medium of lipstick and eyeshadow. Especially lipstick. And eyeshadow. And painted fingernails. Blouses. I believe he once turned up at school wearing a Pierrot doll costume – pompoms for buttons, that kind of thing. They say he was going through a ballet phase. There was a black teardrop on his cheek. What can I tell you? He made Steve Strange look like Charles Bronson. Took pounders off the corner boys, but not to worry. He was an *individual*. He may have been the first New Romantic robot in the whole of Ayrshire. Not a well-contested field, I admit—'

A can of Coke and a poke of chips came flying. Hogg quickly followed, throwing a lousy punch at Clogs before pushing him over. Tibbs opened his eyes for a second, just long enough to see the fists. 'Wallop the bam,' he muttered.

'I say,' shouted Clogs from the rolling centre of his own scrap, 'Duran Duran has gone mental! Get back, you cad!'

'Fuckan hair like Elvis,' Hogg said. 'Cross-eyed, greasy, fuckan loser.' The doctor got up from the ground and wiped his hands. He was happy. 'Ugly fuckan computer geek ponce,' Hogg continued. 'MC5-loving, muso dick . . . I hated Japan and I never once had a fuckan black teardrop.'

'True,' Tully said from our spot by the window. 'It was more grey.'

'Fuck off, the lot of you. I mean it.' And Hogg staggered back, reaching for the girlfriend and her deeper knowledge of him.

'Fade to grey,' Clogs said.

Hogg and his missus stropped off down the street. Tully shook Tibbs awake.

'We're off, Tyrone.'

'Praise Marx and pass the joint,' said Tibbs.

• • •

We pleaded our case to the Hacienda bouncers. From the outside, the club was an old brown tenement with manky windows, but in our heads it was the gateway to a new world. By now, Limbo was a walking Chernobyl. But one of the bouncers was Scottish and we got summoned past the cordon. We had to chip in for Limbo. He'd used the last of his cash to buy some dodgy ticket off a guy in G-Mex.

'What ticket?' I asked him.

'To Salford and beyond,' was all he said.

Once you were past the cashier, before you went into the club itself, there was a cardboard cut-out of Tony Wilson saying 'Welcome'. Tibbs kissed it and we pushed back a curtain of clear rubber. And there it was: the Hacienda, engine-room of the new self, where nothing was taken for granted. With its metal pillars, black and yellow chevrons, it resembled the packing area of a minor industrial plant, yet there was a romantic quality to it, an uncanny rightness. I stood for a moment watching two girls in cascading bangles dancing to the Durutti Column, and Tibbs handed me a Rolling Rock.

There was an upstairs area and Tully went for a walk up there. I had a scout around the ground-floor bar and looked among the crowd.

No sign of Angie.

'If *The Ragged Trousered Philanthropists* was a club,' Tully said, back from upstairs, 'it would look like this. A place for the working man to forget himself.'

'No, remember himself,' Tibbs said.

Clogs and Limbo got acquainted with a Rasta in a sheepskin coat. He had a laminated menu, so we bought sensimilla and were soon introduced to everybody as 'the Scotch'. Tully and I sat quietly on a metal bench while Clogs progressed from a few Ayrshire stabs at the importance of smoking grass to a full-blown denunciation of Babylon, with multiple references to the sacramental properties of ganja, to which Clogs was soon referring, with a mild Jamaican twang, as 'the herb'. Under the lights of the nightclub I could see a few specks of yellow paint on the front of Limbo's boots.

Nag, Nag, Nag . . .

The pulse in that place was like nowhere else. The beat of it and the taste of the vodka and my head was dialling into the tune . . .

'*I dunno, work tomorrow*,' Tully said. He quoted other things, and Albert Finney came floating in front of me, confused with the girl from *Mona Lisa*. I think it was the first time I had ever heard loud guitars mingled with dance stuff.

We were soon on the floor. It was different from all the

places I had known. 'You all right, wee man?' Tully said.

Somebody threw a handful of glitter in the air.

Another Rasta gave me a slug of his beer. Somebody gave me a kiss.

The lights and memory intermingled with all those people up in the balcony smiling down and somewhere in the music Grace Jones sang and a spiky guitar sounded and holy Jesus I was high and never happier and – over there . . . my friends' faces on the other side and Tyrone holding up a glass and what's happening and the beat pumping. All the people and all the times and every single thought catching the light and the beat saying yes and the people saying yes and time vanishing—

'I've divorced my mum and dad.'

'Don't be daft,' he said. 'They'll be back . . .'

'I'm not having them back. It's the solo life . . .'

Somebody passed another joint and I drew deeply and kept the smoke back and then spewed it out in one long puff of enjoyment. On the dancefloor, Angie came past with a huge slice of melon and offered it to me and I took a bite, and I never saw her again. It wasn't a problem and the music was so—

'Jeezo,' I said. 'I'm out of breath here.'

'Take me back to dear old Blighty . . .'

Limbo appeared. 'I went up to the DJ and asked him to play my favourite song.' The song was 'Candyskin' by the Fire Engines.

'Are they going to play it?'

'He told me to piss off to Jilly's, they don't do requests.'

I had to take my time: it was all rushing. I wandered off and sat on my own, just having a breather. I don't know how long. Eventually, Tully came. His eyes were huge. 'This is the best night of my life,' he said, slugging his beer and leaning into me. 'The best weekend of my life. I'm glad we're all here together. Noodles?'

'A million per cent,' I said.

'Candyskin' came on. And somewhere in heaven, in the comical blue or red or turquoise up there, it plays on. Tully clasped me round the neck and tried to speak over the music. 'I'm going to do it. I'm getting out. The world's changing.'

'All the way, Tully.'

'Aye. All the way.'

13

We found it hard to accept the night was over. Maybe it never was. After the club, we walked through the streets and sang in the squares and we found a last drink at a bar called New York, fast by the Rochdale Canal. The bouncer said it was a gay bar and Limbo told him every man should be just gay enough. Inside, it was last orders. We each had a martini because Tully said that's what you drank in New York. (He never made it there.) A drag queen was finishing on a tiny stage but she let Tully take the mic and sing Roy Orbison's 'In Dreams'. All things considered, he did well.

On leaving, I waved to the drag queen. '*Au revoir*, Edith Piaf.'

'Nighty night,' she said. 'Cheeky Bastards United.'

Tibbs went sleepwalking down Portland Street. In the end he slid down inside a bus shelter on Peter Street with his stuff behind his head, not twenty yards from the site of the famous massacre. Clogs slumped down beside him. 'Massacres come in many forms,' he said, 'and I fear the grapeshot of booze and cannabis have done their worst.'

'I'm not sleeping in a bus stop,' Limbo said.

'Of course not,' Clogs said, turning his jacket around to make a blanket and leaning his head on an already snoring Tibbs.

'Shut it, Bobby. I've got asthma. I don't feel well.'

'Nothing to do with the five thousand pints of cider you drank,' Tully said, crushing his last cigarette into the Perspex.

'For fuck's sake,' Limbo said. 'There was a draw left in that. Just as well I stashed a cheeky few tabs for the night shift.'

He pulled out a packet of Kensitas Club.

'All hail the new asthma,' Clogs said.

There was a brown building on the other side of the road. It suddenly loomed like an apparition, a sort of oasis in the stunted night. It said 'St George's House' and the patron saint was high on the building, in an alcove, with his shield and sword. Closer to street level there was a small neon sign that said 'YMCA'.

'Not for me,' Clogs said, alerted to the opportunity. 'I'm in the lap of luxury here and I'll look after County Tyrone. He's passed out.'

It took only a few seconds to cross the road. The guy at the desk was drunker than we were and he said three people in the room was fine. Two beds for nine quid. Limbo and I were skint but Tully paid in pound coins and we were soon ascending in an old caged lift. I dropped my bag in the room and Limbo lay down and fell asleep. I pulled up the sash window. 'Got to get the boy some air,' I said, tucking a blanket around him.

'Too right,' Tully said. 'Old Lincoln.'

'The Liberator,' I said. 'He drank up the whole saloon.'

• • •

Tully and I went off to explore. It was his idea: I was drooping, but for Tully the night could not be over. He wanted further adventures, more time, more everything, and he liked the darkness in the marble halls. We found a huge, weird space at the top of the building, a whole room under glass with a swimming pool. Nobody around, no security guard, just a white fan whirring beside a television set. We could see over Manchester and its strips of neon – Pernod, Askit, Foo Foo's, Bingo – and endless streetlights going, I imagined, to Huddersfield or Halifax. We sat on two plastic chairs in front of the TV. I think it was the first time I'd seen a programme on so late. Reagan was speaking from the Oval Office about the many young soldiers still missing in action in Vietnam.

'Do you think he's unreal?' Tully said.

'He's an actor,' I said. 'He just speaks the lines.'

Tully found the grass from the Hacienda in his pocket. He had papers and a lighter. No baccy. So I was dispatched to rifle Limbo's pockets. He was snoring when I got there, grinning like the air of Brigadoon was in his lungs. I slid a few Kensitas Club out of his packet and I remember pausing by the door, looking back.

Upstairs, Tully was staring into the pool.

'What's old Limbo saying down there?' he asked.

'Nothing,' I said. 'He drank the sea.'

'All those lights,' Tully said. 'It reminds me of those football stadiums abroad – when it's a bit dark and the fans have flares, and they light up the whole place. During the World Cup in Argentina, my dad and I, we watched a game where they did that. The ground had floodlights, but the people lit flares.'

'You watched it with your dad.'

'Argentina versus Peru. They won six-nil, the Argies. My dad was jumping out of his chair. It's the closest we've ever been.'

He ran a cigarette along his tongue and burst it open for the tobacco. He rolled a joint and we took our socks and shoes off, turned up our jeans and dipped our legs in the pool, transfixed by the city.

'*Made it, Ma! Top of the world*,' he said, passing the lighted joint.

'Top of the world, Tully.'

'I'm as high as a kookaburra, and I'm going in.' He pulled off his T-shirt and all his clothes and dived into the pool. I sat on the edge, grinning. I could see the shape of him rippling underwater as he swam to the other side. Then he emerged, circling his arms backwards and treading water for the Commonwealth. 'Stay free, Noodles,' he shouted. 'And get in here.' I turned the lights off and the city blinked to the end of the night. The water was cold but it soon warms up when the boys are made of sunshine.

Autumn
2017

14

There was a dinner that night in Eaton Square. The novelist being celebrated, my eighty-five-year-old friend, was once a state-sponsored journalist in Budapest. Then one day she got up and wrote a beautiful novel about the animals abolishing the zoo. Krisztina Elek: the baker's daughter who fought the forces of indifference in a whole society. She was not tall but always elegant and her coiffed hair was the colour of the Danube. At about ten o'clock, I crossed the room to say goodbye, and she took my hand, not entirely in the birthday mood. 'Come and see me soon, James,' she said, with a comical weariness of heart. 'We can grasp the moment and drink a glass of champagne together.' She liked to make a little drama. 'You can help me fight the forces of self-loathing.'

'I'll take that as a compliment,' I said.

'But champagne, mind.'

I put my collar up and was walking towards Sloane Square when I took out my phone. The screen was quickly wet with rain. A text from Tully Dawson jumped out at me. It was only three words: 'Can you speak?'

'Home in half an hour,' I texted back. 'Are you all right?'

'I'll phone you at eleven, Noodles,' he replied.

On the Tube it was all a smear. I sat in the empty carriage, seeing in my mind the red sign for the Britannia Hotel, years ago with Tully. At home, I took off my tie and poured a whisky. Tully was a teacher now. Head of English. Many long winters ago he had studied at night school, just as we'd planned. He took all my books. And now he taught kids in the East End of Glasgow and was famous among them. I hadn't heard from him in a while and his text worried me. I tried to think of some Highland river or a bright peat fire, then the mobile lit up. 'Tullygarvan, townland of Ulster,' I said. 'What's the script?'

'Aw, Noodles.'

The line was silent for a moment.

'Take your time, buddy.'

'I'm fucked, man. Totally fucked. I didn't want to tell you.'

He began the story.

He'd been on holiday with Anna. They were in Cuba. He was hiccupping and it had happened before, but he thought it was just the drinking. He was also in pain. 'To be honest, I'd been in pain for months,' he said. 'I just thought I had a bad stomach.' When they got back home, his doctor sent him for a scan. He hesitated. 'And that's the results in tonight.' He was breathing heavily on the line. Again, he hesitated, then he said it, the worst sentence in any language: 'It's cancer.'

'Where?'

'There's a lump in my oesophagus, but it's spread to my liver, stomach, and the lymph nodes, whatever the fuck they are. It's a total . . . I'm a dead man walking. I've got four months and that's the end of it.'

'No,' I said. 'We'll get another opinion.'

'It's not a matter of opinion, mate. I'm done.'

I sat down on the sofa. I began to cry and then stopped myself. I told him he'd have every last thing he needed. He said it helped him to hear me say that and I had to stand by him and not let him die like a prick.

'We all die like pricks,' I said.

'You know what I mean. No mawkishness. No crowds round the bed. I hate the humiliation, Jimmy. Get me out when things are bad.'

'I promise. The sky's the limit,' I said, stupidly.

'The sky won't come into it,' he said.

'You know what I mean.'

'Nae bother, Noodles. Maybe we could go back to Cuba. A few of us in Havana. Take a guitar and a few spliffs.'

'Anything.'

I could hear him trying to get his head around the news, using words to find words. 'Just when the band is finally getting a bit of recognition,' he said.

I hadn't kept up with the bands. They'd swapped around. 'What's this one called?'

'Kim Philby. We just made a CD. New singer and all that. I'm on the drums these days.'

'You got it together.'

'Nearly,' he said.

We spoke for over an hour. Barbara was in a nursing home. He'd decided not to tell her. 'What would be the point? She'd just be confused and distressed, and things are bad enough.' He spoke about Limbo McCafferty, who had died fifteen years before. A whole world of hilarity had disappeared with Limbo, a perfect fire, tamped down for a few hours in that room in the YMCA on Peter Street. 'Do you remember he came to the bus station the next day,' Tully said, 'and told us he wasn't coming home. Had a ticket for the Smiths that night at Salford University and he was staying.'

'I do remember,' I said. 'Old Lincoln.'

Tully asked me to come to Ayrshire on Monday and meet him at the caravan. He said Anna was totally freaking out.

'Use the caravan as much as you like,' I said. 'You've got the keys.'

'I want everything to go on as usual,' he said. 'I'll still go to band practice and all that and keep it . . .'

'Normal.'

'*My name is Norman Bates*,' he sang. '*I'm just a normal guy.*'

He laughed. The old style. The old style when it was all fixable. Then we went over the detail again and he cried.

'Go to sleep,' I said. 'We'll make a plan.'

'I knew this was coming. And I've been having these dreams for a long time. White fields that go on and on. Pure whiteness.'

• • •

There are moments like this, when you know nothing. I sat at the table, pouring whisky and seeing clear pictures that I'd thought had faded. My eye fell on a little Mao clock standing on the dresser. It had been a gift from Tully. He brought it back from one of his trips to Cuba. In adulthood, Tully had fallen in love with 'Castro's Island', as he called it, and he would spend weeks of the long school holidays there, going back to the same bars and the same restaurants full of singers and old communists. I stared at the clock. Instead of a minute hand it had Mao waving out the seconds with his little red book. It was difficult to think of the chairman dying and the world ticking on.

I went to bed but I couldn't sleep. Iona was away on a theatrical tour and I just stared into the dark and thought of Tully at his best. Despite distances and whatever, I had stuck with the friends of my boyhood. I had gone off and learned my trade, and so had they, but we never went far from the pond. We liked its elements, it was a lively place to be, and we stayed in touch with the past, the old crowd always in the air. At a single stroke, the phone call that night had defined the year, and several other years, too. One after the other, the images arrived and they lit up the familiar dark of the bedroom.

15

Seamill – on the north Ayrshire coast. I see my father pointing to the Isle of Arran from a tartan blanket on the beach. He held my finger up when the sun was blinding and traced the shape of Beinn Tarsuinn and Goatfell. Forty years on, a caravan stood empty on a ridge above the beach, so I took it over and fixed it up, filling it with cushions and Chinese lanterns. On visits from London, I'd sit at the small table, working by candlelight as the sky grew pink. More than anybody else, Tully loved the caravan, and in the evening he'd sit out and watch the lighthouse on Holy Isle. 'I looked it up,' he said, 'and those rocks out there are called Limpet Craig and the Brither Rocks. It's like a lunar landscape, man. All those rocks. And before you know it the tide comes in.'

He arrived at four o'clock that Monday – the last in September. I heard the car pull to a halt on the gravel outside and then he came through the door like Lord Marchmain from the grouse moor. His face was white and his nose was red from the cold. He said he'd stopped in Saltcoats to get his head together. 'I walked by the sea wall for a while,' he said, 'down by the amusement arcade. I don't mean to be funny but I was nervous about coming in.' He carried a box set of *The Godfather* and a half-bottle of Glenmorangie. Kiss on the lips and the jacket unzipped: the kiss had been the Tully greeting to all his friends for decades, except this time he remained in the clinch, and we rocked in the middle of the kitchen, our foreheads pressed together. Eventually I lifted the Glenmorangie. 'What's this? You only doing half-bottles now, you cheap bastard?'

'I'm worried in case I don't have time to finish it,' he said. 'Got to be practical. I can only leave dregs for you losers.' His eyes filled and we stood by the cooker, nodding to each other and wiping our eyes, trapped in the ignorant present, then I reached up to the cupboard and brought down two glasses. The terrible thing, in a way, was his still looking so healthy and fine. His hair was sparse, the old spikes a feature of memory, and some of the sharpness had gone from his face, but he hadn't gained much weight and the same green eyes twinkled with menace. Tully always had this clear, persuasive expression, like he could back up everything he was saying, and even in our middle years, as we had previously thought of them, now his last year, he showed the same good looks and the same humour, as if cosmic eventualities were of no concern.

We sat down at the table. 'Let's drink some of this stuff and then we can walk along the beach to that diner up on the Ardrossan Road.'

'Magic.'

We ran through it all again. The diagnosis, the shock. He spoke about his sister, Fiona, and her family. How dreadful it had been telling them. His nephews and his niece meant a great deal to him, and his love of childhood, the memory of his own colourful youth, seemed to inform his understanding of them. He spoke about each, how great they were, how talented and how normal in their dramas and indecisions, and I felt for the first time in all the years of knowing him what a sweet father he'd have been. He drank from his glass and stopped now and then to look out at the autumn night. The sea was rough and Arran was a bulky eminence on the other side of the water. Crows collected in the garden in twos and threes and the wire fence swayed with the weight of them. He stood at the patio doors, and then quietly turned back towards the room, pulled the doors shut, and with that he changed the subject. 'You never saw your dad again, did you?'

'He's dead now,' I said.

'I always thought you'd get back together some day.'

'He was in the bosom of another family,' I said. 'He had a second life.'

'So did you,' he said. 'So did we.'

'True. It's one of our tricks. He loved doing favours for strangers. And I never saw him again and that seemed to suit us fine.'

'Strange, though.'

'I told you all this years ago,' I said. 'In our family, we knew how to care for other people, but not each other. My parents just weren't equipped. And I wasn't built to play the part of the neglected son. So we split up. I've never had much reason to question it. I can only remember one real conversation with him. He told me about the Yorkshire Ripper. Honestly, he sat me down and told me about this killer, and how the guy who sent the tape to the police wasn't the real perpetrator.'

'That's definitely weird.'

'Truly. My father was a complete sociopath, when I think of it.'

'And your mum's still living over there, on Arran?'

'That's right. Fifteen miles of ocean between us.'

'Fair enough,' he said.

I opened a spiral notebook and laid a pen on the top page. 'Shall we make a plan?'

'Aye,' he said. 'I want to do this properly.'

I took up the pen. 'What's first?'

'Anna,' he said. 'What am I going to do?'

'You should marry her,' I said.

'We were going to do that before,' he said. 'But isn't it a bit weird to do it now, when she'll be left on her own?'

'You should do it all the same,' I said. 'It'll mean the world to her.'

Tall, beautiful Anna, Glasgow lawyer, gale-force debater, whom he met at a party in the late 1990s. 'She's her own person and she won't take any crap off me,' he told us at the time. They were great together – fun, lippy, well-matched in cheekbones – and they were generally available for the same kinds of adventure. Tully had always been a leader in appearance only. He needed help.

'I love her,' he said.

'Then it's a wedding.' I underlined it on the notepad. 'Do it properly. There's no point holding back and Anna will want a big day.'

'Nothing too naff.'

'Do it nicely,' I said.

I'm sure it's a way of not thinking about things, burying yourself in tasks, but I've always done it. It puts fear on ice. Holds back the dark. We could talk about a wedding. I could lose myself in a country house and a dinner, spend time over trios and cars, instead of facing the uncontrollability of what was happening. It isn't always the fittest who survive, but the people who have the information, those who clock the exits. I could find in relentless occupation what I could never find in helplessness: a way through. And he was asking for a ready accomplice who might marshal reality instead of feeling crushed by it. 'Imagine I'm running for office,' he said.

'So I'm your campaign manager?'

'Totally,' he said.

Our chairs faced each other at the corner of the table. We touched glasses and he pressed my forehead again with his. It was like we were launching a rescue boat, or a scuttling mission. You could hear the waves. 'The wedding is a say-hello-wave-goodbye party,' he said. 'But I don't want a whole lot of sit-downy shite with 150 speeches.' I scribbled. 'Honestly, Noodles. I don't want it to be too big. No grannies-in-daft-hats-style bullshit.'

He took out a small bottle of cannabis oil and put three drops under his tongue. I asked him what the doctors had said about chemotherapy. 'This is the biggest thing of all,' he said, brushing a few strands of tobacco off his knee. 'I want you to help me with this more than anything. So, I'm dying, right? I accept that now. We will all accept it eventually. What I don't want to do is drag the whole fandango out just for the sake of it. I'm not going to lie there like a skeleton, making everybody suffer. People watching you lose weight. Don't let it happen, man. No point delaying the inevitable. They said with chemo I could have an extra seven months.'

'Then take it,' I said.

'I probably will do the chemo. But not to the last. Ending up like . . . just lying there. All changed. Like you never really knew me.'

His eyes brimmed over and he took a heavy pull on his cigarette and wiped his nose on his sleeve. I brought him a tissue and took the rollie from him. I had a few draws myself and I wondered if I should say it.

'*You never really knew me* – Tully, that's the exact same phrase that you thought your dad was trying to say to you.'

'Eh?'

'The day he died. I remember you telling us up in your room.'

'I don't remember that,' he said.

His father died on a Saturday afternoon about three years after the Manchester weekend, his second heart attack proving decisive. When his body was taken from the house, we sat up in Tully's bedroom, just a few of us, and he wept like I'd never seen anybody weep before, sobbing into his hands. That was when he told us that his father had looked up at him from the carpet as if to say, 'You never really knew me and now it's too late.'

I went down to the living room that night, the night Woodbine died, to hug Barbara and to borrow the key to the drinks cabinet. We stood in the middle of the room for a hug and she cried. 'Me and Ewan used to dance at the bowling club,' she said, 'and he would sing, after he'd had a few, you know?'

'Did he?'

'Oh, aye. The old songs. He was a crooner. He wasn't into loud music, not like yous.' We stayed like that for a minute, and she put her hand on my shoulder and I held her other one and we swayed for a minute or so. 'He wasn't always the way he became.' She said I was a good dancer for twenty-one.

I stood up to open the caravan's patio doors. 'There's a bit of America in that breeze,' Tully said. 'And Ireland. Blowing to the wild west of Scotland.'

'Is he on your mind?' I asked. 'Are you thinking of Woodbine?'

'I hadn't thought about him for a long time. But, since this happened, I've been thinking about him a lot. He was young when he died, but I'm even younger. He was fifty-three and I'm fifty-one. Does that mean he beat me, Noodles?'

'He didn't beat you at anything, Tully. He wanted you to win.'

He examined both his hands. In many ways, he had defined himself by being distant from his father.

'I worry this chemo will turn me into somebody I'm not.

There could be three courses of it or whatever, three sets of drugs. I don't know how many visits. People say it's a total nightmare. They say it can give you this extra time, but what if there's no . . . life?'

'You can use the time,' I said. 'You and Anna.'

'With you and Iona,' he said. 'Let's go on holiday. To Sicily. Or we could drive around America.'

A string of bunting over the door was billowing out, giving a hint of summer fête, and Tully poured another whisky and pointed towards the sea. 'It's amazing here,' he said. 'You must miss Iona when she's away.'

'I do,' I said.

'When I first met her, I told her to be kind to you. His choice, I said, but he's gone out by himself, all his life.'

'I've been lucky.'

'There's been love,' he said. He wiped his eyes. 'Let's do what we can, then bring it to an end. I don't want to be some sad sack waiting for pity.'

'You've always had style,' I said, 'so let that continue. Let that be the rule. Take the chemo if it gives you more time. I've been thinking about it all weekend. You've always been your-self, Tully, so make the end like that. In *Antony and Cleopatra*, there's a line, *Make death proud to take us.*'

'I like that.'

We lifted our drinks and the notepad and walked out onto the decking. The lights around the caravan were all burning and a heron rose from the long grass. It made a shrill call and flew at speed over the rocks. 'We must have scared it,' Tully said. 'And who are we to scare anything, eh?'

'Are you?' I asked.

'What?'

'Scared.'

'We'll see,' he said.

The sky was darkening and the clouds disappeared. Like the hour had come and the day was now ending without remorse. Early stars began to blink over the water and the last ferry was crossing on its way to Brodick.

'Promise me one thing, buddy,' he said. 'When it's obviously curtains, you've got to get me the Hitler chow-down.'

'The what?'

'The chow-down. The suicide bullet. When the bad time comes, I want to end it myself and not go skelly. I want control.'

'Have you spoken to Anna?'

'I will. But that's definitely what I want.'

'That means Switzerland,' I said, sitting on the bench. 'You're saying you want to make the trip there and end it yourself?'

'That's totally what I'm saying. In my own time.'

I knew we'd have to get started immediately on that and my thoughts went out to sea. And I remember thinking, 'Anna will never agree.'

'It's what I want,' he said again. '*Make death proud to take us.* You've given me my last quote, Noodles.'

'Assisted dying.'

'You've got to promise me.'

We walked along the beach for a mile or so, using the torch

on my phone, and when I pointed down we could see the rock pools and how the pressure of our shoes darkened the sand. Tully continued to spar with his own dread, like the boy I knew, not letting his guard down very much when sentiment threatened. He wanted jokes, and, if they were at other people's expense, so much the better. A man was coming down the beach with a large Alsatian romping in the dark. He seemed timid, the man, about our age, and he kept his head down as he drew near. 'That's some beast,' Tully said.

'Aye. It's a lovely night,' the man said. He was unsmiling but not unfriendly and that was all the encouragement Tully needed.

'Tell me,' he said to the man, 'are you riding that dug?'

'Excuse me?'

'You and the dug. Are yous at it?' Tully paused and looked fully engaged, as if he'd asked a perfectly reasonable question.

'Come on now, lads,' the guy said. As he walked away up the beach, Tully shrugged, as if no degree of surrealism was uninvited.

When we got to the diner, he asked for cherry pie, making a joke about *Twin Peaks* and the weirdness of the empty diner. He said he supposed he was now in a version of the film *Stand By Me*. 'The narrator-guy was right, mind you,' he said. 'The friends you have when you're young can turn out to be the best you ever had.' Tully ate another piece of pie and then a pizza. He said he didn't know how much longer he'd have an appetite, so he might as well go for it. He was already finding it harder to swallow. We stayed in the diner for hours, the headlights going past on the highway and the moon high and clear over the water. He kept saying, 'Switzerland'. I wasn't sure what I owed him, or what I owed him for, but the sense of duty was there, as well as the love. And as he spoke, I felt for the first time in our lives that our friendship had a final destination.

16

I wrote to a consultant I knew at the Royal Marsden. He replied in three days. 'I've read the medical reports you sent,' he said, 'and I advise you to help Mr Dawson accept the situation, dire as it is, and do what you can to make him comfortable.' I sat upstairs on the 168 bus to Camden Town with the consultant's letter in my lap. The buses were snagged up around Euston and the rain on the windows was dripping neon.

Things had moved quickly since our trip to the caravan. We spoke every day, and the conversation was always about the wedding or the ending, which competed with each other to be the larger field of anxiety. My phone rang on the bus – it was him. 'Anna thinks that if I eat more blueberries I could be all right,' he said. 'She bought a NutriBullet. She won't let me die without a battle that involves new electrical appliances.'

'You'll be cool for vitamin C, then.'

'Shut your face.'

He told me he'd now spoken to all the boys. 'And d'you know what their common reaction was?' he said. 'Embarrassment. That's what it comes down to: embarrassed silences between me and the people I love.'

'They're not embarrassed,' I said.

'So what are they?'

'They're telling the truth. Lost for words.'

He said the chemo would start soon. He'd be confined to the house at first. He said he wanted to get to Switzerland as soon as possible.

'I'm worried, Tully. You need to tell Anna what you're thinking.'

'Thinking?'

'About this end-of-life plan.'

'I will, in a while.'

'No, you have to tell her now.'

'I have told her. She's not listening. She's happy we're getting married. Let her enjoy that for a while.'

'But, Tully.'

'I promise I'll sit her down and explain the whole thing. She'll be fine.'

'She doesn't want it,' I said. 'Iona told me. Anna says it's *you* that isn't listening. I mean it, Tully, she doesn't like it.'

'What's *liking* got to do with any of this, Noodles?'

'You're marrying her; she needs to be involved.'

'She's totally involved,' he said. 'But I can't ask for anybody's permission. That's the reality. That's who she's marrying.'

There was a silent moment, while I took that in. People were coming upstairs on the bus and shaking out their umbrellas.

'Iona's play is coming north,' I said to him. 'She and Anna have arranged to have lunch and talk it all through.'

'Lunch?' Tully said. 'Who invented *that*?'

A determination had been born from the shock of those first weeks, and now, with the kind of brio he'd once brought to living, he was beginning to embody an argument about how to die in his own way. It took me by surprise how that tearful exchange of promises in the caravan now formed into a manifesto. He wanted to be the originator of his last rites and to make a portrait of his own attitude to cancer. Despite what I'd said on the phone, it seemed to me a very natural sort of bravery. The problem was, he did little to prepare the way for it, no unfolding of argument, no open heart. Tully acted like it was merely a matter of taste – like the music you were into – and he wanted to inhabit his own values without explaining them to anybody. It was like a veil had fallen, and all his carnal energy and all his native certainty – everything strong in him – was now devoted to the matter of his own destruction. I didn't understand it better than anybody else, but he needed to believe that I did, and believe that I would help him with all the logistics.

It became joined in my mind to the wedding, as if the marriage would buy him all the credit he needed, all the leeway. The wedding would be his last great affirmation, and he wanted it to be understood that way, as a monumental 'yes' to Anna, after which a steady withdrawal and a silent acquittal could be his. Yet it became obvious, as the weeks passed, that his decisions were having an impact way beyond himself. As an adult, he had a kind of complacency when it came to the opinions of others; he didn't quite believe the world beyond himself could halt his ideas. He felt we could aid his progress, but not hinder it, and it formed a strange human puzzle in that busy period before the wedding. He was making room for death, while, all around him, people arrived with new furniture for a different room altogether, a place of honouring and cherishing, where comfort and light are believed to obliterate the dark.

• • •

Iona's play eventually arrived at the King's Theatre in Edinburgh. She took the train through to Glasgow on her day off and had the advertised lunch with Anna. 'She drank a fair amount,' Iona said to me after the show that night. 'Totally shattered, as you'd expect. The chemo seems to be holding back the cancer, though he's finding the treatment murderous. Really terrible, Anna says. He complains all the time, she said, about Amazon parcels coming to the door, about visitors he doesn't want.'

'I've heard him say that.'

'She thinks he can get a year or maybe longer.'

She told me Anna had burst into tears while saying that and had covered her face with her napkin. 'And she went on again about Tully having secret conversations with you about Dignitas.'

'And what did she say?' I asked.

'Well, she's said it before. She's totally against it. You don't kill yourself, that's Anna's view.'

As she reported their conversation to me, I could tell that Iona more or less agreed with Anna's position. She would do her best to protect me, but I knew Iona thought I should just refuse to talk to Tully about assisted dying. She felt it was natural for

Anna to want to save the man she was about to marry.

The wedding had grown in my mind to be an event riddled with the threat of what it preceded, and I tried, as we all did, to join Anna in her struggle to see it as something joyous. She told Iona she had looked forward all her life to getting married. At the lunch, Iona ordered champagne and tried to reassure her, and promised her the day would be fantastic. She said everybody was excited. But Anna was worried, Iona said, that Tully might not be able to make it through the stress of a whole day like that. She said he would put on a big brave face for everyone and hope nobody noticed.

It was late October, and he asked me to help them with the wedding. But when he was distracted, or in pain, or too depressed to think about any of it, Anna and I would speak alone. He'd wade in now and then and make huge pronouncements, then sleep for a whole day, unable to follow up or revive his interest later on. He was there all the way, but he hated the lacy trivia, the march of obligations. Anna did all of it, and I spent hours on the phone with her discussing the possibility of lacquered chairs. She preferred a posh old house, a humanist minister – 'Why?' he'd asked; 'Just because,' she'd said – and a well-stocked bar and a smoking area were also priorities. The wedding would start with drinks in the drawing room and then vows upstairs in the grand library. There would be readings and a few speeches after dinner, which should be a buffet, Anna said, because Tully didn't want a whole lot of fuss about food, napkins, tablecloths, or candles. One of the boys could do the photographs. Tully's main concern was the music.

'That's all fine,' I said.

'The main event will be the party,' she said. 'The official bit will be over by six. Then it should just be dancing.'

'Right.'

'And that's Tully's bit.'

'No problem.'

'Did he always rely on you like this?' she asked.

'No,' I said. 'When we were young, it was the other way. When my parents stopped being parents, I totally relied on him and Barbara.'

'He says it was all music and comedy.'

'It was. Plus a few films.'

'Now it's all silence and death,' she said. As if to confirm her words, we said nothing. Then I cleared my throat and tried again.

'Come on, Anna. He loves you very much. This is happening to him, and he's just desperate to control it a wee bit.'

'Control me, you mean.'

'No, Anna.'

'Yes, Jimmy.'

We fell silent again. I felt it wasn't our argument to have. Through the phone I could hear her fingers clicking on the keys of her laptop.

'Let's just talk about wedding favours,' she said. 'Yes or no?'

Another day, another FaceTime. Tully was up and about and for a minute or two he wanted to talk. He appeared on my MacBook screen wearing a Delta 5 T-shirt and a frown he couldn't shake. 'If Anna orders any more shite and we have any more Amazon deliveries to this fuckan door I'm going to bomb Seattle,' he said. 'It would be quite a good way to go, taking out a few evil tech companies.'

'You'd better retrain your missiles. Your parcels are coming from Gourock.'

He rolled his eyes. 'Dying is boring,' he said. 'If I don't die soon then I might just die of boredom.' It had been a month since we'd met at the caravan. 'You wouldn't believe how I struggle to get through the day with all this crap. It's so slow. Mainly, I take cannabis oil and learn to hate the dogs in the street, barking all day.'

'What else?'

'Are you sitting comfortably?' He cleared his throat. 'You know how Tibbs says it was a header by Kenny Dalglish that caused the Thatcher revolution?'

'Yes.'

'Well, by a similar logic, I can tell you it was Fred Astaire who caused Brexit.'

'Shut up.'

'I'm serious. I've worked it out. Fred Astaire was in a show in 1926 called *Lady, Be Good*. A girl from London called Maude Wells was in the audience. Because of him, she set up a tap-dancing school in the East End. One of her pupils was Noele Gordon, who went on to run the motel in *Crossroads*. But her first gig, straight out of the dancing school, was doing a test transmission for John Logie Baird's new invention, colour television. He broadcast her trying on a few hats, and he convinced everybody it worked. When Tim Berners-Lee, the guy who invented the Web, was at college he built a computer from an old analogue TV. Without him there would be no internet and no social media, and, without that, the right-wing faction couldn't have spread all those lies and convinced people to vote us out of the European Union. So, there you go – *Fred Astaire caused Brexit*.'

'I actually love you,' I said.

. . .

It was working, as Anna had said, but that first round of chemo went off like a dirty bomb in a deserted city. He said it was beyond description, the feeling it gave you, and he wished all the time for another existence, or non-existence. 'I don't think anything could take my head out of it,' he said, 'although the steroid days are better.' The treatment would fall into three distinct phases. After a week or so, when he stopped throwing up, he said he was keen for some distractions. I asked him if he remembered me talking about this café that was opening next door to me in London.

'Aye. You said the owner wanted records.'

'I've become friendly with him. He's got a vintage jukebox, a 1962 Rock-Ola Princess. It takes fifty singles.'

'Are you asking me to fill it with tunes?'

'Why not?' I said.

'That would be great.'

'What years will you go for?'

'The Eighties,' he said. 'The music was magic. And never, until now, did the country feel so divided.' As we spoke about it, some of his old vigour and purpose came back. 'I'm really tempted to stick with 1979 to '86,' he said, 'but I have to bring a few dance tracks into the mix, so I'll go to '90. If your pal's café is full of London toffs then we'll need to give them something palatable to go with their wankuccinos.'

I was never sure that he wasn't supplanting, with my help, his present self with a previous one, the one his pals knew better, a live wire who was healthy and unmarked and had his whole life in front of him. And that, I'm sure, is what Anna detected and what she objected to as the weeks dragged on. He told me she was often up at night – sitting by their bedroom window, using the torch on her phone to examine the guest list – and amid all these wedding plans they couldn't speak about death. She was in many ways smarter than him, and she saw that he was punishing the present for what it was doing – and she was the present, as well as the devastated future, but he couldn't address it that way. I asked him to slow down and consider her position, but he kept running from the cancer, knowing he'd lose ground to it, and I could only hope that she'd forgive us in the end.

'Can I tell you something, Noodles?' he said one day. 'I never felt like I had much of a self. Not really. Not a proper adult self that gets things done. I got it together as a young guy, and I was somebody then.'

I didn't miss a beat. 'You're still somebody, Tully.'

'It's okay. I accept it. I had a better life than I expected. I met Anna. I just have to control the end, and that might be hard.'

He was obviously talking a lot to Fiona. He was more like

his sister than he knew, as the sea is sometimes like the sky, and reflective of it. He had grown closer to Fiona and her husband as the years went by and their kids grew up. When he got ill, he reached out for her, initially because she was a nurse, I think, but also for a more profound reason, to do with memory. His sister knew his original vulnerabilities, his aches, the ones before cancer, and, alone with a few of his old friends, she knew the world that had existed before Woodbine's death, and he craved that sort of familiarity.

Fiona made trips to speak to his doctors. She read all the notes and the charts. I felt she brought decorum, a well-rehearsed tolerance of life's unfairness, and she wrote to me as if something was still salvageable – from the past, or by God. Fiona and Scott weren't Bible-bashers, but they were that more persuasive thing, quiet believers. We were never in cahoots, but had distant respect. She used the word 'dignity' a lot and began to show me, by a certain silence, that she agreed with her brother's estimation of how it should end for him. I found myself yearning for Barbara's advice, though I knew she wasn't giving advice any more. I made a plan with Tully to go and see her before the wedding. She had no idea what was happening to him.

As the last things fell into place, he was slightly tense, like the guy ropes holding up a marquee. He hated to think he was being exploited by wedding companies. One day, he asked me to join a conference call he and Anna were set to have with a man who ran a limousine company. The man was soon describing white Daimlers with champagne holders in the back. 'Excuse me,' Tully said. 'I don't mean to be cheeky. But do people actually like this shite?'

'Well, yes, sir. A car is a very important feature. We're talking about the happiest day of your life.'

'The most expensive day of our lives.'

'Well, not necessarily, sir . . .'

I could hear Tully revving up. His exhaust was dragging along the ground. 'It's all pish,' he said.

'Em, thank you very much,' I interrupted. 'That's quite a lot to think about. We'll get back to you once we've considered all the options.' I zapped the call and then rang Tully on his mobile. 'What the fuck?' I said.

'Well, no wonder. What a capitalist dick. Why would I want to ride around Pollok in a fuckan bridal hearse? Talk about the opiate of the people. These pricks spend their lives selling junk to brainless neds who think they're on *Love Island*. I'd sooner walk to the wedding or go on the bus. I'm only doing it for Anna. I'm not being drafted into some hellish Bing Crosby scenario just because these creepy bastards say so.' I was entertained all morning by that, and then he phoned back in the afternoon. 'Sorry,' he said, 'coming on all Nutso McNutjob with the limousine guy, but it was good to get it out there. I actually quite liked the idea of the Humvee with the condom machine and the vodka fountain. A man could snuff it quite happily in a vehicle like that.'

17

The wedding was set for a Saturday in November. A few days before, I got the train to Carlisle, picked up a car, and drove across the border. A scattering of white cottages and low cloud brought a powerful notion of home, and then, as I was driving towards the coast, a deer escaped out of the forest and stopped right in front of me, its antlers glowing in the headlights as the snow fell over the Solway Firth. I was on my way to Wigtown. The book festival was over but they'd asked me to do an out-of-season event, to mark the centenary of a First World War battle in which six local men died. They wanted a lecture on the war poets, and what I'd written was stored in my bag.

A song on the stereo – 'Primitive Painters' – filled the car as snowflakes stuck to the windscreen. I stopped at a passing place. It was freezing when I got out, there was wet wool snagged on the barbed-wire fence, and you could make out the sea at the far end of the field, through the salt marshes, beyond the trees. This was the place where Robert Burns took treatment at the close of his life. He waded chest-deep in the sea, under the same cold light, and tried to shock himself back to health. In a last letter to his brother, he wrote that he was dangerously ill and not likely to recover.

'*God help my wife and my children.*'

Caerlaverock Castle. Bridge of Dee. Gatehouse of Fleet. Carsluith.

The car plashed into Wigtown.

Backstage, the organiser was telling me about the town's war memorial. 'We cleaned it up,' she said. 'With the hundredth anniversary and all that, we wanted it to look spruce.' I peeped through the curtain. The hall was a ceilidh of coloured scarves, the floor wet with slush. The people huddled in a hum of low voices. Soviet winters came to mind: the smell of damp scarves and the fog of breath, the fear of unrewarded effort.

I shuffled the pages of my speech. Verse lovers require language that will help them live their lives, and when I stepped out on the stage I could see their eagerness to be reassured, their wish to believe in the war poets as commanders of pity and understanding, pitched in the national key. Looking up at a square of skylight, the snow falling, I felt something go out of me, and all those lyrics by doomed youths and bright officers appeared to melt that evening. When I looked down, the pages in front of me seemed totally blank. This had never happened to me before, and my senses plummeted and I couldn't think, but I relaxed into the failure. I folded away the notes and began speaking without them. 'There is another story of this centenary,' I said, 'not foreign to poetry, but remote perhaps from the idea that young death is an Olympic sport.'

'Shame!' shouted an old man in his medals. He was sitting in the front row and I found myself saying the poets' disgust didn't go far enough, there was no glory in any of it, that to die young was always a waste. I felt an ebbing of pride in the hall.

They wanted Owen and Sassoon, they wanted passing bells, demented choirs, and bugles calling from sad shires, but the swell in those poems seemed too much. I fashioned a whole new lecture out of the cold, thin air, and argued against sacrifice. I spoke about Kandahar. I told them about the child jihadis who blew themselves up and hated countries whose names they couldn't pronounce. I spoke of immigrants unable to reach the other coast, and drowning for want of safety or a job. '*Life, to be sure, is nothing much to lose,*' I quoted from Housman. '*But young men think it is, and we were young.*'

'But people die in war!' the old soldier shouted. 'That's what it's all about.'

'You're right,' I said. 'That's what it's all about. *War and Peace* tells us many small things and one big one, that war is a catastrophe.'

'Every death is a catastrophe, son,' he said. 'But it was nice listening to you.'

The gentleman marshalled his sticks and began to move from his seat as the audience softly applauded, more in politeness.

The skylight was covered with snow.

• • •

'That was something different,' a woman said. 'I came out thinking I'd hear the stuff they taught us at school.'

'It's the old poems that stick,' I said. 'Don't you think?'

'Oh, definitely,' she said. 'I had a passion for rote learning.'

Then, when the hall was almost clear, a person stepped

forward, holding a glass of whisky. It was Scott, Tully's tall, optimistic brother-in-law, with Fiona behind him. I'd spoken to her on the phone, but I hadn't seen her in years, and she had the same vivid face, the same welcoming eyes. I stood up to hug them. 'We saw it in the paper that you were giving a talk,' she said, 'so we drove down the bypass.'

'A bit of light entertainment for a Wednesday night,' I said. They laughed and Scott spun his car key on his finger. 'Tully would've loved the way you tried to turn it away from the whole anniversary-celebration thing.'

Fiona looked at him sharply and linked her arm into his.

'He *would* love it,' she said. 'He's still here.'

'Quite right,' he said. 'A hundred per cent.'

At the pub, Scott accepted a pint and a whisky. The place was crowded and a fire was burning in the grate. Fiona had a quiet determination to be heard, as if years had passed in which she'd said too little. She wanted to do the right thing for her brother and that had been her priority. She reminded me she'd been a nurse, just like her mum, and said she was glad she'd been able to speak to Tully about his treatment and its side effects. I knew this already via Anna, but she said they thought his body had reacted well to the first course of chemotherapy. The second would start right after the wedding. 'It's really hard. You'll have noticed the depression.'

'Will he be able to cope with the weekend?' I asked. 'The reception and the guests and the dancing?'

She shrugged and shook her head. 'He's determined,' she said.

'Yes, he is – always that.'

I could see in Fiona's expression that she wanted to be careful, to watch her words. Although we hadn't seen each other, or discussed it during the phone conversations we'd had recently, I felt she knew that Tully had put each of us in a strange position when it came to Anna. 'We want to support her in every way we can,' she said in the pub. 'Whatever she needs, Jimmy.'

'I think she needs the wedding to be great,' I said. 'And I think she needs him to be less secretive about what he wants to do.'

She ignored the second part, for now.

'The wedding will be great,' Fiona said. 'People are coming from everywhere.'

'Do you know what Tully said to me? He said he wants the wedding on Saturday to show everybody he had a life.'

'Well, he did. He does. You know that, Jimmy – a great life.'

'I hope so,' I said.

Above the fire hung faded Edwardian prints. A few drinks came along the bar from people who'd been in the audience, and I raised each glass to eye level, thanking them. The prints were grouped around an old pub mirror. They would have been strongly coloured at one time, and they showed fly-fishermen casting from the banks of the Esk, the Cree, the Nith, or the Annan, men solid and moustachioed. Inside the frames, under each print, were glued what I took to be proper flies, with violet or emerald plumes, their tails curling into hooks. Maybe it was the event I'd just done, or the vague sense of religious belief coming from Fiona and Scott, but I found myself saying something about Graham Greene and his awareness of the struggle to live a complete life. 'In one of his novels he wrote that people who share your childhood never seem to grow up.'

'That's so true,' said Fiona.

'That's the story,' I said. 'But with Tully it's hard. He's one of those people. We struggle to accept he's not twenty. Him not being twenty means that none of us is twenty. Him dying means we all are. That's what gets everybody – he was always first with everything and now he's showing us how to die.'

'Absolutely,' she said.

I thought I would try again.

'You and I have discussed it before, Fiona. How he wants to end his own life. It seemed to me you got the point of what he was saying.'

She took her time. 'It's so difficult,' she said. 'He hasn't really done it properly, hasn't set it in motion with Anna, and she doesn't want it. Of course she doesn't. She wants him to live for as long as possible.'

'But he's exercising a right,' I said, 'and you're his next of kin.'

'Anna will be his next of kin from this weekend,' Fiona said. 'She'll be Tully's wife and that's a brilliant thing.' She looked at the fire. 'He's relying on you to sort it out, but it doesn't really work like that, does it?'

'They have to make the decision together,' I said. 'And at the moment he's making it a pact between himself and his friends. Well, me.'

'Just let it play out,' Scott said.

'But he's building his hopes on it, he's made me promise, and this thing with Dignitas is taking time to organise. I've applied to them.' The insects above the fireplace seemed set to fly as the light danced over them.

'He has to talk openly to Anna,' Fiona said. 'But we can only take instructions from him. That's the bottom line. I feel the same way about his treatment: if he wants to discuss the details with me first, I won't be asking for anybody's permission before I respond. I'll just do it. It's his life, and, when it comes to ... what he chooses to talk to you about, you're right to go ahead.' She pulled out a fresh tissue from her pocket. 'I think you know where I stand, Jimmy.'

'But can he do it without her?'

'I think he just might,' Fiona said. 'He's got you, he's got us, and for some reason he doesn't want to ask Anna to speed this on and help him die.'

'To ask *her* ... the person he's in love with ... it would probably feel like an offence against what they have together,' I said. 'But there's something more – I think the defiance is bringing him back to his best self. He's taking control of his life. And if you remember Tully in his prime, that was his mission.'

'Control,' she said. 'First of life and then of death.'

Scott nodded. 'But he can't make a secret of it, conspiring with an old pal, or with his sister, because he has a responsibility to Anna.'

'I think we all know that,' Fiona said. 'It's not a conspiracy. We want to help him out of a desperate situation. Anna's bright, she wants to fight with everything she's got to keep him alive, and that describes their relationship perfectly. Just as what we're doing describes ours. Nobody's wrong.' She breathed hard. 'I just hope it doesn't, you know . . . A wedding is hard enough without all this.'

She looked away as if she'd momentarily lost faith in everyone and everything. She appeared to wade through her own thoughts, then she turned back to us. 'You know something? It was quite strange growing up with Tully. I mean, being in a family with him, with the kind of parents we had.'

'How so?'

'Well, he was always treated like a foundling in a fairy tale.'

'Like someone with talent?'

'Yes,' she said. 'He doesn't remember it, but Dad saw it, too. He just loved playing football with him when Tully was tiny. He loved the way he ran at the ball, like a born champion, the look on his face. You got the impression life was a little brighter around him. For a wee while, even Dad got brighter. When you all came to the house as boys, I know it was nice for my mum. She always said those were the best years, when Tully was young. But there was a downside, and it involved feeling lonely when the theatre emptied out.' She checked herself. 'Here's me talking about him in the past tense as well.'

'Being young is a kind of stardom with some people,' I said.

'Until they're no longer young . . .' She took another breath. 'Few people saw how sad and depressed Tully could be.'

'He was very upset about your dad,' I said. 'His first heart attack, the week we went to Manchester . . . Tully didn't know how to feel. I saw it a few times, but especially that weekend.'

'I know it's an obvious comment to make,' she said, 'but I think he's always been looking to get back to the earliest feeling he had for our parents, before life got complicated. Who isn't, at the end of the day?' Fiona's face showed a willingness to say more, to say everything, but it flickered and then it was gone.

I looked into the fire and saw pictures in the red-hot coals. The whisky warmed my tongue but I said nothing for a moment and looked on as Scott's eyes filled up. He offered a sentence and the sob that followed it was lost in his tumbler. 'He's heading for a life everlasting in a world greater than this one.'

'Do you really believe that?' I asked.

He smiled and the answer was there. It was there for both of them. They had faith and they believed Tully was going to another world. 'It's been my good fortune to share a story with him,' I said, 'and that's all we'll ever have. There's no more. Earth is all the heaven we'll ever know.'

'No, Jimmy,' Fiona said with quiet force. 'You're totally wrong about that. After all this, we'll see him again.'

I smiled to show them I greeted their hope with friendship.

Later, when I left them on the street, I felt they had revealed to me in one evening the deep resources of their marriage. Scott kissed his wife's hand and turned to me, walking backwards.

'Hey, Jimmy,' he said, quite drunk. 'It was magic seeing you. Remember the Gospel . . .'

'Right, come on, you,' Fiona said. 'Jimmy's got his bed to go to.'

He turned to her with his finger raised and a sad look on his face, but his words were firm as they walked away.

'*Set your minds on things that are above,*' he said, '*not on things that are on earth, for you have died, and your life is hidden with Christ.*' The town was quiet when they drove off and I stood on my own beside a lighted puddle, watching the snowflakes fall like ashes and melt on the water.

18

The next morning I drove to his old house. Tully had arranged for us to meet there on our way to visiting Barbara. He said he had to pick up some mail and that the house was as good a rendezvous point as anywhere. I arrived a bit early, so I stood looking up at it, the street still dark and empty, and the house, too. From the frosted pavement, it was smaller and greyer than I remembered. Unlit, it was part of another world, but the streetlights at the gable end burned as if nothing in life had changed. Snow lay untouched on the garden and melted and dripped on the wet council fences. I looked up at Tully's bedroom and thought of a hundred nights, laughing in the glow of the stereo. Standing there, I could fill that black window with the colour of past summers, the garden in flower that July, the sound of lawnmowers, while inside the room a pair of boys made their plans for Manchester.

I looked behind me and saw a trail of footsteps and paw prints. My past life was everywhere on that housing estate. It was easy to forget we were near the harbour and the sea and a whole natural world of plovers and seaweed. The modern whiteness of the estate had aged very badly; it seemed tarnished now and damp. I realised I was breathing in the cold air very deeply, feeling almost dizzy. I used to walk down that path from the main road with library books in my bag. Thomas Hardy, with his snow-filled fields and his summer rituals, had once seemed so exotic to me, distant and lovely. Yet now those stories appeared real and very local – familiarly sad and sadly familiar – the litany of small tragedies that matter more to some than to others.

Tully was wearing a coat with a furry hood. He got out of the car and took a little run and slid down the path to his mother's gate. 'Hey, Noodles,' he said, crashing into me and turning it into a hug. 'You're here already.'

'Bloody freezing,' Anna said, coming up behind.

'I hear you were out boozing with my sister last night.'

'Hardly a rave,' I said. 'I was doing an event in Wigtown. It was a surprise seeing them. Good of them to come.'

'Did they do your head in?' Anna said. She caught my eye. We had grown a little closer during the wedding planning, but there were things we just couldn't talk about. She had her pride and I had my promise.

'They were really nice,' I said.

We spoke about the house. Tully opened the garden gate and then hesitated, as if he thought better of spoiling the perfect, unbroken snow. 'You want to go in?' he asked, taking out a key from his coat pocket.

'No,' I said. 'Maybe not.'

Anna took my arm and stomped her feet against the cold. She pulled her woolly hat down over her ears. 'We should get going,' she said. 'We can take your mum down the shore and give her a bit of breakfast. Come back later.'

'You know we're selling it?' Tully said, looking up at the house. 'That's what you have to do – sell the house to pay for the nursing home.'

'That's brutal,' I said. 'She worked hard to pay for that house.'

'That's right. After Woodbine died. She wanted to leave us something.'

There was still the old waste ground to the right of the house. He walked to the end of the path and then stopped and pointed. 'Over there,' he said. 'My best memory. One of them, anyhow. My dad banged in two posts to make a goal. I don't think I ever scored in front of him but he set up the posts and that's something.'

I drove behind them to the care home. It was only a mile or so, closer to the harbour and the shopping centre, near the spot on the river where Tully and I once dumped the leaflets for the Enterprise Allowance Scheme. The reception area was busy with care assistants carrying trays or leading patients. We went up the stairs to a long corridor and I could see her standing at the very end, swaying on her own with a handbag. Barbara was in her housecoat, buttoned to the collar, her hair sticking up. The light in the corridor seemed to know something about her. Tully had said he could still joke with her but that she was confused most of the time. When he'd told her about the wedding she seemed pleased though she didn't even ask about coming.

Anna patted down her hair and took her hand. 'You got your glad rags on, Barbara?' she said. The handbag was crooked over her arm and she seemed delighted with herself, as if she was all set for the dance hall.

'Mum,' Tully said as we went into her room, 'you remember Jimmy, don't you? You must remember Noodles. He's come to see you.'

'Aw, my,' she said.

'He's come all the way from London.'

Her eyes were paler than I remembered. She pointed at me and said it again – 'Aw, my' – and then she fanned herself with a handkerchief and put on her music. Frank Sinatra. She stood up and placed my arm on her shoulder and we began to dance. You could feel how bony she was but the rhythm was still there.

'You're a fair mover, Barbara,' I said.

'Aw, my.'

As we turned around the room, I saw the framed pictures on her chest of drawers. Tully in his graduation gown, 1992. His father in a 1950s suit with a cigarette dangling from his lip. Fiona and Scott with the children, and a wedding picture where Barbara looked like Doris Day.

'You want to go out, Mum?'

'Spain,' she said, and sat down for a moment.

A few times, when Tully made a joke, she'd put a fist up to his face like she was angry. And maybe she was. 'Is it night-time?' she asked. Then she noticed the music again and stood up to dance and stare at the bright window.

'Come on, Mum. Let's get out of here for a wee while,' Tully said.

We waited in the corridor while Anna got her dressed. You could hear them talking behind the door.

The four of us walked past the high flats and down to the harbour. Barbara got excited when she saw a squirrel and Anna patted her arm. Tully went into a routine about how Elvis died from eating a squirrel in the depths of Tennessee. I think he just liked the sound of the words, and we all did, especially Barbara, who clapped.

He wanted to show me the ruins of the Magnum Leisure Centre. 'You wouldn't believe it, man,' he said. 'They pulled it down. And when I look at it, I hear the sounds – all the shouting in the swimming pool during the summer. Before the strike, remember we used to go down to the skating rink, and they played the Clash? All the kids going round in purple hired skates, the weird smell of the ice.' When we turned the corner I was amazed to see the huge empty space. I had once known every hall and every stairwell and every corner of that building. Walking towards the field where the leisure centre used to be, I remembered standing in a Cub Scout's uniform, aged ten, the day the Queen turned up to open it.

'Gone,' Barbara said.

I stood by the road with Anna while Tully took his mother closer.

'He's thinking a lot about his dad,' she said.

Seagulls picked in the mud, the old Magnum. 'We once saw the Smiths play there,' I told her. Tully walked back arm in arm with Barbara and she seemed contentedly oblivious, and only when I said it was time for the café did she look at me. We went to Small Talk because of their homemade cakes. Tully couldn't eat, but his mum ate for two, and Anna had a bowl of soup. I took Barbara's hand and asked her if she could tell us about her own wedding and she sang a bit of 'A Foggy Day (in London Town)'.

She yawned and said, 'Frank Sinatra.'

'Mr Dawson was a crooner, wasn't he? I remember you telling me that, Barbara.'

'Barbara and Ewan,' she said.

There was a swing park by the harbour and Barbara pointed to it as soon as we came out of the café. Anna took her ahead of us and Tully turned. 'Noodles, you remember Stedman, the Jamaican guy who drank in the Glebe?'

'Steady McCalla, the barber. Of course.'

'Aye. He had a kid, right. A wee boy. Well, he once told me that he used to bring the boy down here at night, to play on the swings.'

'At night?'

'Because in the daytime the kids used to say stuff, like racist comments, and the boy couldn't get playing on the swings.'

'So he brought him down . . .'

'When nobody was here,' he said.

'That's shocking, man.'

'That was Steady's life,' Tully said. 'The stuff we didn't see. We thought we knew about Britain, Noodles. We knew fuck all.'

'But you did see it,' I said. 'You called them out for it in the Glebe.'

'Not enough,' he said. 'Never enough.'

His mum sat down on the swing and pushed away with her boots. Tully gave her a little help and then sat on the one next to her. Anna and I took the other two, and soon we were all swinging higher and higher, the cold breeze in our eyes. You could see the abbey tower over in Kilwinning and the old ICI factory and the Firth of Clyde all the way to Arran. *I'm getting married in the morning,* Tully sang as we worked ourselves into the air. Barbara opened her mouth as if to say something and her eyes were wet.

19

When I arrived at his flat on the afternoon of the wedding, I kicked the snow off my shoes on the front step and he brought me inside. He took the red ties in the hall and handed me a glass of Glenmorangie. 'A fair exchange,' he said. We went into the main room, where I greeted the others and we clinked glasses.

The Clash was playing.

I told Tully he had to put a dimple in his tie. 'Just pinch it and push the knot up to the crux of the collar.'

'It's only a wedding,' he said, 'not my testimonial at Ibrox Park, where Kenny Dalglish will bow before the Huns.'

'No, Jimmy's right,' said Mick Caesar.

He wasn't on that trip to Manchester and always had his own habits. Tully had made him best man, along with Ross McArdle, another Manchester absentee, and me. 'Look.' Caesar sniggered and clapped me on the shoulder. 'Jimmy knows zilch about gambling. But he knows about ties. Follow his advice to look like Cary Grant. Or else turn up at your wedding like a plooky schoolboy who cannae tie a tie.'

'Fuck sake,' Tully said. 'It's like *RuPaul's Drag Race* in here. Jimmy, tie it for me while Caesar gets busy with the cheeky water.'

'It's a shame Iona couldn't make it,' Tully said. (She was stuck with the show and had sent her regrets.)

'She's gutted,' I said. 'But she says she'll raise a glass of champagne to you and Anna tonight in Croydon.'

'Can you get champagne in Croydon?' Caesar asked. He handed each of us another whisky and his face gleamed with mischief.

Despite the Glenmorangie and the Clash, we got Tully to the venue in plenty of time, driving through the park and stepping out at Pollok House, a huge Georgian pile with balustrades and chimney-stacks, a house of echoing corridors and servants' quarters, famous for its collection of Spanish art. Tully's pals were waiting outside and they crunched over the gravel to greet him. You could see their breath, the guests all standing in the yard ribbing each other, and, just beyond them, the old house, yellow light shining in the windows, behind the trees.

Detaching from his wife, Tyrone Lennox, postman and general secretary of the Leonid Brezhnev Appreciation Society, came bowling over with the same blue eyes and the same bold grin he had when he was eighteen. The era of male hugging hadn't quite reached Tibbs, so he shook my hand, weighing it for lost sincerity, before leading me inside to a room where the drinks reception appeared to be happening. I hadn't properly seen him in ten years, maybe more. 'How's your work?' he said. 'I see you avoid social media. Good decision. Most of it is just right-wing thinking in left-wing dress, so it is. There's not a lot to choose between Pitchfork

Rabble and Biscuit-Tin Britain.'

'The new authoritarians,' I said. 'They hate any fact that doesn't confirm what they already believe to be true. They hate it even before they hear it. We're all just one observation away from damnation.'

'It's just woke Thatcherism,' he said. 'It all stems from the Eighties. The Decade That Decency Forgot. So, basically it's our fault.'

'You enjoying the EU pantomime?' I asked.

'Embarrassing as hell. Hard to go to sleep at night knowing a bunch of Continental bureaucrats think you're a loser. Britain is done for.'

'You're the scourge of the working classes, Tibbs.'

'Never. But what do you do when the workers aren't on their own side?'

'We'd better stop. We're at a wedding.'

'Working people voting against their own interests,' he said. We paused and looked at each other for a second. 'Ah, who cares. Even happy days are odd at the moment. France must look at us and say, "What happened to poor old Britain? It used to be so brilliant and now it's a complete basket case."'

Looking at his face, it occurred to me that Tibbs had never suited being young. It was something about his head: made for reading glasses and sharp angles and a bit of grey. There are the Tullys of the world, people who are themselves early on, and never better, while others are simply waiting to become the person they really are, and Tibbs now seemed entirely himself and unchangeable. It was as if the insecurities of his youth had been burned away by love and duty, and now he was here, standing up to be counted and ready to shout down the idiocies of the moment.

'The whole thing,' he said. 'It's murder, so it is.' But he was no longer talking about politics and people in power. He nodded towards the wedding party, swallowed a few words, and rubbed his hands. 'I'm finding it nearly impossible, this Tully thing. It's so wrong and so shite. It makes me hold on to my weans, so it does, and Helen. How can a thing like this happen to a healthy guy – not just anybody, but to Tully?'

'I wish I could tell you, Tibbs.'

'I know none of us has a monopoly on grief, but I'm struggling.'

'We each have a monopoly on our own,' I said.

The house was all candlelight and mahogany. As the guests headed up, I waited in the hall for the other best men and Tully. At the top of the stairs, a trio played Debussy, a piano and two violins rushing it. 'Slow down,' I said, as much to myself as the musicians, catching sight of my face in a mirror. Ross McArdle – master of general nonsense – came into the hall, bearing carnations on a tray, with Tully and Caesar walking behind and passing a hip flask between them. 'Everybody is here for the wedding of the year – apart from the fuckan bride,' Caesar said. The hall echoed with banter.

Tully came over to the mirror and asked if I'd help him with the flower. 'Come on, wee boy,' he said. 'I'm trying to look smart for one day in my life. Show me how you do this buttonhole thing.' I stuck the pin through the stem and was fastening the carnation to his lapel when the humanist minister appeared on the stairs.

'Come along, fellows,' he said, beckoning. 'The world is waiting. Or Glasgow, at least.'

'Are you in pain?' I whispered to Tully.

'Aye. In the stomach.' I finished securing the flower and he stood back to examine himself. He looked so pale. The blue of the painting on the opposite wall seemed to reflect back onto his face. 'Carnations, eh, Noodles?' he said. When we walked across the wooden floor it was like knocking on all the doors of the past, and running away.

Upstairs, I stood with him by the French windows in the Pavilion Library, the guests in rows of gold chairs. It was already dark outside, moonlight silhouetting the trees and falling on the snow-filled garden. Anna was late and the jokes wore thin, but the sense of hesitation added a contemplative note to the hour of their marriage. And then, like a cinema bride, her entry was the banishment of all anxiety: every person in the room turned to her, and she carried optimism into the room, as if the whole of time and the whole of hope were hers and his to scatter as they liked. Tully gripped my hand for a second and then watched her as she walked towards him in her white beaded gown, the light making the most of the dress while the Cocteau Twins rang out. She seemed shy of all the attention and at the same time fulfilled by it. All eyes were on her, many of them welling with tears. People craned for a better look and some were felled by the day's formalities. But not Anna. She arrived with self-possession at the windows where we stood, and he kissed her softly. The minister began the ceremony and he spoke slowly of commitment and asked for the rings. As Tully spoke his vows my eyes went up to a painting in the room, a masterpiece. I felt it must have waited for us all our lives, Goya's *Boys Playing at Soldiers*.

. . .

It used to be so natural, dancing. Because the music defined you and the heart was in step. Then it leaves you. Or does it? Saturday night changes and your body forgets the old compliance. You're not part of it any more and your feet hesitate and your arms stay close to your sides. It's there somewhere, the easy rhythm from other rooms and other occasions, and you're half convinced it will soon come back. It's not the moves – the moves are there – but your connection to the music has become nostalgic, so the body is responding not to a discovery but to an old, dear echo.

Some evenings smell of the night's ravages, the ones to come. You can sense the atmosphere of good feeling, the growth of excitement. After the food was over – and it was over very quickly – most of the guests behaved as if they'd waited years to be so at home with their old friends, and they drank heavily. Sure, it was a living wake, and I felt that their gladness, like my own, must have vied with a hinterland of dread, but most of them forgot it all and had a great night. 'Take a bump of this and get jigging,' someone said to me at the bar, holding a little wrap between his waistcoat and mine.

'Go on,' he said. 'You'll be leaping about in no time.' I waved it away and handed him a whisky instead. I told him to fill his boots. He blew a kiss and spun away towards a thumping classic by Eric B. & Rakim.

Among the people I recognised from our past, many of their faces were much the same and others were completely blurred by life, as if time was wiping them. There's nothing rational about people's looks. Some lose them and others improve with age. I saw one shy girl who was hardly noticed by anybody at school, and she now took to the dancefloor with a poised and beautiful realisation about her face. We had friends like Tibbs, who had his life sorted out, who stuck to his values and supported his team, but there were other guys ('for all their pish', as Tully put it) who only cared for their Christmas bonus. Tully called them out in private, but he treated them all equally. He was a friend to friendship itself and never expected people to be better than they were.

Such thoughts give dignity to your average wallflower. Tully tried to pull me onto the dancefloor, but I stood my ground with a glass of Oban. When I went out to the patio, Anna was smoking a vape and took my arm for a second. 'It's the man himself,' she said. It seemed to me she was high on the possibility of life speeded up, and she began telling those around her that I was Tully's 'secret collaborator'. 'You know I love you, Jimmy,' she said drunkenly, before sealing my lips with a finger.

At my elbow, a thin man wearing round glasses appeared.

'Hello, sir,' he said in a theatrical way. He was smoking a long foreign cigarette. 'You don't recognise me, do you, Jimbo?' It took a moment, and it wasn't his grizzled face I recognised, but his intonation, the sense of words like nips. Dr Clogs. His eyes had sunk back and his teeth had come forward, but the old belligerence was in place. He drew deeply on the cigarette and stared at the frosty ground.

'I'm not going to lie, Clogs – you look different.'

'Ah, honesty,' he said. 'We're living in a time of lies, Mr Collins. Best to be honest. You look much the same. Less skinny.'

'Not before time.'

'Well, where's the error?' He swigged his drink. 'Is your wife not here?'

'She's working,' I said. 'One of those jobs where you can't take a night off. People with tickets and all that.'

'You became a writer,' he said. 'A foreign correspondent in your own country.'

'Still trying, Clogs.'

'It's quite weird hearing all this music again,' he said. He made a backwards gesture with his thumb. 'These guys have been listening to the same tunes for thirty years. Maybe forty.' He insisted I take one of his crazy fags – from Dubai, he said – and sparked it up with a mini-blowtorch.

'It was always a struggle to reach the future,' I said.

We both smirked and he took a long drag. 'You remember the time we all went down to see those bands and got panelled for two days?' he said. 'I had a fight with Davie Hogg and spent the night in a bus shelter. They were good times, man. It must have been the last gathering of the old gang, before we all headed off.'

'What a weekend.'

'You in your Marilyn Monroe T-shirt,' he said. 'Tully with his black creps and white socks. There are moments from that weekend, I mean . . . we're talking over thirty years ago. I can be standing at the shaving mirror or sitting at my desk, deep in some corridor of the internet or whatever, trying to do some work, and it'll come into my head – something funny from that weekend in Manchester.'

It all seemed a way of not talking about Tully's illness. Manchester was a byword for who we all were together, and who Tully was in particular, and it seemed easier to evoke him at his best than speak about the worst. 'I hear you've been doing some sterling work on the internet, Bobby,' I said.

'It's a very busy time,' he said. 'I was thinking of making myself a business card, "Bobby McCloy: Counter-Surveillance Mug and General Pest – Holding the Bastards to Account".'

'Address: No. 1, The Dark Web, Planet Earth.'

He chuckled and got a fresh cigarette between his teeth. 'Thing is, Jimbo, there's a centre of world power in every box bedroom.'

'You saw that coming, with your BBC computer, then your Apple II.'

'There's a depressing drift to it, though . . . I leave off now and then. I hardly turn my laptop on at the moment. It's an addict's world.'

'You mean the trolls?'

'I mean all of it. Trolls. Supremacists. Abusers. Fundamentalists. Conspirators. Cryptocurrency nuts. Tech companies.

Shopping websites. They'll do away with you.'

'Jesus, Clogs.'

'Punk was right about everything,' he said. 'About society, I mean. And about people. We are poor slaves in a constant state of co-exploitation.'

'A swindle.'

'That's right, cobber. *Facebook*. You must be kidding.'

'All right, doctor. It's just us here. I want your top three hacks.'

'Of all time?' He took a slug of his drink. I had written about this kind of subject and the gleam in his eye told me he wouldn't reveal the best.

'The three most delightful ones,' I said.

'Okay.' In the traditional way, he counted them off on his fingers. 'One – we spent a whole day rearranging the traffic in Brisbane. We controlled the traffic lights. We broke into the system and ran it for kicks. Tailbacks, perpetual red lights, green on side streets, people getting out of their cars, cursing the system. Beautiful. We could see it from a window at the university and it was sort of perfect.'

'You're the Dr No of Dreghorn.'

'Two – I made all the TV sets in Kilmarnock come on in the middle of the night.'

'Certain TVs?'

'Most of them. They all have smart TVs. I did it twice, and the second time I was in the vicinity and it was a fantastic light show. Four a.m.'

We nodded and I stared at him for a moment. It was the

continuing joy of Clogs and his secret mission to interrupt, and was so consistent with the person I once knew, with his cowlick and a metal pencil case. 'And three,' he said. 'It could be so many. But the gun people are always the best fun. Many long nights.'

'The NRA?'

'Naturally. One time we moved $100,000 out of their New Mexico account into the account of a shooting victim's mother, then moved it back, leaving one dollar behind, just for the poetry of it. Then we emailed a picture of the mushroom cloud over Hiroshima to millions of NRA addresses.'

'I love it, Bobby.'

We got more whiskies and settled in at a freezing garden table.

It took a minute.

'What do you think about Tully?' I asked.

'Shocking business,' Clogs said, lifting his glass. 'Can't get it out of my mind. We went for a few games of pool. He says he's depending on you.'

'He said that?'

'To pull him through. To get him out.'

'It's complicated, Clogs.'

'I'll bet it is. It must be.'

'We went to see Barbara two days ago. She's in a nursing home in Irvine. All she knows is the music she likes.'

'That's all anybody knows, Jimbo.'

'And the films.'

'Them, too. It's the stuff we found, isn't it?' I must have

looked a little faraway because he nudged me. 'It's the whisky talking, Jim.'

The patio doors swung open and I saw Tibbs coming towards us. He was dragging someone by the arm, a huge bloke in a baseball cap.

'You'll never guess who turned up,' Tibbs was saying. 'Totally out the blue, and the bastard wasnae even invited.'

Tibbs was smashed.

'Ah, come on,' the guy said. There was a hint of an accent and he lifted his cap as if to help with the recognition issue.

'It's Davie Hogg!' Tibbs shouted, still holding him by the arm and pointing at him. 'Look at the fuckan nick of him!'

I stood up and put out my hand. 'Davie,' I said. 'It's been a long time.'

'He ate every pie in Europe, so he did!'

'Tibbs,' I said. 'Go easy.'

'Go easy, my arse,' he said. Tibbs was in his element. Banter was banter. 'I just saw him in the corner. He's a fuckan baldy bastard.'

'I had to come over for Tully,' Hogg said. 'I had to say hello.' He was quieter now, his sharp edges worked away by foreign necessity, I suspected, and he seemed a bit shell-shocked by the old energy and the shaming and all that. He had changed enormously, but each of his sentences still sounded like a question. Tibbs handed him a whisky and I noticed he didn't take a single sip the whole time he stood with us. Looking at this shy man, it was impossible to believe he had ever thrown yellow paint around a room. His conversation was stilted, but I guessed he was putting the past to rest. 'I see nothing changes over here. You're all exactly where I left you.'

'He's got six weans!' Tibbs said.

'And three ex-wives,' Hogg said, nodding.

'That must keep your nose to the grindstone,' said the voice behind me. Clogs was still sitting in the garden chair.

'Who's that?' said Hogg, squinting.

'It's your old friend in electronics,' Clogs replied. It took me a second to realise that their mutual dislike had survived thirty years.

'How you doing, Bobby?' Hogg said.

'Ah, still alive. For the time being.'

'Good . . . great.' He really had nothing to say. He began, painfully, to make remarks about the Scottish winter.

'Somebody told me you live in Copenhagen,' I said.

'That's correct. Denmark.'

'It must be weird,' Clogs said, warming to his opportunity, 'living in a country famous for its fried pork?'

Risky strategy for verbal abuse, I thought – in Scotland.

'*Flæskesteg*,' Hogg said.

'We were talking about Manchester,' I said. 'The trip we made that time.' He looked from one of us to the other. 'To G-Mex,' I added.

He shook his head like he didn't want to talk about it. 'There were so many gigs back then,' Hogg said. 'It was a bit of a gong show, if I remember.' Tibbs heard what he said and stood apart from him and screwed up his face.

'A gong show? What the fuck you talking about? It was the

best weekend in history.' Hogg looked at Tibbs and couldn't see what he meant. The past was not only a foreign country, it was a whole other geology. He suddenly looked like he regretted coming back, and I felt sorry for him but understood it, the wish to see Tully one last time. I stepped forward to shake his hand again, but there was no reaching him.

'It was good seeing you fellas again,' he said.

Hogg turned with a sort of resigned smile and walked down the frosted path towards the car park. No one could accuse him of living in the past. He wiped the past off his new shoes and called it success. 'There he goes,' Clogs said when Hogg was beyond the gate, 'a one-man argument for Brexit.'

Soon we heard applause and whistling inside. We took it that Ross was about to give his speech, and rushed in. He was a tall bloke, the tallest of us all, and when he stood on a table at the end of the dancefloor he loomed over everybody.

'Tully has many different bits to his life,' he began, 'and stories in each. But this evening I'm going to concentrate on his shocking delinquency. That's the duty of a best man. I know this feels like a wedding, but in fact it is a convention for all those who have had their lives blighted in some way by the madness of Tully Dawson.'

'Show us your arse!' Tibbs shouted.

'We'll come to that, Mr Lennox,' Ross said, unperturbed. 'As you know, the name Tully is short for Tullius. His mother just liked it. In later life, Tully would deny that the name suggests a certain tinker nobility. We won't go into it. Let me just say he can sniff out a beer tent at several thousand yards.

And, as we all know, Tully has always been very handsome. His youthful good looks have, unfortunately, been sustained, and he's in that insufferable group of people that includes Rob Lowe and Jamie Redknapp. Speaking of footballers, it was in 1979 at the playing fields on Irvine Moor that I first met Tully. Like his dad, Tully was an avid footballer. We were introduced by Freddie McFarlane, who I was at school with and who played on the same football team. Freddie wanted these two young footballing punks to meet, as he was certain we would get on. And that has occasionally happened, once or twice over the years.'

The crowd roared at every turn. There was energy in it, and truth, and a mass of unsayable things, but the crowd heard them. Ross put it out there in a blaze of brotherhood and loyalty. 'Every honest man and woman is a juvenile, too,' he said, 'and the old humour is always at your elbow. Some people in life are just stars, and this geezer is responsible for some of the biggest laughs I've enjoyed in my life. I know that might sound like a small thing to say, but think about it.'

Tully was standing on his own. He glanced over at me and shrugged. 'The humour he provides is difficult to explain,' Ross went on. 'But I'll always remember him on our many journeys, rolling down the window of the car in some forgotten town in Scotland or England, shouting at some self-conscious, innocent passing teenager, "Stop walking like that!" The funny thing is, no matter how normally they had been walking, the shout would throw their co-ordination.'

The room convulsed and he shuffled his cards and began his

list of thanks. 'Anna,' he said, 'is the one I really want to thank. She's the one we all really want to thank, Tully included. She's bossy, she's tenacious, she's loyal, she's got beautiful taste in her husband's friends, and she has loved him like no person could hope to be loved in their lifetime, and that's a fact.'

We all cheered and she hid her face with her glass.

'He's a difficult bugger,' Ross said, 'and she's kept him right. She will never know the complete reprobate he was as a young man, and that is a mercy. Let me just say that we thank her and her family for organising this perfect day.'

And then the dancefloor was pounding for hours. People came and went from the bar, and we island-hopped the malts. As it grew late, the night began to feel pressured, as if the guests knew it was to be the last of its kind. I believe we all felt it, and when the music finally stopped there was a freeze in the heart of the room. The lights came on and the carnage was revealed: men slumped on their wives; bridesmaids overcome with emotion. Tully was standing with his oldest friends, and, signature gesture, he wiped his nose on his sleeve and sniggered as he put his tumbler down. He understood inebriation, he always had, but he seemed embarrassed by the emotion in the room. 'You can all fuck off now,' he said, the disco ball throwing squares of light on the floor.

• • •

The second course of chemo began a few days later, when the alcohol was out of his system. It was another kind of treatment, a mitotic inhibitor called Taxol. He went to the hospital at nine in the morning and didn't leave until 7 p.m. He phoned me in the afternoon to say the stuff being pumped into him was making him feel sick. 'I have to try this for a while longer,' he said. 'People want me to. But please tell me Switzerland's going to work out.' He spoke strangely during that call after the wedding, as if embarking on treatment instead of a honeymoon had filled him with disgust. He said one sad thing in particular and I dwelled on it down at the caravan. 'I've always been kind of repulsed by people who are ill,' he said, 'no matter who they are.' He recalled giving his dad the kiss of life. 'I felt he was passing something on to me,' he said, 'like poison, from his mouth.' Then he whispered, 'I'm not saying it's a sensible thing to say.'

'You're not required to be sensible, Tully.'

'I just feel so horrible.'

'Can I bring you anything?'

'Yes,' he said. 'Bring me the pills that will end this.' He paused. 'I had a dream last night. You sat down and wrote a book about us. And I woke up this morning hoping you had and I wanted to read it.'

I was walking across the rocks a few days later when he Face-Timed me, saying he was feeling a bit more human, though not fully. He asked if I could reverse the camera and show him the Arran hills. 'Holy balls,' he shouted. 'The sea is silver and Arran is like lilac or something. That's nuts.'

'It's never the same way twice.'

He asked me to hold the phone low so he could hear the sound of the waves. 'I'm coming back down there tomorrow. Will you stay?'

'I have to go to London for a thing,' I said. 'One or two days, then I'll come straight back.'

'That's good,' he said. 'Try and get some of that Hitler chow-down in Brixton. I'm sure you can buy suicide pills down there.'

'I'm not doing time for you,' I said.

'Come on, buddy. It'll be *Angels with Dirty Faces*. And when they're taking you to the electric chair and you turn yella to save the boys, I'll be Pat O'Brien, standing there with a tear rolling down my fuckan cheek.'

'That would make you a Catholic priest,' I said. 'I might be willing to fry for that.'

'On second thoughts.' He paused for a bit, then asked me to hold up the phone and show him the view again. He said he was trying to put his mind on the positive but he wasn't sure he could sustain it. 'When I woke up this morning, I was thinking of that Bob Marley song, "Waiting in Vain", and I was like, "I don't want to wake in pain no more." You know, like singing my own words.'

'Speaking of which, how you getting on with the jukebox fifty?'

'I'm getting back to it,' he said. 'Nearly there. I promise you I'll have it finished before you get me the chow-down. I'm not going to embarrass you.'

'Better not,' I said.

Speaking on the phone that night, my friend Krisztina said she was finding it harder and harder to write anything that wasn't true, and we often spoke about Tully. She had no trouble comprehending his wish to go peacefully. 'I have an old boyfriend who lives in Zurich,' she said. 'He deals in antiquarian books and has made a life in Switzerland. You must go and see him, when you finally take your friend. Let me know your date when you have it.'

'It's hard to think about,' I said, 'but it's coming closer.'

'All the important things are hard to think about.'

20

Above my desk is a small sketch by Madame Mohl, who had a famous salon in Paris in the 1860s. She attracted writers and painters to her apartment, which overlooked a garden off the rue du Bac, the same garden you find in Henry James's novel *The Ambassadors*. It is in this 'spacious, cherished remnant', this garden, that a young character receives some advice, and we are told of faces appearing like ghosts at the windows above. James was a frequent visitor to Madame Mohl's, and one of those faces had to be his own, looking down and seeing the people of his imagination, and those characters turning, through the ether of time, to look up at their author standing there at the window. The sketch hung on the wall through everything that took place that year, and I would glance at it, feeling it said something true about all of us.

The process with the people in Switzerland had been slow. I wasn't sure it would work, or that Tully would be found suitable, but he'd consistently asked about assisted dying since his diagnosis in September, and I'd written to the organisation before the wedding, and filled in the forms. Then, on 10 December, a Dignitas official, Matteo, rang me to get the whole thing moving. 'Is his wife supporting it?' he asked, during that first conversation. 'Why isn't she the person applying?'

'She's against it. They're newly married. She believes he may get better.'

'That is impossible.'

Even in English – or perhaps more so – he had a tendency towards economy of speech and Swiss accuracy. 'Yes, the prognosis is terminal,' I said. 'And my friend is preparing to die his own way.'

Matteo sent me a number of articles he'd written, papers for conferences. He rang me up several times and with each of the calls he would offer a little more detail, which I carefully wrote on scraps of paper before pinning them to the bookshelves. 'Well,' he said one day, 'strictly speaking, we do not need his wife's consent or anybody's consent but his. The reports are clear, he will die in the short term. But timing is important in the management of people's feelings.'

'Yes.'

'Please take him through what we have discussed. I will be in touch with him soon, and several times before any appointment, to ensure consent, and check his mental state. That is our job and we will liaise with him and the doctors over that.'

'Of course.'

'But you are the one he has chosen as his sponsor. So you must do what you can to monitor the issue of timing and steer his loved ones.'

When I spoke to Tully that same evening I told him he had to talk to Anna again. It wasn't a matter of consent, it was a matter of decency.

'I will,' he said. 'I totally will.'

The thing I was never able to discuss with him – at this stage, or later – was my own ambivalence. He had made it a condition of our friendship, an aspect of our history, that I should support him now as he had once supported me. I'd needed his kindness once, and I'd always helped him through the years, but this was really it, so far as he was concerned. My own ambivalence was for me to suffer alone. *Live all you can*, the character is advised in Madame Mohl's garden, and I looked up at her sketch.

• • •

Before Christmas, he sent me an email:

> Dear Noodles,
> Do you mind if I have a night at the caravan on my own? Everything annoys me, Anna tidying up, washing, cooking, asking if everything is okay, looking anxious. She's doing everything she can but most stuff annoys me now. People making a noise, parcels arriving at the door. I can't switch off. The daily round of pills and these smiling arseholes on TV spouting shite, stuffing their faces with food. The Christmas Capitalism Ball starting up. Second course of chemo done. This one was worse. Much worse. I think we should go for a week's holiday in Sicily. Can you and Iona book it?
> Love you,
> Tully

Iona was at the Lowry in Salford. Her play was in its last weekend. When I called her that night, I found myself depressed. 'I'm sorry I've been away so much,' she said, tearful herself. 'You just can't prepare for something like this.'

'It's probably been for the best,' I said. 'I've had time with him on my own.' I told her the theatre she was in rang a lovely bell. 'It used to be just canals and docks where you are now. Tully and I sat there once, down by the water. I'm sure your theatre was just abandoned warehouses then.'

'It's such a *hub* nowadays,' she said. 'All shops and restaurants, and we're getting full houses every night.'

'It's all changed,' I said. 'And we saw the change when it began.'

'For Salford?'

'For all of us.'

I told her about Tully's request for Sicily. She started checking rental properties on her laptop while we were on the phone. 'There's a really beautiful villa in Taormina,' she said. 'I'll talk to Anna. It has two huge bedrooms and a balcony looking over the bay.'

'They'll totally love that.'

I could almost smell her bath oil through the phone, feel the towelling of her dressing gown, and see the candle flicker on the nightstand.

'She won't budge on this Dignitas question,' I said. 'Mainly, she just won't discuss it. Well, I don't think Tully is discussing it with her – and she certainly won't with me. She makes jibes about it, like at the wedding – Tully's *secret collaborator* – as if it's a private joke between Tully and her and me, but it frightens the hell out of her.'

'She has a way of storing her anger,' Iona said.

'I know. But she has to release it. Just for the . . . for the ethics of the whole thing . . . for the management of it.'

'She won't, babe. She'll hold on to it. She thinks it's wrong of him to forge a pact about something so fundamental to their relationship.'

'It's not about their relationship, Iona. It's about his relationship with the fuckan universe and with . . . I don't know . . . free will.'

'She's a lawyer, James. She doesn't believe in the universe. She believes in people and she believes in procedure.'

'You sound like you're on her side.'

'Don't be defensive.'

'She thinks that by seeing it as a kind of boys' game, it can be dismissed and will somehow disappear. But Tully's in agony about it.'

'Well, there is a boys' game aspect to it,' she said. 'And that's the way Tully has chosen to articulate it, or not articulate it. She's not wrong. But just let her come to terms with it in her own way. You can't write the script for her.'

'No, I see that.'

'Let it unfold in its own way. She's a brave person. And if they want to erase it with silence and holidays, so be it.'

'Tell me about that villa,' I said.

'It has lemons and rosemary by the pool,' she said. 'Marlene Dietrich and Truman Capote. All kinds of people stayed here.'

• • •

A new sense of smell came with the new year. Everything was too ripe. A strange, psychosomatic music was playing in my head, raising the threat level. Standing at the open doors of the caravan, I could taste sulphur and my throat hurt. The sea roared onto the beach, and as the foam spread up the sand I could smell the rotten seaweed and pulverised shells. Tully said he felt the caravan was a safe house. He said it should only be safe houses from now on, like the one Iona had booked in Sicily for June. He wanted places perched on the lip of a good time, places safe from pity or the evil of the chemo, and he wanted to pretend, he said, that the pain was only a state of mind. The treatment had given him months. His moods went up and down, but he had periods where his strength returned, and his face was fuller, his head clearer. In the months from winter to spring, we were often at the caravan watching *The Godfather*.

At four in the morning one night, I found him sitting on the edge of the sofa bed. The curtains were drawn back and the red coal of his roll-up was fierce against the black of the coast outside. 'My mouth is sore,' he said. 'And I had a dream I was sleeping with the fishes. A man swam down to meet me. He was wearing a cardigan. He swam down and blew me a kiss and tried to touch my mouth.'

'Do you think it was your dad?'

He didn't say anything but his eyes glittered.

I stayed on at the caravan by myself, and spoke to Matteo again later that week. 'Well,' he said. 'We have now gathered all the latest medical information and have spoken to the doctors.'

'Tully said you'd rung him.'

'Yes, we spoke to Mr Dawson. He is a clear candidate for the clinic. And everything you reported to us is correct.' Matteo changed a little on that call. His tone moved to being more pastoral, and I felt the test was over. The precision was still there, but he wanted now to talk books and philosophies of dying as much as practicalities. Probably more, actually. The phone call was long and he said the main issue remaining was not a medical one, but what he called a 'social problem'. 'It's unusual,' he said, 'to be this far forward and still have no involvement from the spouse.'

'I think Tully imagines I can just fix it.'

'I doubt if you can,' he said, quite abruptly. 'There will be . . . what is the phrase? There will be hell to pay. His family should all be included. It is not a matter for us. This is what my experience tells me and I am passing it on to you.'

'Didn't he suggest you call Anna?'

'Mr Dawson's wife? We're not permitted to do that.'

'Why not?'

'We have only one task. It is to assist people who are terminally ill who wish to die. It is not our task to assist the loved ones. But this is also a huge job, and your friend ignores it not so much at his own peril, but at theirs.'

'Yes, of course.'

'He will be leaving them behind, in more ways than one.'

'I understand. Thank you.'

'Don't thank me,' he said. 'This is our work. We will speak again.'

There was a pause and he asked me if there was anything else.

'Matteo,' I said. 'Is she right, his wife?'

'Yes and no,' he said. 'He is going to die. But people's expectations around death are very strange.'

I texted Anna from the train to Kings Cross. 'A. Can we speak about Tully's wishes? I'm not comfortable.'

I could see she'd read it, but she took two hours to respond.

'Hi Jimmy. To me, it's not a thing. And discussing it just makes it a thing. It won't happen. Treatment is going well. He's better. I know he goes on about it and thank you for being a friend to him, but I'm not going there. Can't wait for Sicily. Love, Anna.'

'He's talking to the clinic, Anna.'

'It's not a thing. xx'

Past Darlington, the world was blurred. I put my head against the window and dreamed for a hundred miles in black and white.

• • •

One day at the beginning of April, my mother's name came up on my phone. It doesn't happen often and I was surprised to see it. I picked up, and it was like a pinch of salt sprinkled in the open wound of that year – a sting of egotism, carelessness – to find her talking to me in the same old way. She was calling from Arran. She spoke for a minute about troubles she was having with her phone.

'What can I do for you?' I said. It wasn't a phrase I knew

how to use. I hadn't used it since the last time she'd called me, some years before. She immediately gave me an account of her own situation on the island. 'We need a radical healthcare plan for the ageing population,' she said, going on about some recent therapy training, 'and mindfulness is part of this amazing effort. I'll be setting up a new practice in Lamlash.'

'Good for you.'

'Oh, it's essential. And much in demand. I put up a stand at the summer fête at Montrose House. Wonderful response, I can tell you. People need much more support than they're getting.' She went on about the new emergency unit at the hospital and about the strawberry tarts available at the fête. She used the word 'tombola'. Somebody had made a huge trifle. There were raffle tickets and a very interesting discussion about future housing needs. A new pub in Brodick was dog-friendly. And on it went. There were dog-obedience classes in Whiting Bay and many of her friends had benefited greatly.

'But that's not why I'm telephoning you,' she said at last. 'I know you don't like to be disturbed, so I'll keep it short.'

'Right.'

'Maybe you won't remember her, a teacher of yours. I think English was her subject. Susan O'Connor? She taught at St Cuthbert's. She died this week. One of her old colleagues lives on the island and she said the family wanted you to know. Apparently the teacher kept up with your writing. So that's why I'm ringing.'

I took a moment or two, turning it over and picturing Mrs O'Connor.

'Are you still there?'

'She saved my life, that teacher,' I said.

'Well, I'm sure she did what she was paid to do.'

'No, Norma. She did much more than that.'

I saw it as fresh as the tulips on my desk: the image of Mrs O'Connor standing by a darkened window reading from W. B. Yeats. 'Thank you for telling me,' I said, 'and let me know if there's anything you need.'

'What would I be needing anything for?' she said. 'I'm too busy.' She rang off with a curt 'goodbye' and the advice that I should come one day and see all the wonderful improvements she was bringing to Arran.

I got hold of an address for Mrs O'Connor and wrote to her husband saying what my old teacher had meant to me, and that in my head she was eternally young. While writing the letter, I heard a few lines from Yeats in her Glasgow voice, and I typed them carefully from memory at the foot of the page, the scent of pine floor cleaner drifting in the air of the London afternoon.

Once out of nature I shall never take
My bodily form from any natural thing,
But such a form as Grecian goldsmiths make
Of hammered gold and gold enamelling
To keep a drowsy Emperor awake;
Or set upon a golden bough to sing
To lords and ladies of Byzantium
Of what is past, or passing, or to come.

21

If spring is always a reprieve, a return, then summer's a blessing. He was eating again and the bloom was back in his cheeks and the cheek was back in his remarks. He had gone quiet on the endgame topic. He came to London for my fiftieth birthday in May and sat on the sofa watching the Mao clock. 'Maybe it won't last,' he said, 'but the sores in my mouth have gone and I feel good.' He had morphine on standby. Anna was plotting a future on the promise of these successes, and she even considered, for a week or so, that they might move house. She'd looked at Rightmove and thought Largs was nice. Tully loved her enthusiasm and her life-improvement goals but saw it for what it was.

We went to Sicily on 10 June. Iona managed the whole thing so beautifully and we arrived like double honeymooners in Taormina. From the swimming pool you could look through a grove of lemon trees and see Mount Etna. Iona changed into linen trousers and a blue shirt and I laid my books by the bed as she walked over.

I kissed her.

'Are you okay?' she asked.

'I'm glad we're all here.' I walked onto the balcony, taking in the view and the tonic warmth of the sun. The smell of jasmine hit me and Iona came up and put her head on my shoulder and squeezed my arms. 'Listen to that,' she said. 'What a sound.' There were goats on the hillside with their bells tinkling.

'Do you get that scent?' I said.

'Lemons and chlorine.'

'Something else. Jasmine. There's something sickly about it.' She squeezed me again more tightly and said nothing.

Sitting on the patio at the front of the house, surrounded by cypress trees, Tully was reading with his sunglasses over his specs. When I came down he placed his book on the table between us, and I lifted it up to examine the cover. It was the familiar old Penguin Classics edition of *David Copperfield*, the one I used to own, thirty years ago. 'I'm reading it for the umpteenth time,' he said.

'Mr Peggotty working on his old boat at Yarmouth.'

'*And all that David Copperfield kind of crap*,' he said.

Around 4 p.m., the four of us walked down to the Piazza IX Aprile. We were shadows on the black-and-white tiles, and drank Aperol Spritzes, huge tumblers of amber that seemed like distillations of the sun. Anna held Tully's hand. We sat looking at the volcano while the ice melted in the drinks. Turning our heads, we saw the broken pillars of the Teatro Antico. Tully wanted to go up the steps of the Church of San Giuseppe and asked Anna to take a picture of him and me on the balcony. When we got up there, standing and facing out to sea, he put his arm over my shoulder and pointed to where Anna and Iona stood in the piazza below. 'We are all in heaven,' he said. 'I will now face my people like Eva Perón and tell them how I suffered for them.'

'Not yet,' I said. 'There's wine to be drunk.'

'That's true,' he said. 'This country's full of grapes and papes.'

We explored the town. In a shop stacked with soaps and dried herbs, I bought him a bottle of Acqua di Parma. And when I told him it had been Frank Sinatra's favourite scent he bought me one, too. 'That's a bit of the local magic right there,' he said. 'It smells of lemons but it also smells of public enemies.'

'Vegas crooners,' I said.

'Handsome bastards.'

After the shops, Tully announced that we would go on a mission to find the best glass of red wine in the whole of Taormina. Anna and Iona were up for it, and we went to place after place, eating up the bread and olives, drinking. 'What's this one called?' Tully asked, holding up a glass by the stem.

'Le Casematte. Nero d'Avola,' the waiter said.

'Strawberries and coffee,' Iona said. She made a fuss of sniffing it. Tully took a large swig and settled back in his chair.

'Lorne sausage, with a hint of HP Sauce.'

It made me emotional to see him eating better, and for a moment I was caught in Anna's programme of hope. It must have been 6.30 or so when the waiter got us a car. He'd noticed our interest in the wine, and maybe he perceived something of the special occasion, or was just good at marketing. In any case, he suggested to us that we visit his friend's vineyard high on the slopes of Mount Etna, and then he made phone calls to arrange it. We drove down the hill and then up another one, bumping along a dirt track and disappearing behind a row of eucalyptus trees. Our table overlooked the sea. We had boiled eggs and slices of fennel with dark red wine. Tully stopped the conversation after a while and held up the bottle of the Petto Dragone. 'This is it,' he said, 'from the house of Gambino. I want it recorded by you, Noodles, that this is the world's best wine.' We were all drunk. We ordered another bottle. 'Rhubarb,' he said, sniffing it.

'Go fuck yourself,' I said.

'Let me just die here,' he said.

The conversation petered out for a minute and the light began to fade along the coast. 'There are plenty of medical treatments,' Anna said eventually. 'I want you all to know that. It's going very well and there's lots more they can do, a plan of care all the way to next year.'

'Let's not talk about it now,' Tully said.

'I *spoke* to them,' she said. He drained his glass and looked impassive and Iona tried to change the subject, talking about *The Godfather* tour—

'*Make death proud to take us.*'

He said it very clearly and Iona stopped. I'm not sure if he said it to goad Anna, or to establish authority, or just because he was drunk, but the use of those words was the closest he had ever come to vocalising his wishes with all three of us present.

'What?' Anna asked, swallowing hard.

'From Shakespeare,' I said.

'Words you gave him, I suppose?'

'Tully's his own man, Anna,' I said. 'He's an English teacher. He knows his Bard.'

She stared at me. 'I don't know about making death proud,' she said. 'It sounds like poetry to me, and reversible. Make life proud to preserve us.'

'Good point,' I said.

Tully went off, under the pretence of studying some vintage bottles displayed in glass cabinets, and it somehow lightened the atmosphere. Iona spoke to the manager about getting a case of the Dragone sent back to Glasgow.

We returned to the villa late that night. It was warm and mint-scented and the muslin curtains were billowing into the rooms. Etna looked Japanese under the moon and Tully went into the kitchen to pour brandy. I sat on a sun-lounger out on the balcony and suddenly felt overwhelmed with exhaustion. It wasn't ordinary sleepiness: it felt stored up, and it went all the way through me and made my bones feel heavy. The months of tension, and the corrosive, draining business of acting for people who wouldn't speak. I felt I could have closed my eyes and slept until it was all over. Anna and Iona were talking about the stars. My wife pointed out a constellation and Anna blew vape smoke over the railings. 'I love how you know your stars,' I said, opening my eyes.

'You get bored when I point them out at the caravan.'

'Circumstances,' I said.

'I don't like them much,' Tully said.

Iona searched his face. 'What do you mean?'

'They have no role,' he said, 'except to hang about out there, freezing cold, watching us disappear.'

'It's funny,' Iona said, 'how we feel watched by them.'

· · ·

We had sore heads the next morning, but it was hot and we drove to Savoca. Tully said there must be a bus we could take, but I ignored him, making an argument for air-conditioning and taxis in general. The driver missed the turning and drove too far towards Messina, which Tully saw as clear evidence that we were being robbed. Then, noticing the driver spoke English, he asked about the history of the local area. The driver didn't know much, so Anna read something off her phone about Italian mercenaries in the year 288 raiding Messina and killing the men and marrying their wives. 'The usual,' she said. Everything brightened as the car went up the hillside, houses and vineyards slowly revealed. Rain started falling out of nowhere, and just as suddenly disappeared. In a few minutes it was scorching and the road ahead was bleached white and we could see the rooftops of Savoca.

The driver dropped us off in the centre of the village and we walked over to the viewing platform. I held Iona's hand, watching the ships out in the bay. In the other direction, facing inland, the haze was incredible, but you could see all the glinting promontories, towns, castles, and the windows of far-off hotels. Bar Vitelli was next to us. They served us Cokes and cannoli, then lemon granita, and Tully said he'd dreamed of coming here. We stayed as long as we could. We moved on to beers and the sun shone down and Anna took photographs with her phone. 'I can't believe it,' Tully said. 'This is actually *The Godfather*.'

'Where Michael speaks to the girl's father.'

'Right here,' he said, banging the arm of the chair. He was the ultimate movie aficionado, sitting in his black cap and plaid shirt, happy as a game-show winner, smiling under a metal sign that said 'Itala Pilsen'.

Anna and Iona went down the road to buy postcards. Tully clasped my arm and shrugged his shoulders like Brando, before sliding into an impersonation of Sonny Corleone. '*Nice college boy like you. Now you want to gun down a police captain. You gotta get up close like this and, badda-bing, you blow their brains all over your nice Ivy League suit. C'mere.*'

We sniggered and the waiter came out waving flies away. 'You guys know all the movies,' he said, and encouraged us to come inside and look at the little *Godfather* museum they'd set up. They had film scripts and props. Tully went round taking pictures with his phone and sending them to his nephews, and the waiter snapped us next to the beer sign. After that, he brought out more cannoli and an ashtray and told us about a woman who lived over the road. He pointed to a balcony overflowing with bougainvillea. 'She was in one of the films,' he said. 'Mr Coppola, he hired the whole town. You see them at the church, all the people of Savoca. The *signora* is in a white dress, walking with Mr Pacino.'

'This guy here,' Tully said, pointing at me. 'Is boss of the Primrose Hill Mafia. You wouldn't know it, to look at his nice side-parting, but he runs one of the baddest gangs in the whole of North London.'

The waiter flicked the air with his towel. 'Am I safe?' he

said, laughing. 'If I go in my car tonight, will it blow up?'

Tully touched the side of his nose and winked. He asked for two more beers and licked his fingers after lifting one of the pastries.

'Almonds,' he said. 'Different from the other one.'

'That was ricotta. This is sweeter.'

He seemed the most relaxed he'd been in ages. The waiter came back with the beers and joked with me again, *Il Capo dei Capi*.

'I'm sure they get this shit every day,' I said, when he'd gone. But Tully was pensive, still playing with the pastry.

'They say cyanide smells of almonds,' he said.

I looked across at him and slugged my beer and waited.

'I think we're there now, aren't we?' he asked.

'With what?'

'The chow-down.'

So, no: he hadn't budged an inch. 'Everything is still in place,' I said, tentatively, 'as they told you. But you do seem better, and Anna's programme—'

'Anna is dreaming,' he said.

'But, Tully—'

'Listen,' he said. 'She's dreaming. And I love her for it. I might be eating better and I'm glad the bastard chemo has given me more time. But I'm dying and one day soon it will get much worse and I haven't changed my position. You're my wingman and I'm telling you it's going to start. The guy said everything was checked and they're ready. He said nothing will change at their end.'

'Matteo,' I said. 'Yes. He told me the same thing he told you. When it gets bad again and you feel ready, they can offer you a date. But it's important to remember you can pull out at any time.'

'And let nature take its course?'

'Whatever,' I said. 'You have the alternative.'

Switzerland stood sharp in his mind and you could see he didn't want survival-talk wearying the plan.

'Stick with me,' he said.

'And Anna? I asked you to discuss it properly with her, Tully, and you didn't. The Dignitas people said it was crucial.'

'I've told her the basics, Noodles. That's it. What else is there to say?'

'It's just upsetting for her.'

His eyes darkened. It was unusual to see him grow angry. 'Upsetting? None of you know what you're talking about.'

'Tully, you can't—'

'Don't fuckan tell me what I can and can't do! Who I need to talk to, and how!'

We sat in silence then. I felt I could hear the bubbles rising in the beer bottles. He looked at me like I was on the brink of a total betrayal.

'You have me in a bind, Tully.'

'And what do you think I'm in? You'll get over it. *She'll* get over it. It's me that has no future and controlling this is all I have left.'

'I hear what you're saying.'

'Do you?'

'Yes, I do,' I said. 'I'm sorry.'

'Set me free. That's all.'

When the others came back we walked along the road to the Church of San Nicolò. Part of the way there, Tully stopped and leaned his back against one of the trees. 'Wait a minute,' he said, catching his breath. 'I'm like an old man. One minute you're skanking all hours to the Specials, chugging cider and snorting speed, then, before you know it, you can't make it up a daft wee hill.'

At the door of the church my companions searched my face for signs of resurgent Catholicism. I could see them nudging each other, preparing for mockery, so I dipped my hand in the water font just to satisfy them, and crossed myself. Had I been on my own I would probably have done it anyway, if only out of hope. When I got to the far end, in a cool plaster alcove only yards from the Sicilian sun, I took out a coin and lit a candle. 'Fancy gaff,' Tully said, appearing at my back. 'I see they're charging you. Bring back John Knox. Bring back Pastor Jack Glass and Henry VIII and Ian Paisley and King Billy.'

'Ah, shut it.'

'Silence is overrated,' he whispered, walking off. He had no awareness of sin and stuck his tongue out at all the paintings. I'd once heard a poet say something about religious belief, that it gave you a 'structure of conscience'. I couldn't really accept it, yet the phrase stayed with me, and it came to mind, edging out other thoughts, as I tried to keep up with Tully's comic engine, reigniting at the church in Savoca. For him it was nothing but a big tomb full of plastic flowers. He needed humour, just as he always had when we were boys, to tamp down the darkness, and to cover his embarrassment at having ever given in to seriousness of any kind. He was the same man who once made jokes about colours in a Salford car repair shop, minutes after sharing his fear of stagnation and death, his fear of life passing from him like breath from his father.

'I smell opium,' he said. Then he reached into his back pocket, extracted a blister pack and popped out a white pill. 'A wee drop for Our Lady.' He put his hand into the grotto and laid the pill by the chipped painted roses on her feet. It was morphine. He loved the perversity of it, and I stood still, wondering if a bit of the hard stuff might indeed have helped the poor woman through Holy Week. For some reason, Tully adopted the accent of the Irish mammy, staring into the statue's upturned eyes.

'Have you anything for a crown of thorns now, doctor? . . . Oh, no problem, Mary. We have these newfangled pills, you know. A distillation of the old scag. All the rage with the young ones . . . Oh, doctor. That would be a mercy now . . . Ah, away with you, Mary. You just take the prescription into the chemist, so. A wee something for the lad up on the Cross. Sure, he'll hardly be feeling the spear. The whipping must've been a shock to the system. And the vinegar. The nails. Oh, for the love of God.'

He went off in search of more mischief. I reached in and removed the pill, worried about leaving it there. It felt powdery and I licked my finger. By this time he was standing on a wooden chair by the altar, intoning Joy Division in a pure voice. I walked into the aisle and looked up at Tully Dawson, that font of earthly presence, singing 'Atmosphere' to a high window and all the gods.

22

When we left them at London City Airport, there were dark circles under Tully's eyes, and I sensed his healthy revival had already ended. In the transfer hall he hugged Iona and me and then all four of us hugged, spontaneously, as if to pool every last molecule of the Sicilian sunshine, and then they were off to Glasgow. In the taxi home, I remember staring out at the wet streets and thinking of other last sightings. I knew I would see him again, but the feeling gave rise to memories of Limbo. He'd shone in Manchester, but he'd given signs of a difficulty with himself that only increased with the years. Eventually, a certain lost quality took over with him and he began running with a new, rougher crowd. The last time I bumped into him it was 2002 and I'd stopped when I saw his unmistakeable shape standing at the counter of Missing Records in Glasgow. I went into the shop and tapped his shoulder, and, as Limbo turned, I saw the old anarchic face dimmed with exhaustion. He had a bag of badges in his hand and a signed poster of Iggy Pop.

'Heavens to Betsy, it's Jimmy Collins!' He rummaged in the bag and held up a badge. '"Coal Not Dole"?'

'Jesus, Limbo,' I'd said. 'Great to see you.' We stood there catching up and he showed me other badges: '999', 'Down with Trident'. He seemed under pressure, but Limbo was

Limbo and he couldn't help but tell stories.

'It might be a bit shady,' he said, 'but I can prove to you that the novelist Evelyn Waugh is personally responsible for 9/11.'

'Go for it,' I said.

'Okay. In 1945, right, Evelyn Waugh published *Brideshead Revisited*. The book was adapted for television in the early Eighties and brought fame to the actor Jeremy Irons. In the years following his initial fame, Irons was in a series of rubbish films, including *Die Hard with a Vengeance*, where he played a psycho who wants to set a bomb off under Wall Street in a passing subway train. The film was screened by the film club of Hamburg University of Technology in the mid-1990s, and one of the nutters who attended at that time was Mohamed Atta, an Egyptian student who was becoming radicalised and thinking of a big crazy plan. He mentioned the film to his pals in the Hamburg al-Qaida cell and together they later carried out the attacks on America, Atta flying his hijacked plane into the North Tower of the World Trade Center. So, I rest my case – Evelyn Waugh caused 9/11.'

I remember putting my bag on the counter and clapping. 'Very good, Limbo,' I said. 'Not sure it'll stand up in court.'

'It needs some work,' he said. I slapped his back and we went for a few drinks at the old Rock Garden, and I'm glad we had those hours. What a wonderful, loving man. As the taxi drove on, I saw him very clearly in my head, sitting by the window saying everything was coming good.

• • •

A few weeks after our holiday in Sicily a letter came from Tully. He'd been sending me packages of singles for the café jukebox – I now had the complete fifty ready for my neighbour – and then this serious and formal letter arrived. 'I want you to know, James,' it started, 'that it's all beginning to get bad, and I refuse to die in a hospital in an undignified state. I have always said this. They want me to start a new kind of treatment, immunotherapy, and I feel like offing myself just thinking about it.'

'Who's they?' I asked myself.

Then I answered my own question: 'The doctors, Anna.'

'All the arguments are over,' he wrote. 'Please push the people in Switzerland now for an actual date.' His letter went on to talk about various difficulties he had endured over the last few years. He wrote about an argument with the head of the school he'd been teaching at. Tully had been the union rep and had been disciplined, him and another guy, over some emails they'd sent which appeared to criticise their boss. 'Why am I telling you this? It really got to me and I've been thinking about it a lot recently. I was accused of being aggressive to a member of staff and behaving unprofessionally. It's as if this illness, fuck knows – as if the illness is part of a judgment made against me.'

I went to my desk but I couldn't give him answers. Fear doesn't have an answer. I wrote sentences of solidarity filed as paragraphs. Over the next few days, we emailed back and forth, speaking about approval and compassion, mothers and fathers, the stories that never end. The idea of 'judgment' was strong in him at that time. One night we FaceTimed. He looked thinner, beginning to break.

'What does it mean that I got this?' he asked.

'Illness has no meaning,' I said. 'It's just illness.'

'But it's as if I did something terrible.'

'You did nothing, Tully. You are a human being. And that's an unstable condition that ends badly for all of us.'

Changes of mood were abrupt. The next day we talked about the jukebox and the selections he'd finally arrived at. 'I don't see,' I said, 'how you can justify going from 1979 to 1990 and leaving out Prince.'

'Sorry, man. It's clearly my fault, but I refuse to pander to your interest in cross-dressing nymphomaniacs in silver boots.'

And so it went on, the gentle alternation between the serious tone, goading me to take the lead on his wish to die, as I had at the beginning, regardless of anyone's opinion, and our usual banter, where we cut most things down to a joke. On the phone, Tibbs Lennox told me that he found it hard to keep off the big subjects when he was with Tully. They'd met up at a bar in the Gallowgate.

'We end up talking pish,' Tibbs said, 'when in my head it's all life stuff and crushed hearts.'

'Did you say Karl Marx?'

'Him as well.'

• • •

But he was definitely beginning to fail as the summer peaked. His eating declined and the doctors spoke of putting stents into his oesophagus. Tully wanted his date. I called Matteo. 'I'm having trouble feeling secure about the volition issue,' I said. I worried that Tully was only capable of taking this action because I was behind it, because it had been offered when we spoke about it at the caravan that first night, and accepted as a token of friendship. But was that the same as him deciding for himself to take his own life?

'Then I must speak with Mr Dawson.'

On 2 September, Tully emailed me. 'Heard from the dude again about the chow-down,' he wrote. 'I told him I was in constant pain. He wants a letter. I wrote to him in Zurich. Told him my body was failing and that I definitely, one hundred per cent want to go. Sent it off to him today. I put on double the number of stamps, just to be sure. And I emailed it as well. So that is definitely that, so far as I'm concerned.'

'Did you show it to Anna?' I asked him that night.

'Yes,' he said. 'I put it on her desk. It's still there.'

From Zurich on 15 September, a letter came by courier. I opened it that evening at the front door then stepped back into the house. The same letter had gone to Tully. My hand shook because it was suddenly there, as I knew it would be, printed in bold, the date of the 'appointment'. I called Iona at work and cried down the phone. 'I'm not sure it's right, helping him to do this,' I said, looking at his stack of singles on the dresser. She carefully went through all the reasons. It was what he wanted. He had never wavered. I toyed with the arguments – Anna's arguments. What if he suddenly got better? What kind of friend arranges your death? But Iona gently talked them away and brought me back to earth again: Anna would begin to see the sense in it. Anybody would.

. . .

A few days later, I brought my unease to someone else, Gemma the believer, the stalwart of God, a recently elected bishop I had become friendly with after a book panel discussion we did on the radio. 'Good for me to talk to a person of faith,' I said to her by text, suggesting we meet for lunch in Edinburgh.

'Good for me, too,' she replied.

On my way to the restaurant, I stopped at the Portrait Gallery. I'd woken up thinking about J. M. Barrie and I knew they had a painting of him. Beyond the chieftains and the captains of thought, it hangs in a little corridor, and I stood there. He had a tinge of green about him, with his worried face, the loose necktie and the dowdy, brown coat. He seemed old, and what is it for the author of *Peter Pan* to seem old?

Walking in St Andrew's Square, I halted at the scent of hops, something in the air of burned porridge. *Old winters. Schooldays.* From the corner, I saw Gemma arrive at the restaurant and hand over her coat to a smiling girl. Tall, and wearing her purple blouse and dog collar under a black jacket, she threw a brightly coloured scarf over one shoulder and strode through the Art Deco palm trees of the Ivy. I gathered myself at the crossing before heading over the road.

'Crusty bread,' I joked when I reached her. 'Why such reckless extravagance in one so young?' She half stood to kiss my cheek.

'Hello, you,' she said.

'The Right Reverend Fisher.'

'Isn't it grand?' she said, smiling and swatting me with her napkin. We sat down and she told me she was in battle costume because she'd been opening a food bank that morning. 'One of the less joyful modern necessities.'

'It's great to see you,' I said. She was one of those Anglicans who liked wine and the menace of conversation, interested in everything, old books, Shakespeare, European films, sudoku, as well as the salvation of the masses. I think she enjoyed bandying doubts with people she wasn't likely to bump into on a Sunday. 'I saw a whole lot of faces in the National Portrait Gallery a minute ago,' I said, 'rows and rows of them. Faces full of the mind's construction, as you might say.'

'They have me in there,' she said. 'A likeness, they call it, from when I was warden of the Episcopal Institute. A real child-frightener. Like Joan of Arc after the conversion therapy. Sculpted by some Glasgow genius.'

'I wish I'd seen that. I was looking at Barrie. The Nicholson portrait. It's haunting, actually. I've never seen a picture of a person more alone. He's only forty-four. It was painted a dozen years before the tragedies began.'

By the time the food arrived I'd already updated her on Tully. She asked me more about our past and formed a few sentences, the kind only she would deliver, that invited science and faith into a circle of common sense. 'Everyone has a person like Tully. The thing we know is that humanity has a hundred per cent mortality rate. We all die. But the facts don't matter – we can't bear to lose the people we love, and it doesn't quite register about the billions who die, or even about our own coming deaths. We don't experience our own death the way we experience the deaths of those we love.'

'Yes, that must be true.'

'His dying is now part of your life.'

'And that's . . .'

'Disappointing. Heartbreaking. Confusing. It's one of those events that will appear to reorder your whole past. That's the story of life, if you're open to life, and affected by the reality of death. And one death will do it. By the sounds of it, you and he spoke about the future and believed in its power.'

I pondered for a second and lifted my glass. 'I allowed myself to forget it was all ephemeral,' I said.

'We all make that mistake.'

I felt that was precisely what I'd seen in J. M. Barrie's face. 'He lost himself,' I said, 'because he forgot that time had to pass.'

'He was the Scottish Proust,' she said. 'He lent his own childhood a myth. And he seemed really to hope for a changeless world.'

'There's this shadow beside him in the painting,' I said.

'That's what I'm talking about. That's the brother.'

'The lost brother?'

'David, yes. Died in an ice-skating accident. He was a student at Bothwell Academy. Of course, the better-known tragedy came for Barrie with the deaths of those Llewelyn Davies boys. One of them in the trenches and another by drowning, I think. But there was that earlier loss, too – the brother.'

I told her I'd spent one summer, a few years ago, writing a story about Jack Kerouac, who also lost a brother in his childhood. While I was working on the story I found the widow of his old friend and stand-in Neal Cassady. She was ninety years old and living in a caravan park near Reading. She'd survived all the friendships. 'I sat with her and we smoked cigarettes into the evening,' I told the bishop, 'and she spoke of those times as if they were perfectly ordinary. "They were just boys," she said, "and the romance of it all lay in knowing they'd seen the sun together."'

'That's fantastic,' Gemma said.

'It was the end of her life. She's dead now.'

We slowly got around to the difficulty. She had another glass of wine and I weighed the words before trying to say them.

'Is it murder,' I asked, 'to take Tully to Switzerland and pay the assistants there to end his life?' She took a swig from her glass and wiped the rim, as priests do.

'No,' she said. 'It's that other thing beginning with 'm' – mercy.'

'I made him a promise.'

'Then you must keep it. What you said about him makes it clear – your friend is too young to die but he has lived a wonderful life and he will be remembered, and the love he expressed will multiply. That is what I believe, what I encourage you all to believe. Follow your instinct and make his exit a thing of dignity and peace.'

'Thank you, Gemma. That's—'

'You were all young together. New to the world. Now help him leave. That will be the measure and the grace of your friendship. Others will understand. The medieval Church left us a Latin text, *Ars moriendi*, "The Art of Dying". It's a masterpiece of preparation, written by a couple of unknown Dominicans. The world will be less without him, you have said as much. Now help him get his house in order.'

'He was the life and soul.'

'Then turn up the music,' she said.

. . .

I was due to see Tully's band in Glasgow that evening – Kim Philby, his four-man combo, just starting to gain recognition. I was worried about his strength, but that was pure Tully, too: it somehow suited his case, his nature, that he'd go out of the world trying to make music. I was driving out of Edinburgh a few hours before the event when the phone rang. It was difficult to hear but I could tell he was upset, so I pulled over. He was calling from his mother's house. He said he was in the living room and had told the removal men to leave him alone for a minute. The house was sold and the men were trying to take everything away. 'It's as if the world collapsed,' he said, weeping.

'Get up and leave, Tully,' I said.

'We put the dining table on Gumtree. Nobody wants it. Anna's out there asking the neighbours if any of them wants it. Even for nothing, nobody'll . . . Jesus fuckan Christ, Noodles.' His voice cracked. 'The table. Remember we sat there that time, my dad was being a pure prick?'

'Honestly, mate. Just leave. It's too hard.'

'He told you to watch out for the Soviets. Accused my mum of giving me more food than him, because I was working. Remember?'

'Of course,' I said. 'Findus Crispy Pancakes and mash.' We were silent, calmer, just breathing peacefully.

'I've been thinking about Limbo,' he said. 'Why did we let him die, man? He was only in his thirties. Only a young guy. In a hotel, on his own. There was powder by the bed. Did you know that, Noodles?'

'I did know it,' I said. 'You told me at the time.'

'But we've never really discussed it, have we? How did that happen to Limbo? How come we didn't get a hold of him, and bring him back?'

'Nobody could, Tully. He just had a run of bad luck.'

'But we could've changed it,' he said.

'I'm not sure. I'm really not sure.'

He sobbed, and eventually his voice settled.

'But we had a great time, didn't we?' he said.

Sitting in the lay-by I choked up and couldn't say anything else.

'Noodles?'

'I'll see you at the gig in a couple of hours,' I said, eventually. 'Don't look back. Go to the car and don't look back.'

'Looking back is all I've got,' he said.

We could all live side by side, like in Brookside Close. That was the thought I had driving past those Scottish new builds by the motorway. It had occurred to me on many of the long drives during those months: this thing was all a mistake. In time to come we'd talk about that terrible scare when Tully nearly died, we'd make fun of it, have dinner together, and watch old films and then he and Anna would go home to the house opposite. We'd switch off our lights at night knowing we were all safe at last, Iona and me, them, everyone. We could forget all the interim parts, the careers, the houses elsewhere, the made life. If he would only survive, we could give it all up and go back to the start, to those houses along the bypass. I have never forgotten them, the box bedrooms, the lofts that smelled of putty and fresh paint, the tiny gardens and their rotary washing lines. And with this, I continued driving. Only the motorway ahead, only miles of facts and Glasgow in the rain.

I parked near the site of an old bar we used to like. Bar 82. It wasn't really a building at all, but a kind of Nissen hut. They gave out drink like medicine, or cod liver oil, or Communion wine, or poison. Tully loved it in there, thirty years ago. So did Tibbs Lennox, sitting in a corner with a music paper. Usually loveless himself, along with the rest of us, he would read out the keepers from the Lonely Hearts. '"Catcher in the Rye, Come Share My Smithdom. Female and Ill. Box No. 7951."'

'Circle that one,' I'd said.

'"Lonely Male, 20. Likes Weddoes, Mondays, Roses, Peely Bands, Autumn, and cuddling cats. Seeks Lovely People."'

Tully looked up. 'Take his number. Any port in a storm.'

'Not *cats*, Tully,' I said.

The rain continued as I walked to the entrance. I went

down a mineshaft of peeling posters. Greasy tables and no ice, different bands every night. The chairs hadn't changed since I was a student and neither had the bands, not really, though half the musicians were now surfing on statins. Bass players, men with paid-off mortgages, nodding off during their own set, thinking of tinned pie and programmes on Netflix, while the younger singer shrieked his way past the curfew.

I met Tully at the crowded bar before they went on. He was wearing a T-shirt that said 'Socialism'.

'You're packing them in,' I said.

He rolled his eyes. 'The fuckan *NME* died before I did,' he said, 'and I want my money back. Thursday after Thursday, year after year, boring interviews with bands called Meat Whiplash or the Shrubs, and not one of them had a single thing to say. Now, just as I'm about to kick the bucket, the BBC wants us in for a live session with that knob from Radio 6. No justice. Why didn't it happen when I was young and handsome and could've shagged two million people?'

I caught sight of Anna at one of the tables. She was sitting in a group and one of them was talking to her, but she just stared at us and didn't move. I raised a glass in her direction and she nodded almost imperceptibly.

I waited for Tully to finish speaking.

'Have you told Anna about the date? Does she know?'

'Aye,' he said. 'She'll come.'

'So, it's all clarified?'

'She'll come. That's all she's saying. You know what she's like.'

I didn't have anything to add. There would be more to come on that front, and I thought I was ready now to accept it when it did.

'You'll be with me in Zurich, won't you?' he said. 'And Iona, too. The four of us. Just like another holiday.' And at that point one of his many friends came up to hug him, so the discussion was closed for now.

Later, while the band played, I could see he was in pain and still upset from the house clearance. But he always wanted these gigs to be great, and needed his playing to seem unhindered. The venue was filled with the kind of people who hadn't had a stamp on the back of their hand in thirty years, and some of them – lawyers, teachers, social workers now – had forgotten how to hold a pint. Tumblers perched on their palms, they leaned forward to hear what their old friends were trying not to say, exchanging looks from the angst-scape of youth. Bobby McCloy was still in Glasgow and he headed towards me with an air of experience. 'I must commend the management,' he said, 'for their sterling effort in maintaining the venue's traditional standards of awfulness.'

'Don't lie. You love it, Clogs,' I said.

'I'm not sure, captain,' he said. 'I believe the talent is unquestionable. But nothing ages you like a halo of dry ice.'

23

I came down Pall Mall to meet an American woman. It was the first week in October by then and all had been quiet for a week or two. She texted to say she'd gone into St James's Park and would be sitting on a bench near the pelicans. I found her there with a notepad in her lap and she fanned herself with a theatre programme. She had read something of mine and wanted me to write a story for her pages, but I couldn't really concentrate. Her words floated into the daylight and I tried to listen, thinking normal life should be maintained. She said it would be a long reported story about scent and memory, looking at the perfume industry in Grasse and the search for the ultimate fragrance. It would be for a special issue. They already had a title: 'The Manufacture of Nostalgia'.

'It's a good title,' I said. But I wasn't thinking of Grasse, I was thinking about the reality of being eighteen and its strange afterlife. I told her the title might suit another piece I had in mind, a profile of a cigarette-paper factory in Belarus. 'It used to supply cigarette papers to the whole of the Soviet Union,' I said.

'You speak Russian?'

'Rusty now, much like the factory.'

'You could write about Putin's men,' the editor said.

'I think I'll stick to cigarette papers. Much less toxic. But I'll look into the business of Grasse and the fragrances and see if it might work.'

'We like writers with many subjects,' she said. We spoke for a while, then I thanked her for taking the time to meet me and she stood up and shook my hand. I remained there after she'd gone. Squirrels were running along the boughs of the thinning trees, and one of them froze halfway, keeping vigil on the sitter.

My phone pinged, announcing a series of long texts from Anna. Tully was in hospital, something to do with the wrong medicine, the wrong doctor, but really it was a turn for the worse and she was feeling confused. While I was reading the texts, she rang me. 'He's out of his skin today,' she said. 'The worst I've seen him. And he's started going on about this date. He told me he has a date to go to this place in Switzerland.'

'He's only just told you?'

'About the actual date – yes.'

'But he told me he'd shown you the letter.'

She sniggered, as if in disbelief. 'Come on, Jimmy. You know fine well he isn't giving me the facts. He wanted to keep it between you and him.'

'I told him not to do that. So did the Dignitas people. He said you'd agreed to come and I went ahead and got tickets.'

'But it didn't occur to you to tell me yourself? Or the people in Switzerland didn't think it was necessary to give *me* the information?'

'They're not allowed. It's Tully's job—'

'But you and Tully had it all sewn up.'

'Stop it, Anna.'

She put the phone down on me. I'd felt it coming – felt it coming all year – and there wasn't a part of me that didn't sympathise. But I was resolved. After Edinburgh, after Gemma, my only task was to help him reach the end.

'Jesus, Noodles,' he said when I rang him five minutes later, 'it's a fuckan catastrophe. You've got to get me out of here, buddy.'

'Are you on a ward?'

'Aye. I keep throwing up. A few old guys next to me. One of them worked in the shipyards and now he has a colostomy bag and there's shit all over the floor. My immunity is down to nothing – and we're sharing a bog. The cancer in my stomach has grown and I'm in pain all the time. They started the immunotherapy, but . . . I can't.'

'Take your time, man.'

'I hate putting this on you. But . . . when . . .'

'You know when, Tully. You got the same letter as me – 20 October.'

'Can't they bring it forward?'

'It's only two weeks away,' I said.

Through the trees I could hear a marching band. 'It's the downward spiral, this,' he went on. 'The same questions again and again and all I can say is I feel terrible. The doctor came round. He goes, "How are you?" and I'm like, "If I had a gun I'd fuckan shoot myself." And he goes, "Oh, so you're having suicidal thoughts?" And I'm like, "Shit, brother, don't worry about it. I don't have a gun." But the guy goes off and speaks to some psychology team, and they rush in for a talk and now I'm on Whack Watch.' He said they were giving him a room with a TV and a clear view of Ibrox.

'As if things weren't bad enough,' I joked.

He coughed the air out of his lungs.

'I've got the date imprinted on my mind,' he said.

'Yes.' He was silent for a long time. I didn't try to fill the gap and we sat on the line, saying nothing.

'We've got flights and everything?'

'It's all done, but remember it can be undone. I just spoke to Anna. She's furious, Tully. She didn't know about the date, the tickets, nothing.'

'I need this to stop. I'm ready to go.'

I kept silent.

'Come up,' he said. 'If you're not too busy.'

'Fuck all that,' I said. 'I can be there tonight.'

• • •

When my train was outside Preston that evening, he texted to say he was going home. 'What about the view of Ibrox?' I replied.

'It can't end the pain,' he wrote. 'Even on current form.'

The train took its time to Glasgow. I sat thinking about a trip we once made to a Soul Weekender in Skegness. It must have been 1990 because the World Cup was about to happen. Ross McArdle was there that time. So was Tibbs, and Mick Caesar, who drove us down in a second-hand Saab that he loved. Caesar was funny about his car – he always thought people on the road were trying to cut him up – and his willingness to drive his mates to gigs might have been considered masochistic, given he was sober. 'Listen, soap-dodgers,' he said on the way past Grimsby, 'don't get mashed in my motor. If any of you throw up, you're getting ten rapid to the forehead and dumped at the bus stop.'

'Come on, wee boy!' Tully said, leaning over from the back seat and offering him a slug of his Buckfast. Not unreasonably, Caesar swerved into the slow lane and told him to resist interrupting the driver's concentration, or words to that effect.

Images came back to me on the train. The holiday camp and the boys diving into the pool. The monorail. There was a neon sign on the front of one the buildings, the dining hall or something – 'Our True Intent Is All for Your Delight' – and it was the last of the great trips to England. We would never go like that again as a group, the halls full of druggy fools, the mornings filled with unwanted breakfasts and daft conversations. I could see the faces and hear the words: Tibbs cracking us all up in a pub by the boating pond. 'Yeez are full of shite,' he said to a bunch of boys from the inner workings of Suffolk.

'No. Listen,' one of them said. 'You asked me for the three best football songs of all time and then you won't hear past this New Order nonsense.' Tibbs was pointing to a paper, in this case the *NME*.

'No, you listen,' he said. 'I gave you a challenge and you came up with dross.' The paper lay sodden under a forest of Budvar bottles. The headline, if I'm not mistaken, was 'Love

Will Terrace Apart'. Tibbs waved the new East Anglian best-chums-for-life away with a firm hand chopping the air. 'I never said "Ally's Tartan Army" was any good. No Scottish World Cup song was ever good. What I'm saying is, none of yours have been any good either, until now, because of John Barnes and Barney Sumner.'

'He's right,' Tully said. 'You're sound guys. But we can't accept your pathetic attempt to raise 1982's "This Time We'll Get It Right" from the dustbin of history. It was an aggressively shite song of zero value to mankind.'

'*They think it's all over*,' Ross said.

'*It is now*,' Caesar said.

• • •

I rented a car near Central Station and drove up the ramp, turning into a bleak precinct under the railway, west of Jamaica Street. Empty booze bottles stood on the pavement and rain dripped from the girders. I pulled over by an abandoned club called the Arches. I could still see Tully in its darkened rooms, dancing in dungarees and high as Ben Lomond, some night in our youth before the advent of distance.

Driving up the rise to Tully and Anna's flat, I thought the trees seemed protective of the houses underneath. I passed a group of spray-painted shops. I hadn't noticed them the previous November when I came for the wedding. In one way or another, the shops signalled the life of the place, and reminded me of the young Tully. I drove on and parked, stepping out of the car to find him sat on his doorstep. I hadn't seen him for over two weeks and he'd barely eaten a thing in that time. His arms were bony and he seemed delicate. He had a cigarette going in the semi-dark and was reading the sports pages under the porch light. I came walking up the path and I pointed to his sandals with socks. He smiled. 'It's all one to me, buddy,' he said. 'I don't care what I look like any more.'

He folded the newspaper away as I asked him all the medical stuff. 'Whack Watch,' he said. 'They can see you're about to croak but all they care about is whether you're going to tan your wrists on the premises. So I just said, "Fuck it," and got out of there.'

'Do you think you can manage here?'

'Aye, Anna's been amazing. She does everything. I'm going to finish the last of this immunotherapy, but I'm just doing it for her sake. Switzerland is the only good news I've had this year.'

'I think the road is clear now.'

'I honestly don't care if people don't like it, Noodles. It feels like a godsend to me. I was in that hospital shitting myself about shitting myself. Think about that. I was scared about what humiliating thing was going to happen next.' He opened a fresh pouch of tobacco and rolled a cigarette as we walked into the house. He made me a cup of tea in the white kitchen and Anna came through from having a nap.

'Ah, it's you,' she said, rubbing her eyes. She seemed distant and she cast a nervous glance at Tully.

'Are you not going to give Jimmy a hug?' he said. 'He's come all the way from London without any notice or anything.' He clearly knew nothing more than I'd told him about the conversation between Anna and me earlier that day. She kissed my cheek and stroked my arm and said she'd go and check her email: the nurses at the hospital might have been in touch. Tully coughed and bent over the sink for a minute. When he came up, I noticed his eyes: the thinness made them seem bigger. Not since he was a boy had they looked so green. We went through to the living room and he pointed to a painting above the sofa of *La Pasionaria*, a statue on the north bank of the Clyde, very near the car hire place and the old nightclub. He and Anna used to visit the monument when they were first dating. 'That's what it's all about,' he said from the sofa, craning his neck to read the words.

'*Better to die on your feet than live for ever on your knees.*'

'That could be Arthur Seaton,' I said.

'And we thought they were just quotes, Noodles.'

He told me there was a constant pain in his stomach and in his back. 'I never really thought about my body before, you know that? Never once. I went to the gym but that was to clear my mind, more than anything.' He hesitated. 'Do you remember all those remains in that crypt in Sicily, up in the mountains? Round the back of Savoca. The place the driver took us to after we'd been to the church?'

'Of course,' I said. 'The convent, with all those mummies.'

'I know this'll sound weird,' he said, 'but after seeing them I thought – it doesn't matter. It doesn't matter if it's today or tomorrow or a few hundred years ago, or next month. When you're done, you're done.'

'Those old Sicilian princes and monks.'

'That's right,' he said. 'They had their time. If you'd given me a pill in that crypt, I'd happily have taken it and gone to sleep. The same mad coupon as them. I would have stretched out there and then in one of those boxes and you and Anna and Iona could've shut the door and walked down the hill to have a few drinks. Me: just another goner up there in old Sicily with all the dead godfathers.'

'In that story,' I said, 'why do I have to be the one giving you the pill? Why can't you have it in your pocket?'

'Oh, don't you start.'

Anna came into the room, wearing her coat. She heaved a sigh and told us she was going to see her mother. 'Jimmy, don't let him drink too much,' she said. 'It's me that has to stay up with him when his stomach's killing him. That's *my bit.*' She said it with emphasis and looked at me. What we couldn't say now could be said later. 'Try to eat something, Tully, and don't go mental on the whisky.'

When the front door clicked shut he sank back in the sofa. He was playing an album by Run the Jewels. 'They are the pain I can trust,' he said, tapping his knee and staring into the fire.

'Remember Limbo's flat?' I said. 'When we stayed there and Davie Hogg painted the living room bright yellow?'

'You went to sleep cuddling a bottle of cider.'

'If being young is a crime scene,' I said, 'the evidence from that night is everywhere.'

'How come?' he said.

'For years afterwards, I'd find spots of it, like on the edge of

243

zippers and on the soles of my trainers. When Tibbs phoned to tell me about Limbo, I went to the shelf and took down a book I'd had with me that night at his flat – Keats's *Letters*. And there it was, still bright and everything, bang on the spine of the book – a splash of yellow.'

'The past isn't really the past,' Tully said. 'It's just music, books, and films.'

'Right.'

'It's every day of your life. The songs. The quotes. Down at the caravan recently, I thought to myself, It's been a life of quotations. That's why we liked some of those bands so much in the Eighties: they sampled as much as we did.'

I stood up and walked to the window, rubbing the condensation. 'I'm glad you've used the caravan,' I said.

'It's my favourite place. That and Cuba.'

'It's not really a dwelling,' I said. 'It's an idea by the coast.'

'I'd live there happily,' he said. 'Anywhere, to be honest, if living was an option. But we're going all the way to Zurich and that's what the good doctor ordered.'

He tapped the side of his head. 'The doctor in here.'

He stood up and swiped a bottle from the fireplace. I followed him outside. The patio was wet, so we sat on the bench under an awning in the proper dark. He loved looking over Glasgow. 'Just the feeling it gives you,' he said, 'that we're all here together at the same time . . . the city going on for miles and all the lights.'

'I can still see them,' I said, 'the city lights from the top of that building in Manchester.'

'Some things are like that,' he said. He leaned over and hugged me and we rocked on the bench for a while in silence.

He poured two more glasses.

'Make it a wee one,' I said. 'I've got to drive down to Ayrshire. And Anna's right about the stomach, Tully.'

He handed me the glass. 'When I went to night school to get the Highers,' he said, 'the first thing I read was *The Great Gatsby*. And the copy I read was in that shelf of books you gave me. It had all your pencil markings on it, images underlined. And all this time later, it's still my favourite book.'

'The green light.'

'That's right. To me you were always the narrator – Nick Carraway. And I was the guy who'd end up face down in the swimming pool.'

'Don't say that.'

'It's true. But you know what, buddy? We had the party. We had our story.' He lifted his glass and walked to the garden wall for a better view of the city. 'That's it – the whole mad thing.' He looked at the miles of buildings. 'It's like an explosion of life happening and then it's gone,' he said. 'We had our time, buddy. I've come to terms with it and I've never been to Switzerland and I'm ready.'

24

Laughter is the obvious policy in a time of strife. Anna had said as much to me the morning we left for the airport. She had been silent and stoical as the final arrangements were made, and I never learned exactly what she and Tully said to each other, though I knew she blamed us both equally for Switzerland. She ended her silence when the day arrived and came on the phone without much hesitation.

I was sitting on our front steps in London with my phone to my ear as she said none of this was her choice. 'You two were planning this for months,' she said, 'despite me not wanting it to happen. It's only a fortnight since he explained it fully, and I've had to prepare myself and my family in that short time.'

'I'm sorry, Anna.'

'The whole thing has made me sadder. I just want you to know that.'

I felt I had to take it on the chin and not defend myself – not that day, not on the phone, and perhaps not ever.

'But he is adamant,' she said. 'He's dying and nobody can stand in his way.'

'He's got to own it,' I said.

'You gave him that idea, Jimmy, of owning it. You, with your Shakespeare. And once it's out of the bottle, that's it. I

246

don't know where you've been, but it's handed you the ability to think you can invent your life and own your death.'

'That's harsh, Anna.'

'I'll try to smile and feel it's merciful. We have all the details now and he wouldn't let me speak to you about it. So, here we are. I'll try to step back and let him have the ending he wants to have. Iona will help me.'

'She's right here. We'll be at Heathrow in two hours.'

'There wasn't much else you could do, Jimmy. I know that.' Her tone was balanced between pity and anger.

'So let's get the jokes going,' she said. 'It's the only policy. Hasn't he always been famous for scoffing in the face of adversity? I'll lose it otherwise.' Their flight to London was announced and she ended the call.

Before I ordered an Uber, Iona went through a checklist. We had the documents, the shirts and ties. I packed a sheaf of letters from the boys and Iona handed me a packet of Xanax, just in case. We locked the front door. The driver turned down his talk-radio programme and checked our destination.

'How was she?' Iona asked as we drove along.

'Furious,' I said. 'Who can blame her? We didn't do it properly.' She nodded and held my chin and kissed me on the lips.

'I'm on your side, James. We can air our grievances in life, or we can try to understand other people's. Anna's a smart person. She does the really hard work with Tully and then he goes off and makes a plan with somebody else. It's a thing men do. Not the end of the world, but you can't expect her to like it.'

'I don't expect her to like it. Maybe I was hoping she'd see beyond it.'

'And that's what she's doing.'

'Not quite yet,' I said.

'Go gently with people's pain. It's the same as yours.'

After a moment I took her hand and held it and looked out of the window as we drove over the Westway. It was late October once again and the clouds were scattered over West London like nothing mattered.

• • •

In the afternoon, Tully held his lower back and chuckled as we stood outside a café at Heathrow. 'Stop with the gags,' he said. 'It's too sore.'

'That's my humble opinion,' I said. 'Every death should involve an airport. The clue's in the name – Terminal 5.'

'Shush, James,' Iona said.

We were waiting for the gate number. Iona and Anna wandered off. In the days running up to our departure, Tully had become grave, like a boxer or a fighter pilot building to the task. Now he was ready, on form. He stood with a small rucksack at his feet, taking in the signs for Harrods, Burberry, Jimmy Choo. 'I'm no tycoon,' he said, 'but if I was Anna I'd spank all my credit cards today. I've got two. She could say I went berserk on my last day and bought a hundred pairs of high heels.' He delved into his bag for gum. 'Do you think they'll mind,' he said, smiling from dimple to dimple, 'the security dudes? Will they mind that I've brought a loaded Uzi and a bowie knife, just in case the chow-down doesn't work?'

'They love a challenge,' I said.

'I wasn't sure what to pack, actually. I mean, it's not exactly an overnight bag, is it? More like an over-life bag.'

When they returned to us, Anna held up a gift box. 'Something for you, Jimmy.' She pressed her lips together. 'For giving us the caravan, and for . . . all your help with the wedding. Coming up and down to Glasgow . . .'

'For everything,' Tully said.

Her eyes sparked with irritation. She looked briefly at him and then handed me the box. 'We thought you might like a decent pen.'

'Montblanc,' he said. 'None of your cheap shite.' I took it out of the box and marvelled at its weight and the gold nib.

'That's crazy,' I said, hugging Anna. 'Thank you so much.'

'What about me?' he said. 'It's my dough she's spending.'

'In your dreams, James Cagney,' she said.

'*Top of the world, Ma.*'

The passengers formed a pointless queue when the Zurich flight was called. They seemed like the sort who roamed the world, men with sunglasses propped on their heads, brandishing their fat watches like badges of prodigality. Women – slim wrists and noses upturned – listed to one side as they escorted their huge handbags through the gate. As we stood up I saw Anna dabbing the corners of her eyes.

In the glass tunnel the daylight was piercing and Tully stopped to look down at the broad ordinariness of the tarmac. He put his hands on the Perspex, seeming to take in the workers down below in their yellow vests, the catering vans and baggage trucks swooshing back and forth. We were only a few steps from the door of the plane. I went over and put an arm around him. 'When we left Scotland this morning, I looked down and saw Paisley,' he said, 'and it was weird, you know, to think I'll never be in Paisley again. Now it's the whole country I won't see again, the whole of Britain. I suppose I should be glad to see the back of it, but it's hard to think of it here on its own.'

As we departed, it seemed separate, the old country. We all knew Tully was leaving for good. 'Before he became a postie,' I said to him, 'Tibbs once applied to study journalism at Napier College. And when the tutor asked him to suggest a title for a newspaper column, he said, "Britain is a Ropey Old Cow".'

'No way,' Tully said. 'Did he really?'

'Yep. "A Ropey Old Cow." And then he proceeded to dictate the column there in the seminar room. He goes, "British Steel is dead. British Coal is dead. British Rail is dead. Britain is a ropey old cow." And he mooed.'

'That's Tibbs all right.'

'Staggeringly, they didn't offer him a place.'

'Silly bastards.'

He slept on the plane and I thought of his mother. She'd be sitting in her care home back in the parish, oblivious to all this. Anna held his hand and she kissed the back of it now and then as the journey passed. The ambience of travel seemed to take over somehow, and, when he woke up, I imagined he might have entered the pure, white zone of otherness he told me he'd dreamed about for months. Switzerland lay under the jet stream. It wasn't winter but there was snow on the mountains and by and by the whiteness gave out to brackish forests and chalets with brown roofs. That neutral country glinted under the sun, the blue roads like veins carrying poor blood to the heart.

· · ·

Tully led us straight to the escalators. He was holding on to his prejudices about taxis and big hotels. It was a matter of character. He said he'd concede to the fancy dinner that was booked for that evening, but he wasn't about to waste money and he'd heard the Zurich trains were better than any taxi. So down we went, the four of us, into a gleaming underworld of sporting goods and luggage retailers, the escalator humming its clean sound. We boarded a train full of commuters. 'Do you think Switzerland is a den of vice and the scrubbing is like a clean-up operation?' he asked.

'Almost certainly.'

'It's the Fredo Corleone of countries,' he said. 'So naive and so corruptible.'

I laughed as we passed Hardbrücke station, and Tully did, too, the expression spreading like good news over his face. 'Fredo should never have gone to Vegas,' he said. Images appeared to flicker in his eyes. '*I know it was you, Fredo. You broke my heart.*'

'You two should have your own show,' Anna said.

Tully looked out over the streets and buildings. 'You have

to rip it up in a city like this – what do you think, Noodles?'

'I'm hazarding a guess,' I said, 'but this is probably not the time to take up indifference and passivity.'

'Nope,' he said.

. . .

The Hotel St Georges is by the River Sihl. Across the bridges and beyond the trams, it sits on a corner of Weberstrasse, in a pretty square with a fountain. We checked in and handed our passports over to the receptionist, who asked Iona, in faultless English, if we'd like to settle the bill for the rooms right then, or 'on departure'. Iona quickly dealt with it, but when I glanced at Anna I could see the thought of it was too much for her. Everywhere she looked, I imagined, there was a provocation or a further unwelcome surprise, and she was mortified by it, while trying to keep it all light for Tully.

Late in the afternoon, he was in his room watching a French football match on television. He sent me a text to say he'd just seen a local doctor, as required by the organisation. The surgery was only around the corner and he'd walked there with Anna. 'It was all fine,' he said. 'Wanted to know I was of sound mind.'

'And are you?'

'No less than normal.'

The hotel had a smoking oasis outside, a bench with a furry rug, a brass Moroccan table with wooden legs. That evening, when I came down from our room – single beds, sink, powerless shower – he was out there, staring into the fountain and the twilight hour of the square. He looked smart, ordering two Cuba Libres. We clinked glasses. 'This is it,' he said. 'Let's show those two a right good time tonight.'

'Absolutely. You're in charge.'

We sat down on the bench.

'That's what they say.' He tilted his glass. His head went back. He'd always had this way of drinking, like he was putting it away. He'd taken steroids and all sorts, he said, and would be able to eat and drink, with any luck.

He'd asked that we dress up – he didn't usually do ties outside of work, so I'd gone to the place in London where I'd got the wedding ties and bought two knitted ones, and shirts as well, and we were both wearing them. He had on his wedding suit. The shirt was too big but when he got up to order more drinks he stopped and winked at himself in the glass door, smoothing his eyebrows and making like Albert Finney. '*I dunno, work tomorrow,*' he said, before turning towards the bar. When he returned and sat down he told me he'd stopped watching them, the old kitchen-sink dramas.

'Why?' I asked.

'I think we wore out their nostalgia,' he said. 'Maybe that's what happens. Realism starts to seem a bit too romantic once reality kicks in.'

'That's a big thing to say, Tully.'

'We just liked the images, didn't we? The talk. All made up. And everything that's happened in the last year, it's . . . well, it's not made up, is it?'

'I wish it had been,' I said. 'Reality's got a lot to answer for.'

Halfway down his second drink, he said the British working class had changed so that it was no longer the natural constituency of the Labour Party. 'It's like the policies are good but the times are not,' he said, 'and the majority of the people who might benefit from those policies don't want them.' He paused and checked his phone. 'Technology has knackered our sense of the common good.'

'I wonder if it ever really existed,' I said. 'Like the world of those films. Maybe it only ever existed in the imagination, and that's what we liked.'

'No, it existed,' he said. 'Like Manchester existed.'

He began coughing and I got him some water. He had a sip and then waved it away, wanting to get back to the conversation. 'Do you remember when my dad died?' he said. 'My mum was sitting in the living room for days, just lost really. Devastated. Then you came over and sat with her and started telling stories about Glasgow moneylenders and how one time the family dog bounded in and scoffed your dad's wage packet, and she picked right up. Just like that. You were twenty-one. I don't think you ever had a dog but you had the room in an uproar. She never forgot it.' His voice was steady. He was calm. The air appeared to carry the spirit of what he was saying, and I breathed it, too, and when Anna and Iona came down it felt like our first evening on a new island.

25

Tully and Iona did a slow Buzzcocks medley on the way to the Kronenhalle. The squares were filled with people and you could hear the ringing of the trams and see reflections on the surface of the Limmat. The churches were lit up and the bars along the quay had fairy lights hanging outside and from one of the bridges I saw 'Lindt Chocolate' glowing in blue neon at the top of an office building. We made our way through the lanes by the cathedral and I stopped to look at a bookshop, but Tully grabbed my arm and pulled me along, saying he was hungry for the first time in forever. Arriving on Rämistrasse we saw the grand building in front of us and Anna fixed her lipstick.

The sound came first in the Kronenhalle, then pictures and chandeliers. A great brightness fell from the ceiling as we were ushered through. Coats hung in iron cages and a silver samovar glinted on the bar. Our table was in the corner, with paintings all round, a beautiful red Chagall dominating. Sitting down, the women high-fived over the table. Anna kissed Tully's cheek and wiped it clean. Behind his head, framed in flaked gilt, a small Bonnard showed a girl with an umbrella and a dog. 'So, Noodles,' he said. 'Is this where socialists come to die?'

'No,' I said. 'Only to dine.'

'What's a consonant between pals?' When each of our glasses was filled we held them up and Tully looked at the label on the bottle.

'Fancy restaurants. You'll be the ruination of him,' Anna said, and I let it go with a sip of champagne.

'I love it here,' Tully said, twisting his wedding ring. 'Maybe I was wrong and the bourgeois pigs had the right idea all along. Great booze. Cracking pictures.'

'I like it, too,' Anna said.

Six Galway oysters.

One prawn cocktail.

Blinis with smoked salmon.

Clear soup with herb pancakes.

The restaurant of the 1920s rose out of the chatter and the tinkling glasses. And somewhere beyond the buzz, I could hear Ravel.

They talked but I didn't hear them, because of the music. I watched the waiters coming and going with their red faces, their green gloves, seeming like they too had been painted in oils. I wondered about the patrons who had come before us, those historic eaters of oysters and clear soup. The heraldic shields around the walls seemed to recall families and tribes, and it was helpful to think of them, with their own fears and regrets, present again for a minute or two in this pulling of corks.

'Where have you wandered off to?' Tully asked.

'Checking out the people at the tables.'

'Come the revolution,' he said, 'they're the first to go. But not yet. What's this music you're tapping to?' He looked over at Iona. 'I once knew him in Manchester. He was mesmerised by northern workers and a million jangly guitars.'

'Long ago,' she said.

'I know you're younger than him,' he said, 'but take my word for it. Jangly guitars and *Coronation Street*, writers with a few memories and a dole card. He loved every one of them and so did we all, and now it's pianos.'

'Get lost,' I said.

'Big fat pianos,' he went on. 'And nobody nowadays to stop him with the opera-loving and the Beethoven whatever.'

'Every now and then he'll play the Smiths at full volume when we're getting ready for a night out,' Iona said, 'but usually it's some Russian pianist. He wakes up in the morning and is quiet for a minute and then he says, "Alexa, what time is it?" And then he says, "Play Shostakovich's Fifth Symphony," and suddenly the whole house is rattling with wind instruments and tam-tams.'

'Stop with the ganging up,' I said.

'It would drive you mad,' she said. 'Every morning. Rise and shine!'

'I suppose you think it's easier waking up to fourteen tracks by the Fall,' Anna said. She grinned and Tully spread shallots on his oyster.

'So, what is this music playing now, then?' he asked.

'It's by Ravel, a nice little Catholic Frenchman,' I said.

'I'm sure he did a Splash One Happening in Glasgow in

the Eighties,' Tully said. 'Possibly supported by a wee punk from East Kilbride named Debussy. It was some gig. A guy from Castlemilk called Chopin with a papier-mâché head was crushing it.'

'He knows much more than he pretends to,' Anna said.

'It's terrifying what a man can do with one O-grade,' I said. I put down my spoon and looked at him. 'Ravel was the punk of his time.'

'Here we go.'

'The piece you are currently abusing was dedicated to his mates—'

'What, he had *mates*?'

'A bunch of rebels called the Apaches.'

'I told you!' he said.

'They were called the Apaches, or the Hooligans. Stravinsky was one of them, and the painter Paul Sordes.' Iona started cheering when Tully suddenly went into a routine about gangs of European artists and intellectuals running wild on the housing estates of Glasgow. He did the routine in full dialect, picturing the Apaches armed with clubs and machetes, high on glue, 'doing some serious damage to the Cumbie, a group of experimental poets from Easterhouse'.

Tully looked at Anna with delighted surprise. He was enjoying himself and seemed pleased to find he had the energy. 'That Beethoven,' he said, 'what a nutter. Pulls a blade on some geezer at the bus stop. Turns out it's Mozart frae the Garngad. Ludwig tried to slash him and the wee man shouts for handers—'

'Oh, *handers*, is it?'

'Reinforcements to you,' he said. 'Next minute, Ravel and the Apaches and the Garngad Vambo are pelting it up the hill, writing a symphony and picking up bottles and all sorts of shite and pure lamping him, what a rammy.'

He seemed suddenly to run out of steam and looked up at the pictures. The Chagall had a curious mood, in tune with the restaurant, in tune with Tully and his aides-de-camp. He focused on a second picture hanging above Iona. 'That's a Miró,' he said. There was an inscription beneath the drawing, a dedication to the one-time proprietors of the restaurant, and, nearby, a note to them from James Joyce. 'It's hard to take it all in, like,' he said, and I muffled the echoes in my own head. Not until that day, not until Zurich, had I known such a combination of exhilaration and dread.

Anna signalled to the waiter. He soon came over.

'*Geehrte Damen, Geehrte Herren* . . .'

He was holding up a bottle of the Petto Dragone. He nodded to Anna. 'The lady called ahead and requested a special bottle,' he said. 'A favourite from Sizilien.'

'From Sicily,' she said. 'From Taormina.' I put a thumb up and saluted her as a maker and a keeper of stories. She had planned the wine despite her doubts, creating a moment for Tully, even though her eyes, beautiful and violet and clear, would always be holding out for a miracle. She took a deep breath and exhaled. The red wine lashed into the glasses and she held hers up.

'*Sláinte.*'

'Down with propaganda,' Tully said.

'Spoken like a true Apache,' I said.

Rock lobster with garlic and parsley.

Calf's kidney with rösti.

Chateaubriand and Béarnaise sauce.

Rack of lamb Provençal.

Once the Sicilian red was gone, Anna and I looked at the wine list and ordered a bottle of Château Chasse-Spleen 1990. 'This wine,' I said drunkenly, 'was loved by Lord Byron and Baudelaire.'

'Late,' Tully said, 'of the Govan Young Team. Or was it the Possilpark Toi? No, wait a minute – I think your pal Byron was definitely in the Gallowgate Mad Squad. Used to twirl a stick. Famous for his knuckleduster.' We all spluttered and the waiter came over to see that everything was all right.

'Very good,' I said to him. 'I'm making a splendid speech about the wine.' The waiter offered a nod of recognition, topping up our glasses. He was familiar with the British custom of turning everything into a drinking experience.

'Go for it,' Tully said.

'But Byron's not the reason. The reason we have this wine from 1990 is because that's the year Margaret Thatcher was deposed.' I clinked his glass and the smile on Tully's face was as wide as the River Clyde. All the light in the room and the light of our shared history were on his face.

'Bringing it all back home,' he said.

A short time later we went to the gents. He stepped into a cubicle and I could hear him being sick. I waited by the hand-drier. He came out, waving away my concern. 'I can't really eat,' he said, 'but I'm going to, and that's that.' We stood outside the restaurant for a smoke. There was cold air coming from the hills and a disco could be heard along the river. Tully suddenly wanted to talk to the boys in Scotland. He concentrated on the phone. I could see he was scrolling through the numbers and then he looked up, blowing the air out of his lungs. 'I can't face it, bud,' he said.

'Don't worry. They're all with you.'

'I'm just going to stay here for a minute.'

At the table, Anna and Iona held hands. I saw them from the door and could tell Anna had been crying. I felt I couldn't yet enter the circle, so I returned to the bathroom and had a breather at the mirror. When I came back, Anna at first seemed keen to recuperate the merriment, but since Tully was outside she took the opportunity to ask what time they wanted us at the clinic the next day. As happens, in drink, in crisis, the resentment that had been put to bed was suddenly awakened.

'Tully doesn't seem to be aware of *precisely* what's happening.'

She said it formally, expressing her frustration and igniting mine, with the implication that he was somehow not in control.

'He knows exactly,' I said. 'He's spoken to them many times. And I've confirmed the information they gave us. We arrive at eleven.'

'And then what?'

She was right. This was her moment to ask for the information as if it might still be subject to her revisions. While he was away from the table, she could turn to me and register a little of the feeling she'd been holding back.

'You can take the whole day if you want,' I replied. 'There's no rush.' She rested her hands on a small, clear bowl of roses. As we spoke, she picked petals from the top flower and rolled them between her fingers.

'It's up to Tully,' she said.

Iona reached out for her hand again, as if to mime the effort Anna was making. 'But if he changes his mind, can we go home and it'll be like normal?'

'Of course,' I said. 'He can stop it at any time.' She lifted her hand to push the hair out of her eyes and a scent of roses came with it.

'I think you could stop this, Jimmy.'

'Why would you say that? I don't have any special power. You keep returning to this, but it's not my call. I have no authority.'

'Maybe you do.'

'I'm not his father.'

'Interesting choice of words.'

'This isn't a court case, Anna.' I felt confused. I said the wrong thing. 'You don't get it. You're not yourself.'

'Don't pathologise me for disliking Tully's methods, and yours, like I don't "get it". I get it perfectly well. It's the old game of men rescuing each other and being rescued. While we watch. The two of you helped each other years ago. It makes you think you're two sides of the same coin. Game over.'

'That's not fair, Anna.'

'You're going to talk to me about fair?'

'Anna.'

'I'm not part of that story, Jimmy. I'm his wife. And I wanted to keep him alive because I can't stand to lose him.'

Her chin trembled.

'But, Anna. We have to go with his choice.'

'Once you put it like that, there is no other choice.'

'But it was put like that – by him.'

'He didn't have the words, Jimmy. You gave him the words. *Make death proud*, you told him. Remember? People talk about the power of old friendship. I'm interested in that power, Jimmy. He's speaking through you and you're speaking through him, and there's no room for argument.'

'Look, I tried. The two of you should've been having these discussions from the beginning.'

'It was all sewn up,' she said. 'By the boys from the 1980s.'

'He's an adult, Anna. He asked me to make him a basic promise. And I'm honouring it.'

'Always efficient.'

'You can't say that,' Iona said, responding to my hurt glance. 'This is Tully's decision. He may not have handled it brilliantly, when it comes to you, but it's what he wants.' Anna took a slug of wine and looked unsparingly at Iona, as if there were things about life and men that Iona might never understand. Anna's lips were pressed together and she wrapped her hands around the base of her glass.

'Thing is, Iona, you won't be a widow tomorrow.' There was an unspeakable force in the way she said it and Iona caught her breath.

'There's nothing I can do, Anna,' she said.

I shook my head and stared into the tablecloth. 'He wants to go with grace and I want him to have that choice.' I must have flushed, or maybe it was all tremendously clear to her at that moment, but I could see she was also provoked by the ebbing away of all diplomacy from my tone of voice.

'And men tend to get what they want,' she said.

. . .

The birch trees along the Stadthausquai were white and bare. The summer had been hot and now they stood in the dark like the Dry Salvages, as if the good weather had restored everything but had left the trees in ruins. The Fraumünster clock showed it was just past eleven and Anna was buoyant with a complex new energy. She took the lead in finding somewhere for a nightcap and even suggested a club. 'Nah, babe,' Tully said, 'let's stick to the drinking places. Noodles is a shocking dancer.'

'Not true,' I said. 'I am the Gene Kelly of Ayrshire. It's a well-known fact. I follow the moves on *Strictly* while others lag behind.'

'He does,' Iona said. 'He has a freakish memory.'

Anna stopped by the church and let the others walk ahead. She turned and suddenly gave me a hug. 'Nobody has to be right, Jimmy. Nobody has to win. You've tried your best and so have I. And we're here, that's all.'

I kissed her on both cheeks and then she took my arm as we walked into the cigar bar at the Hotel Storchen. They all spoke English. We sat in a corner under mullioned windows and Tully seemed relaxed. The barman knew everything about Havana and Anna asked him to bring champagne and the best Cuban cigars in the house.

'These are not the most expensive,' he said, 'but they are the best.' Soon, behind a glowing tip, Tully was conducting one of his famous quizzes, blowing executive smoke between large statements. He asked me to name the top three smoking scenes in cinema. We all pitched in with submissions.

'That bit in *Grease*,' Iona said, 'when Frenchy shows Sandy how to smoke. That's one of the best.'

'Acceptable,' Tully said.

'The scene in *Pinocchio* where he smokes a giant cigar,' I said.

'*Now, Voyager*, obviously,' Anna said.

'I don't want random films,' Tully said. 'And there's no point saying "the whole of film noir". I want your personal Top Three.' None of us could satisfy his ruling, so he stuck the cigar in his mouth and counted them off. 'One, Tatum O'Neal smoking in bed in *Paper Moon*. Two, Rita Hayworth smoking at the roulette table in *Gilda*. And three, De Niro smoking and laughing in the cinema in *Cape Fear*.'

'You win,' Iona said.

We got lost crossing the rivers on the way back to our hotel, repeatedly passing the same idle roadworks, though none of us cared. We stopped at the Brasserie Lipp on the Uraniastrasse because Tully said he'd never tasted schnapps. 'Just want to say I've tried it,' he said. Once inside, we shared the pictures on our phones that we'd taken around Zurich, and I found one of

Tully under a sign for Cabaret Voltaire. 'A great band in their day,' he said, hanging his head in a familiar way and drumming the metal surface of the bar. In a muffled voice, he said, 'Tell us the top three things you've never done.' Anna looked at me and shook her head, as if the game wasn't up to that.

'One,' he said, sitting up straight, 'I never ate an avocado. Two, I never visited Graceland. And three, I never got round to reading *Ulysses*.'

'I can't speak for Memphis,' I said.

'I can,' Anna said, 'and that house is a dump.' We liked the Anna-ness of that and we snuggled up close, drinking plum schnapps.

'You know Joyce died here, Tully?' I said.

'How old was he?'

'Fifty-something.'

'Same as me. I should've read it,' he said. 'Too many films and football matches and too many tunes.'

When we left the brasserie I resorted to the map on my phone and we were soon back in District 4. We were in the square and were about to enter the hotel when Tully suddenly shook both his arms out by his sides, like someone shivering. He pointed up at the moon and said, 'I want to buy you all just one more drink.'

'Are you sure?' Anna said. 'You're tired, babe.'

'Never tired,' he said. 'Never in my life.'

The Penalty Bar had gingham curtains and big screens. Tully barrelled in and asked for four glasses of Hürlimann. He spoke to the barman about players and transfer fees and told him he loved Glasgow Rangers. Iona said he was like a sailor on leave. There was now an expansive, talkative, intimate vitality about him, as if he wanted to put himself out in the world one last time. But he had always been like that. Even when he had all the nights and all the years to play with.

He paid for the beers with his card and then handed his wallet to Anna.

'It's totally like the Glebe in here,' he said. 'The boozer we used to go to when we were young.'

There was a recording of a match on TV and he shouted at the referee and appealed to the strangers in the bar over the ref's decisions. He always loved a stranger. After a while he said his phone had run out of charge and asked if he could borrow mine. We walked outside, lit two cigarettes, and I asked him if he needed any numbers. He sat on a bench and asked me to ring his sister.

'Hold on a second,' I said, scrolling for her name.

'How late is it in Scotland?' It was the only time during the whole ordeal that he seemed afraid. His hand was shaking.

'An hour behind.'

He said he'd posted me a bag of photographs. 'They'll be waiting for you at home when you get back. Loads of good pics. Including a cracker of us all hugging and laughing that time in Manchester.' Fiona's number was ringing. I handed him the phone and he took a deep breath. 'This'll be hard,' he said. 'I miss them.'

26

The fresh cotton of her pyjamas. Even on such a trip as this, Iona would bring her nightwear and her special creams, her scented candle. For all we'd drunk we weren't tired and we faced each other on the single beds, holding hands across the gap and talking as the light from the street fell into the room. 'Nobody expects anything like this,' she said. 'And she's doing better than I would.'

'It's a shame she feels singled out for defeat. We all feel defeated.'

'Don't take it personally.'

'Everything is personal. I just wish he'd spelled it out to her.'

'Maybe he's too much in love with her to do that,' Iona said, 'like he's embarrassed to be ill and feels he's let her down.'

I stroked her hand. 'I hadn't thought of it like that.'

'Men have a way of writing themselves into each other's experience and placing it away from the women they love.'

'Wow,' I said. 'Do you feel that?'

'Everybody feels that. And she's got to let it out. She hates feeling coerced, and that's been obvious all along.'

Lying there, listening to Iona, I felt close to her, and that closeness now seemed for the first time to include all of the past, hers and mine, a last gift to us from Tully. 'He used to collect groceries for the miners on strike,' I said. 'Him and Tibbs Lennox and Limbo spent the winter of 1984 gathering tins of food.'

'Was it really like that?'

'Pretty much. He never mentioned it to his dad, who was on strike himself. But we'd all come, Dr Clogs and Ross and Caesar, who was in his first year as a welder on the YTS. We'd all arrive at the community centre and make up these boxes from what the boys had collected, then load them into a works van and drive to New Cumnock. We had a list of striking miners we'd got off the union. Tully would knock on their doors and shake their hands and tell them he was proud of them, the whole family, telling them to stick it out. He knew something at eighteen that the government never knew, that closing those industries would murder those people, and it did.'

'Some people live to be ninety,' Iona said, 'but they never know such things. It's no comfort right now, but he really lived.'

• • •

The church bells began at seven across the city. You could hear them every fifteen minutes after that, until they stopped at eight. I could smell toast and hear the bumping sound of the elevator and the metallic drag of the trams outside. I hadn't slept. Anna had sent several long texts in the night while Iona was sleeping. She said Tully had vomited a few times more when they got back to the room. He shouldn't drink, she said. He needed his own doctors, and I replied that it was in her hands. We could wake Tully and Iona and we'd all be on the first flight back to London, then to Glasgow. The day should not go ahead as planned if she opposed it to the last. It was her decision now. Her tone changed. It had broken her heart to see him suffer, she said. Zurich was his last hope. 'This is for Tully,' she texted. 'We've been through everything together and I'm not going to let him down.'

'I'm sorry,' I wrote. 'I'll be sorry all my life.'

'He needed you,' she said.

· · ·

After breakfast I went for a walk. I wished the walk would last forever, yet it took less than ten minutes to reach the shop on Holzgasse. 'Welcome to Schumann's,' said the friendly, bearded gentleman who met me inside. 'It's much too early for serious work,' he said. 'But any friend of Krisztina's is a friend of mine, as they say.' The man was Hungarian and he'd known her since she was in her early twenties. They had once been colleagues and lovers in Budapest. 'We worked for the government,' he said, rolling his eyes and pushing his glasses up his nose. 'Krisztina graduated early from our very special illusions.' He went to the corner and returned with a pot of tea on a tray.

'How long have you lived here?'

'Oh, a lifetime,' he said. 'It's a long story. Krisztina will tell you. I left the country in her brother's bread van. True, you know.'

'It's in her novel *The Stone Lions.*'

'Yes. I'm Benedek in the book. I would never have dreamed there was so much comedy to be found in us, and such sadness, such history.'

'But it's not worth it, is it?' I said spontaneously. 'Just for a story. You wouldn't have chosen to live through all that just for a story.'

'The choice is not ours to make. The book is the book.' He gestured to the packed shelves going all the way up to high windows. 'And the people who write these things wish to keep the essence alive.'

I felt I knew the room. I had a strong sense of déjà vu, and as I looked at the man's face something about my own life seemed clear and settled, and I suddenly wanted to tell him everything that had happened. 'I'm here in Zurich because my friend is dying,' I said. 'He's come here to end his life today.'

'I'm sorry about it. Krisztina said, on the telephone.'

I think my eyes filled with tears. He put a hand on my shoulder and a few sentences tripped out of me. 'He loves music,' I said, 'and football. We were young together.'

He squeezed my shoulder. 'With luck,' he said, 'you have time ahead of you. And the future will still involve him.'

'I can't imagine it.'

'You will,' he said.

He took his cup and saucer and went to the back of the shop and returned with a volume in his hands. 'Our friend wanted to give you something. It's quite rare,' he said, pushing his glasses up again and opening the book. 'I've only ever seen a few complete copies at auction.' He laid it on the table.

Ephemeri Vita: or the Natural History and Anatomy of the Ephemeron.

'Eight engraved plates,' I read. 'And the date, 1681.'

'A beautiful publication,' he said. 'Swammerdam believed that no being was higher than any other being, a revolutionary thought at the time. He wrote this book one summer in Sloten, outside Amsterdam. He filled it with poetry and visions as well as anatomical observations.'

'It's really wonderful,' I said. 'Mayflies.'

'It's yours,' he said. 'Don't ask me the price. Krisztina bought it for you. A token of friendship.'

. . .

Tully appeared in the hotel lobby wearing a Joy Division T-shirt. We hugged and he told me he'd spoken to everybody he wanted to speak to. A doctor had come to the hotel while I was out and had seen Tully in his room, where they signed papers. Anna came straight up to me in the lobby and took my arm, and Iona took Tully's. When I saw Anna place her room key in her bag my stomach lurched, but Tully lifted his thumb in front of his chest and looked at each of us. 'Let's do it,' he said. He wanted to walk a few streets and then take the first of two trams. 'I think we blew the budget last night,' he said, 'and anyway it would be nice to mingle with folk going to work or whatever.'

We walked to the tram stop. 'Do people actually come from here,' he said, 'or was it just invented for strangers?'

'That's a big question,' I said.

'It doesn't feel real – Switzerland, I mean. Like a place in a snow globe. Remember that glass thing I gave you, Noods?'

'A paperweight. It's on my desk.'

'Found it in a junk shop in Glasgow, for his thirtieth birthday. It's a dandelion clock preserved in a ball of glass.'

'I love it,' I said. 'That and the Mao clock.'

We got on the tram and passed all the big shops on the way to Stadelhoferplatz. Tully turned to Anna. 'Last chance to hop off and spank the credit cards,' he said. 'After that, it's fraud.'

'It's always fraud,' she said. 'By the card companies, I mean.' He liked that and leaned over and held her face for a kiss. The people outside were walking with purpose and the shop windows gleamed in the sun.

'Eat the rich or die trying,' he said.

We changed trams onto an orange one that climbed up the hill. It came away from the city like a ski lift and the trees looked fresh and cold. I imagined those brown roofs were the ones we'd seen from the plane. At a yellow crossing near Zollikerberg a party of schoolchildren were passing and one of them dropped his rucksack. Anna was holding Tully's hand and he pointed with the other. 'Look, the wee man's dropped his stuff and his packed lunch is all over the road.' He seemed fascinated by the scene. Two other children and a teacher came to help the boy recover his things, and soon they got off the crossing and Tully looked back as we proceeded up the hill.

'He's all right,' I said.

Everything was made of weightless glass, these modular offices and wide chalets that seemed unoccupied.

We got off and headed down to a roundabout, as instructed, then took the third turning on the left and walked along a vacant street without saying a word. A series of low-rise houses, a group of white doors opposite a tractor factory, Matteo had said. And when I texted him from outside he appeared at the middle door, wearing a philosophical expression. 'Happy to see you in person,' he said to Tully, then shook our hands and brought us inside.

'I've had dreams about this place,' Tully said. He sniffed and rubbed his nose. He seemed embarrassed now to be the centre of attention. In another room, Matteo introduced us to a pair of young women in sweatshirts.

'Okay, Mr Dawson,' Matteo said.

'I'm just Tully.'

Matteo nodded, his head to one side, as if nothing was ever a problem to him. 'Zoe and Giorgia will be your companions,' he said. They made small talk for a minute and then they sat us down at a round table in the conservatory and someone brought in a tray of tea, the white mugs seeming new.

'It's all about the biscuits,' Tully said, as if to relax everybody. He turned to Anna. 'You all right, babe?' She nodded and held his arm with both her hands and I could see she had no resistance left. She'd done her best to forestall this hour and now it was pacified by her gravity. At one point, he reached into her handbag and took out the bottle of Acqua di Parma and gave himself a spritz. Anna took it from him and did the same and passed it to me, and I took some and gave it to Iona. The staff poured the tea and began laying out the procedure and the rules. He could go home now if he wanted. Was he sure this was his decision and of his own free will? Tully looked at me across the table and said very clearly that it was, and there was silence for a moment.

'A Top Three,' he broke in.

'Oh, here we go,' I said.

'What's your top three biscuits of all time? And don't say Wagon Wheels, because it isn't a biscuit.'

'One: McVitie's orange Club,' I said.

'Fair play,' he said.

'Two: the Garibaldi.'

'That's a bit London.'

'And three: the humble custard cream.'

'Ah, the true taste of Ayrshire,' he said.

Everyone laughed. 'He's being polite,' I said, turning to the companions. 'Normally he wouldn't give my choices the time of day.'

'Don't worry,' he said, 'I'll be pondering them in eternity or whatever cosmic tea room I'm going to after the chow-down.'

He was like that the whole way. I couldn't say what bravery is, but it must resemble something like the way Tully remained himself. He gestured to Anna and suggested we all have a drink. She brought out a bottle of Havana Club and some Cokes and asked for ice. 'No problem,' Zoe said.

When she went to the kitchen the other companion messaged Matteo and he brought in more papers. Tully put on his glasses and read them over and then asked me to come and look at them. With a hand on his shoulder, I suggested Anna read them first. She flicked through the pages and patted my hand. 'Go ahead, Jimmy,' she said. 'Make sure they're okay.' I borrowed his glasses. Matteo came back in a few moments and checked again that the decision was Tully's.

'Before you drink any alcohol,' he said, 'is everything clear to you? Your medical information states you will die within three months. You are electing today to end your life and making an autonomous decision to do it here.'

'I am,' Tully said. I had to turn away. 'It's my last vote, buddy.'

He signed the papers and they told him to take all the time he wanted. The rum went round. He said no to music. Anna had stored a lot of his favourite tunes on an iPod but he said it would be better if we could just talk. He sniffed his glass and held it out for us all to clink with him. 'Remember Steady McCalla?' he said, looking over at me. He turned to Anna and Iona. 'Brilliant guy who drank in the pub back home. I wonder where he is now. Wish he was here – old Steady, the calmest guy we knew.'

The helpers came in and out but Tully said he didn't want anything else. He spoke about his mum. He spoke about Fiona and Scott and the kids, how proud they made him, and he went on to talk about the times we'd had with our old friends, and the one who died young. 'Limbo always thought I was the lucky one,' he said, 'and he was right. But I wish we were back in Manchester for one night only. Just to tell him we'd stick together and make everything okay.'

'He'd tell you to fuck off,' I said.

'Too right,' he said. 'He was always good like that.'

'Cheeky Bastards United.'

'It's been a hell of a ride, Noodles.'

There were two small cups. He asked for the first. Zoe had explained it was to line his stomach, and the second, thirty minutes later, would be a dose of pentobarbital. We walked into the bedroom, and he stood like light and air.

The bed had a yellow sheet and Indian pillows.

He drank the first cup.

Along the windowsill there were votive candles and we could see a football pitch outside. It had white goalposts, a ball sitting on the grass, and a small lily pond in front of the house. He asked if he could go out to the playing field, just for five minutes by himself. But when he reached the door he held out his hand for Anna. From the window we watched them walking the touchline and the sun was hazy and the pond was perfectly still. He stood for a moment, looking back. Then he hugged his wife and blew us a kiss, before running onto the field with his arms outstretched. He stormed towards the goal and booted the ball and when he turned round the champion's smile was on his face again.

Acknowledgements

The author and publisher gratefully acknowledge permissions granted to reproduce the copyright material in this book.

Page 28 *A Taste of Honey* by Shelagh Delaney (1958/film 1961): reproduced with permission from the Estate of Shelagh Delaney, courtesy of Sayle Literary Agency.

Pages 28, 29, 37, 64, 98, 127, 253 *Saturday Night and Sunday Morning* (1958/film 1960) by Alan Sillitoe. Published by HarperCollins, 2008. Copyright © The Estate of Alan Sillitoe. Reproduced by permission of the Estate c/o Rogers, Coleridge & White Ltd, 20 Powis Mews, London W11 1JN.

Page 29 *Mona Lisa* (1986): reproduced with permission from D. Leland, N. Jordan and Handmade Films.

Page 37 *The Exorcist* (1973), screenplay by William Peter Blatty, reproduced courtesy of Warner Bros. Entertainment Inc.

Page 54 'They Shall Not Pass', *1936, The Spanish Revolution*, 1986. The Ex. © 1997 The Ex/AK Press © 1997 The Ex. Reproduced with permission from T. J. Hessels and The Ex.